AN EXCELLENT NIGHT FOR MURDER

Virginia Rath

AN EXCELLENT NIGHT FOR MURDER

VIRGINIA RATH

COACHWHIP PUBLICATIONS
Greenville, Ohio

An Excellent Night for Murder, by Virginia Rath
© 2019 Coachwhip Publications

Published 1937
No claims made on public domain material.
Cover image: Rain © emarto

CoachwhipBooks.com

ISBN 1-61646-474-7
ISBN-13 978-1-61646-474-5

AN EXCELLENT NIGHT FOR MURDER

PART ONE
ROYAL FAMILY

I

His last match flared damply and went out before he could light the rain-soaked cigarette between his lips. Rocky Allan threw cigarette and match into an overflowing gutter and shrugged philosophically. Rain trickled down his neck from a sodden hat brim and he turned up his coat collar and swore mildly.

A voice from the wet darkness said: "I entirely agree with you and I can think of some words you have omitted."

"So far. Give me time. Do I know you? I can't see you."

"Nor I you. Might a stranger in this town inquire what has become of the lighting system? Or is there one?"

"Don't insult our local pride." Rocky took a cautious step forward. He put out one hand and touched a wet, fuzzy coat sleeve. "I don't want to bump into you and it's funny, talking to just a voice . . . The lights went out as soon as the storm began. Some trouble at the plant. They may come on any time or not for the rest of the night."

"How jolly!"

Rocky frowned. The fellow had an English accent that somehow wasn't quite right. He sounded like an American playing the part of a stage Englishman. Rocky smiled at himself; it was none of his business if this man he couldn't see had a phony accent.

"Are you lost?" he asked. "I can show you to where-ever you're goin'."

"I want to go to the hotel. As I remember the town, I should be somewhere near it."

"Yes, but you're goin' the wrong way. Turn aroun'. We can cross the street here. See those dim lights over there? That's the hotel. They must have lamps burning. There should be a driveway about here."

"There is. I feel gravel underfoot now."

"They've never paved the driveway. Be thankful it's not just plain mud," Rocky said.

The man laughed: short and, for some reason, an unpleasant sound. "A little more wouldn't matter," he said. "I'm smeared with it to my knees. But there's more than one kind of mud. . . . Thank you, Mr. . . ."

"Allan. Uh—are you goin' to be here long, Mr. . . ."

"Cooper. No, I don't believe I'll be staying very long. You said your name is Allan? Well, thank you. I can find the hotel now and there's no need of your getting any wetter. Good night."

"Good night," Rocky said. He was turning away when a sudden flash of lightning split the black skies. The eerie light faded quickly but it left him with a picture of a slight dark man standing in the road, lips drawn back from white teeth in a sardonic smile. The voice bridged the darkness between them again:

"Has it occurred to you, Mr. Allan, that it's an excellent night for murder?"

Rocky started forward involuntarily. "What—what makes you say that?"

"Don't worry. I am not murderously inclined"—the voice moved slowly away, blown back by the gusty wind—"but it is, isn't it? Good night."

For an instant Rocky stood still, forgetful of rain beating against his face. He might, he thought, follow Cooper into the hotel and talk to him again. But after all, what the man said was perfectly true. It was a fine night for a murder: black as velvet, no street lights, constant roll of thunder drowning out lesser noises.

Cooper had said he was not murderously inclined. Did he mean someone else might be—toward him? The fellow was plenty mad about something, Rocky decided. He might talk, but, on the other hand, he would very likely tell Mr. Allan to mind his own business. No harm done if he did, but . . .

Rocky took one step toward the hotel, then turned about with an impatient movement of his broad shoulders. If he didn't get home pretty soon, Eleanor would be waiting with a thermometer in one hand and a hot lemonade in another. Nothing, apparently, would ever convince her he didn't catch cold. And since Andy Duncan hadn't turned up at the office, he was probably waiting at the house.

Rocky went quietly up his own front steps; stopped and looked through the porch window. Eleanor had lighted an old lamp with heavy brass base and was sitting with her hands clasped about her knees, looking into the fire. Andrew Duncan occupied the other big chair before the fire. Rocky sought for a term to describe Andy's expression and finally murmured:

"He looks kind of like a moon-struck calf."

More than once, just lately, he'd noticed that vague, moony look in Andy's eyes. He hoped fervently that the kid wasn't beginning to imagine

he was in love with Eleanor. You'd think her mat-
ter-of-fact, sisterly air would shrivel romantic
notions.

But Andy wasn't quite twenty-one and Rocky
had an amused remembrance of a blonde and bux-
om waitress in her thirties whom he'd fancied—at
eighteen. And he would hate to have to act like
an injured husband and lose the only satisfactory
deputy he'd ever had.

Eleanor said Andy was a perennial Boy Scout.
His nickname, among his former schoolmates, was
Handy. What made him useful to Rocky was the
fact that he'd always been an enthusiastic amateur
detective.

At sixteen Andy learned how to "be a detective,
by mail, in ten lessons", and began to study fingerprinting, criminal psychology and toxicology.
With a small camera he produced extraordinary
photographs. He could type, achieve an erratic
sort of shorthand, and was incredibly neat with
official documents and correspondence.

Rocky was not, and from the last sheriff he had
inherited an elderly deputy who was not even a
competent office boy. Cy Rand still dozed his life
away in the office but Andy did the work he had
once pretended to do. If Andy's academic ideas regarding murderers did slightly exasperate Rocky,

he still wanted to keep his useful jack-of-all-trades as long as possible.

He would not have had Andy's services at all if he had had money enough to finish his college course. Eventually Andy would put by enough money to see him through to a degree; whether legal or medical he was undecided. He even, being a great admirer of Dr. Thorndyke, talked grandly of medical jurisprudence.

Now, as Rocky came into the room, he got up quickly. "I didn't get back to town till the lights had gone out so I suppose you weren't at the office," he explained. "Eleanor said I'd better wait—"

"An' here I am. Of course the car would have to be out of order on a night like this." Rocky sat down and began tugging at his wet boot laces. "Honey, I'm goin' to be real nice to you and wear those slippers you gave me Christmas—"

"If I can find them," Eleanor said. "I put them away with the other gifts you never wear."

"Well, Christmas ties are pretty bad, aren't they?" Andy said. "I got one with yellow and purple stripes last year."

"Then a man gave it to you. All my life I have heard of the loud ties women choose, but to my certain knowledge," Eleanor said impressively, "no woman could possibly buy a more flamboyant tie for a man than he would pick out for himself. I'll get the slippers—"

"And a drink?" Rocky said.

"And a drink. Just a minute."

With some difficulty Rocky got his boots off. "Well," he said, "what happened?"

"What . . . Oh, at Indian River? The squaw don't want her old man arrested after all," Andy said. "She figures he can't work when he's in jail and says he didn't hurt her much."

"What's she call 'much'?"

"He hung a peach of a shiner on her. I wouldn't know about the rest of it. He must have been pretty drunk because she weighs about two-fifty and ought to be a match for him. I don't see why they don't get a decent jail over there. My trip was wasted."

"I was afraid it would be." Rocky accepted the slippers and hot toddy Eleanor handed him. "They're too broke—they say—to build a jail that'll keep folks in."

"Wasn't there a murder over there once?" Andy asked.

Rocky chuckled. "The squaw that carved her old man up with an ax? They acquitted her an' then she wanted the ax back. So the court told the sheriff to have it sharpened, first, because it'd got rusty, lying aroun' without being cleaned. Jake

Thompson said he was damned if he'd clean it: she could take it dull or not at all."

"Oh. Well, there wasn't any mystery to that," Andy said disparagingly. "Nothing worthwhile has happened since I began working with you. I suppose nothing will, in Brookdale."

"I reckon not," Rocky said dryly. "It's mighty peaceable and you'll just have to put up with it."

"Oh, I didn't mean I wanted anyone to be murdered! But I would like a little practical experience."

Rocky grinned at Eleanor but he said: "The last 'worthwhile' affair—up at Slacktown—will do me for quite a while. It's the only case I ever had come to trial and I didn't know what a damn unpleasant thing a trial is."

He leaned over and patted the big black cat curled up before the fire: souvenir of the "affair" at Slacktown.

"Unpleasant? Gosh, I thought it was exciting."

"You didn't know the murderer—before you knew he was one." Rocky reached for the telephone. "What's the hotel's number?"

"Six-nine," Eleanor said. "Why?"

"The usual reason, sugar. I want to call 'em. . . . Six-nine, please. . . . A man said a funny thing to me tonight. It bothers me— Clarence? Say, did a small dark fellow named Cooper come in a few minutes ago? . . . He did? Well, will you go up and see if he's all right? Make some excuse and I'll hold the wire. . . .

"Did either of you," he asked, "see any strangers in town, yesterday or today?"

"A traveling salesman," Andy said promptly. "One or two people whose faces I know but not their names."

"It isn't hard to pick out strangers here—in November," Eleanor said. "What was this man like?"

"I only got a glimpse of him. He had an accent like some of these movie stars born in the Middle West and tryin' hard to hide the fact. I'd like to know where he'd been walking from."

"How do you know he'd been walking any distance?" Andy said.

"He told me he was mud to his knees. But we do have paved streets in town. There isn't any night train, so he didn't just get in on that. And he said he was a stranger, but he knew about where the hotel should be. Also, he was plenty burned about something."

"The mud?" Eleanor said facetiously.

"I imagine," Rocky said soberly, "it was just that."

"But what did he say that worries you?"

"He asked me if I knew it's a swell night for a murder."

"Oh! Did he know you're the arm of the law here?"

Rocky looked at her approvingly. "I wondered. I told him my name but I don't know if it meant anything to him."

"Well, that's a harmless remark," Andy said. "I mean: like saying, 'Pity the poor sailors on a night like this,' or something like that."

"Maybe." Rocky rested the telephone on his chest and admired the effect of firelight and lamplight on Eleanor's red hair.

Andy's hair was red too; not a shimmering orange red like Eleanor's but a subdued copper tint. He had a thin freckled face, and his usual expression was one of alert and friendly curiosity toward the world in general. But now he was staring at the fire again and frowning unhappily. Rocky glanced toward Eleanor and found her regarding Andy with a look of motherly amusement. Well, of course she'd know if . . .

"Hello! Yes, I'm here. . . . Oh, he's all right? Thanks for your trouble, Clarence. . . . Oh, I just wanted to know if he found the hotel all right. Good night."

"What a very lame excuse," Eleanor said. "Clarence probably thinks Mr. Cooper is a desperate character. Satisfied?"

"I reckon I'll have to be."

Andy got up abruptly. "I've got to go. See you in the morning?"

"Please. When the power went off I couldn't find anything but candles to work by and it was too hard on the eyes. There's a lot of letters to get out. Good night. . . . What," Rocky demanded, "is the matter with that kid lately?"

"He's in love. No, not with me. I don't know who and—naturally—I wonder. Not with any of the girls I thought of at first. But I wouldn't mind guessing. Tonight he was telling me what a fine man his father was."

"That's true. He was well off at one time too. He had that box factory, but the depression and his investments cleaned him out before he died."

"Andy's point is that his father was one of our leading and respected citizens. And he is going to make a name for himself," Eleanor said. "He's going to become so famous he can come back here someday and snub all his old friends."

"That's a very worthy ambition. But what," Rocky said, yawning, "has that got to do with your guess as to who he's in love with?"

"Darling, you are very clever about some things but not so bright about others. This sudden harping on his claim to be counted in with the first families . . . Oh, never mind. You're half asleep and your feet are wet. Come to bed."

"With the greatest of pleasure. Only I'm not half asleep. Do you know you get prettier ever' day of your life?"

"That," Eleanor said, "is a very sensible remark." She put her head against his arm and smiled up at him. "Go on from there."

II

"Well, that's all for a while," Rocky said. "There's nothing else to do when you get that stuff typed."

The telephone rang and he reached for it. "You might as well go eat, Andy. . . . Hello . . ."

After an instant he said: "Don't go, Andy. . . . All right, Clarence; we'll be right over. Don't touch anything. . . . Go ahead and call Doc Bradley and have him c'llect the cor'ner. It'll save me time."

He put down the telephone and looked at Andy. "Don't ever ignore hunches, kid. Though I still don't see how I could stand guard on a fellow I never saw before and didn't know anything about. And still don't—"

"That one you met last night? You mean he's dead? Murdered? Gosh!"

Andy tried to assume a look of frowning gravity but he reminded Rocky of a dog waiting eagerly to pounce on the stick he expected someone to toss in front of him. Rocky said:

"Well, here's where you get that practical experience. Get your junk together."

"Camera? Fingerprinting outfit? Chalk . . ."

With a gleam of amusement Rocky watched Andy turning out the contents of his desk drawers. "Anything you want," he said tolerantly. "You can take pictures. If," he added, "you still feel like it after you get there. . . ."

The man who had registered as Walter Cooper of San Francisco was most unpleasantly dead. Rocky grinned briefly as Andy gulped and backed involuntarily toward the door, freckles standing out on the greenish pallor of his face.

"Let the pictures go for a while," he said.

Andy gulped again. "I'll—I'll take 'em. But there's—there's a lot of blood."

"Um-hum." Rocky stood looking down at the twisted figure on the floor. The man was in his shirt sleeves and the edges of the cuffs were badly frayed. His necktie was carefully knotted to conceal a worn spot. Rocky bent and looked at the soles of the still-damp shoes beneath a chair.

"They've been half soled," he muttered. "I don't reckon he was exactly rollin' in wealth. . . . Well, Clarence?"

Clarence Monson, stooped and sallow, with thinning hair and Woolworth spectacles balanced halfway down his long nose, sat on the edge of a chair. It wasn't at all "well", he said. Though he couldn't see how he was to blame, Mr. Derby would probably think he was, when he got back from the city.

"Derby's away?"

"Yes, and that makes us shorthanded. I have to work about eighteen hours," Clarence said resentfully. "I was on duty when this fellow came in. When you phoned I came up and asked if the lamp burned all right. He said some things about the electricity being off. That was nine-thirty.

"Well, I wondered why you wanted to check on him, but he looked all right to me. I was on duty all night and didn't expect anyone to come in so I planned on sleeping some."

"Of course," Rocky said soothingly. "You can't stay awake forever."

"That's what I tell Mr. Derby. Well, when I sit down behind the desk, I can't see over it. Anyway, I did sleep. No one used their phone. The front door was open, in case somebody traveling late in a car might come in. I'd count on hearing that. But I didn't hear anything or any shots."

"Not surprisin', considering the storm. The lights were off all night, weren't they?"

"Till I dozed off, about eleven. I just had one lamp, turned low. When I woke up, about five, the lights were back on. So then I sat at the desk till six-thirty, then got Ella to take my place till noon. I had a bite to eat and went to sleep.

"I meant," Clarence said regretfully, "to look in at that fellow but I was so tired I forgot. When I woke up it was the first thing I thought about. I asked in the dining room and he hadn't had breakfast there. So then—"

"Just a minute," Rocky said. "I think I hear Doc and the cor'ner."

Whenever you heard noises like a small steam engine warming up for action you knew that Dr. Bradley was approaching. Brookdale people said he was a fair-to-middling doctor when he was sober and a crackerjack when he had half-a-dozen drinks in him. He lumbered into the room, his ancient hat over one eye, vest proclaiming that he'd had gravy for dinner. Lorenzo Sloane drifted in behind him and stood looking like the undertakers of all the world compressed into one typical specimen.

"Well, this is nice," the doctor said. "Very nice. What's wrong with you, Andy? You're green around the gills. Have to get over that if you're aiming to be a detective or a doctor. Like to see you watch your first operation."

Andy was more red than green, now, but you couldn't talk back to the man who'd spanked your first breath into you. He set his lips and began to examine his camera. Rocky drew Clarence out into the hall.

"Go on with what you were sayin'."

"Well, when I found he hadn't been down for lunch, either, I wondered if he'd sneaked out without paying his bill. So I came up here, found the door unlocked and him just the way he is now. I locked up and phoned you."

"Not many people stayin' here now?"

"You know what business is after summer's over. There's just the two schoolteachers, Mrs. Gray from the bank, and Mr. Cronin and Mr. Arney. You know all of them."

Rocky nodded. Cronin was the latest editor of the Brookdale *Sun* and Arney the town's only lawyer. He knew the women by sight and was willing to believe, temporarily, that none of them had known Walter Cooper.

"Anyway," Clarence went on, "the women were all gone, it being Friday. The teachers go away a lot over the week end and Mrs. Gray went to Merton for the night."

"That makes it nice. How many besides you on the hotel staff?"

"Just the cook and two girls, now. The girls wait on table. Ella sleeps at home; she's got a mother here. She didn't get around to doing this room because she was at the desk, for me. The others sleep downstairs at the back and they won't know anything about it."

"I b'lieve you. How much coal oil was in the lamp you put in his room?"

"Well—it'd been used a little since it was filled, so it wasn't quite full. It was burned out this morning, though, so no one turned it out."

"I noticed the wick was pretty well charred," Rocky said. "Well, you don't need to stick aroun' any longer, Clarence."

"I suppose when Mr. Derby gets back he'll—Oh, there is just one thing, Rocky."

"What's that?"

"Why, that fellow's face bothers me. Last night the lights were poor but, now I get another look at him, I'd swear I've seen him before. Here, maybe. I don't know where else. I've been here fifteen years and I only go to Sonora for vacations at my sister's."

"He wasn't at all unusual looking. You see his type in the movies."

"No," Clarence said stubbornly, "it's not that. I don't go to the movies. If I really have seen him, I'll remember where. But it must have been quite a while ago. I'll keep thinking and let you know."

"Did you think he was mad about something last night?"

"He certainly wasn't very pleasant. I said I hadn't heard a car drive up and he laughed, real nasty, and said: 'There wasn't any car.' I said that was too bad and he laughed again and says: 'Yes, it will be.'"

"He said 'will be' and not 'is'?" Rocky asked quickly.

"Yes, he did. That's funny, come to think of it. When I showed him up here I saw how muddy he was and spoke about it. He just scowled and didn't say anything. I wondered how he got all that mud."

"So do I. He didn't say where he'd come from?"

"He signed the register as from San Francisco, but you know there wasn't any train or bus for him to come in on. I did say, seeing how muddy he was and remembering he said there wasn't any car: 'Have a breakdown?' but he didn't answer, so I gave up. But," Clarence repeated, starting down the hall, "I've seen him before—some place."

Rocky returned to the bedroom in time to hear Dr. Bradley's: "I don't know how you think those pictures will be any good, Andy, taken inside."

"He's taken good ones before now," Rocky said. "Well?"

"Oh, he's dead," the doctor said unnecessarily. "Quite a while. Ten to twelve hours. Shot three times."

"Three!"

"Yep. Two of them mightn't have killed him. But the other would, so what the hell? Shot at close quarters. Looks to me like it was a small gun. Tell you more when I get the bullets. They're all in him. No gun in the room, I see. Anything else you want to know?"

"How old would you say he is?"

"Oh, about thirty-five. Maybe younger, maybe older. Anything else? Well, pack him over to my place. I'm going to finish my dinner."

"I'll go with you," the coroner said. "Would four suit you all right for the inquest, Rocky? Might as well get it over." Lorenzo Sloane considered his only responsibility as coroner was to hold inquests immediately, get them over quickly—and, if possible, give the deceased a "high-class funeral" from his own undertaking parlors.

Rocky hesitated, then: "That will do," he said. "You'd better send your hearse over here, Lorenzo."

He sat down on the bed and lifted Cooper's one piece of luggage, a worn Gladstone bag, up beside him. "You can look for fingerprints if you want to, Andy. You'll have to take Clarence's and the maids'. Find out how many of 'em have been in here lately."

"Sure." Andy was beginning to feel quite at home in the room since he had recovered from the

shock of discovering violent death to be even ug-
lier than he had supposed. "Say, he was shot from
the front, wasn't he?"

"Yeah—at close range. You heard what Doc
said."

"Well then, he must have known whoever did
it. He must," Andy said eagerly, "have stood here
talking without being afraid—or he wouldn't have
let 'em get close."

"Colossal, Sherlock. Someone's been through
this bag," Rocky said, frowning into its jumbled
contents. "I think some labels have been soaked
off it too. There's a piece left but I can't make out
any name. Well, that means he traveled."

He laid on the bed a scanty stock of worn un-
derwear, half a pint of whisky, one soiled and two
clean shirts, a cheap leather shaving kit, an un-
opened pack of cigarettes, and Thursday's early
morning edition of the San Francisco *Examiner*.

"It looks like he left the city on Wednesday
night's train."

"It's Thursday's paper," Andy objected.

"This is the mornin' edition that comes out
the evenin' before. And the only eastbound train
leaves Oakland about 9 P.M. Also, he's changed
his shirt once. Say he put on a clean one when
he got in, Thursday, and the one he's got on now,

yesterday . . . I'd like to know where he's been these last two days. Hand me his coat."

Andy brought the coat and vest that were hanging over the back of a chair. "Think these have been looked over?"

"Probably. You can't tell." Rocky tossed the contents of coat and vest pockets onto the bed: cigarettes, a cheap watch, soiled handkerchiefs, a knife with broken blade, a small comb and nail file in a green case, a wallet containing four five-dollar bills.

"No," Rocky repeated, "he wasn't rollin' in wealth. Not to take a trip like this. No checkbook, either, or any return ticket. None of the junk men carry, like old letters and bills. No identification cards—"

"Maybe he didn't bother with things like that."

"Most people have something of the kind on 'em in case of accident." Rocky bent down and went through the man's trouser pockets, finding only a small box of aspirin and several dollars in silver. He straightened up as someone tapped on the door.

"Oh, it's you," he said to Lorenzo Sloane's son and assistant. "Yes, you can take him away."

He walked into the bathroom and Andy followed quickly. "It's funny," he ventured, "that he'd take a room with bath if he didn't have much money."

"He probably thought a hot bath might keep him from catchin' cold. Besides, being mud all over—"

"There's an awful lot of mud in the bedroom."

"Yes, but you can't prove there's more than he tracked in himself."

Andy glanced about the bathroom. "Golly, what a mess!" he said, looking at the dried brown sediment in bowl and bathtub.

"He washed off his shoes and some of the mud off his pants. Used three . . . They do just give you three towels here, don't they?" Rocky said slowly.

"I never stayed here."

"I have. One dinky bath and two hand towels is the rule. And there's five here. Turn on the water." Rocky emptied the contents of the container by the washstand into the tub. "They're so dirty you can't see the names on 'em—and I want to."

"Gosh, look at the mud roll out of them," Andy said, leaning over the tub. "There's one with Brookdale Hotel on it."

"And two more." Rocky turned the water off and went fishing. "Here: this says Hotel Warren. Well, that might be any place but I'm hoping it was where he stayed in the city."

He hung the towel over the rack at one end of the tub. "And here's another."

He stood still, staring at the square of white linen; fine, smooth linen with a beautifully worked monogram. He pronounced its letters slowly:

"'L.M.G.' Does that mean anything to you?"

"Why, how can we tell?" Andy said. "If he was in the habit of collecting guest and hotel towels—"

"Some fellows are. I wonder if he left anything else in here." Rocky searched the room with a methodical thoroughness that met with Andy's approval as much as his lack of interest in fingerprints did not.

"Nothin' here," he said finally. "You look through the bureau drawers in the bedroom again while I take another look at his things."

"Are we looking for something definite?" Andy said.

"I'm not. But he may 've collected something else interestin' or had some things with him that whoever searched his grip missed."

"He may have mussed up his suitcase himself."

"Maybe. Nothing in the bureau? Well, try to pry open the back of his watch. I put it over there. But even if he threw things into his bag in a hurry a man don't usually mess up his only clean shirts like these are—"

"I got it open and—look!" Andy said. "It's a picture in the back of it! See . . ."

The snapshot was of a plump blonde with ridiculously infantile curls, smiling toothily. She had inscribed herself in a flowing hand: "To Wallie. Yours Forever, Pearl."

Rocky said: "Nice going," and for a moment sat looking at the sheet of note paper in his hands. It was expensive paper, the color of rich cream. At its top was engraved a picture of a pioneer blockhouse and underneath, in square letters, The Stockade.

He held it up, finally, so that Andy could see it. "This had slipped between the pages of that newspaper. Does that monogram mean anything to you now?" he said.

Andy's jaw sagged. "Lucilla Mary Graydon! Oh gosh, Rocky—there's got to be some mistake! The Graydons—"

"Yeah, I know. The royal fam'ly of Brookdale. Sanctified an' sacred," Rocky drawled. "But just why it's got to be a mistake is somethin' you'll have to explain to me: carefully and in words of one syllable."

III

The Graydons, Andy said, were—well, they were the Graydons. They had made Brookdale what it was.

"And what," Rocky inquired amiably, "*is* Brook-dale?"

Andy ignored this. Perhaps Brookdale was only the county seat of a small mountain county but it had a very impressive courthouse which probably would not have been built if it hadn't been for Joshua Graydon.

"He used his influence an' the taxpayers put up the money," Rocky said. "He helped get this hotel built too—and sold 'em the lumber for it."

Well, Andy said, since Rocky had mentioned the Graydon Lumber Company . . . Of course they'd lost money after '30, but they were getting along all right now. It was one of the oldest companies in the county. Of course it was a small concern but it had always been well known.

And besides dabbling in mining, hadn't Joshua Graydon built the branch line from the main railroad, from Brookdale Junction into Brookdale? The Graydon Southern: one of the shortest independent roads in the United States.

"Six miles of the worst track ever known to man, which nobody who can help it ever rides on because it's been known to take an hour to get here from the Junction. Another thing old Josh sold for a profit. He was quite a lad but he's dead, so what's he got to do with Cooper—who is also dead? Stop talkin' like a Chamber of Commerce, Andy, and get down to facts."

Well, Andy asked rather heatedly, wasn't Rocky ignoring facts? The Graydons never mixed with Brookdale people. They lived one mile and might as well have lived one hundred miles from the town. Of course they had guests from the city and gave formal dinners among themselves: Lucilla Graydon and Bertha Graydon Hobart entertained the Ellis Hadleys and the Earl Graydons and Dewey Stinson . . .

"Spare me the society notes of the Brookdale *Sun.* I know there was never in the world a tighter-closed clique than that bunch. I've never seen the women, except sweeping through town in a closed car. Which one of the bunch," Rocky said pleasantly, "is a friend of yours? The only one you didn't mention: the girl? What's her name?"

"Melinda Graydon. Well, what if I do know her?" Andy said sulkily. "She—if you knew her, you'd see she proves what I've been saying. That the Graydons are—are cultured people."

"I begin to see, now, what Eleanor was guessin'," Rocky said obscurely—to Andy. "How'd you meet Melinda Graydon? She didn't go to school here. As the *Sun* had it, Miss Melinda Graydon recently graduated from Miss Somebody-or-other's School in Piedmont."

"I met her when we were kids. Dad had to see old Mr. Graydon on business once and took me with him. Linda had run away and was playing outside the mill. Of course I'd forgotten all about her—till she came to the trial and we met there."

Rocky raised his eyebrows. "Was she at a vulgar affair like a murder trial?"

"Twice. She didn't tell anyone where she was going. She's not like the others; not high hat, I mean. She wanted to take a business course but they wouldn't let her."

"And since the trial?"

"Oh—well, I see her sometimes. She goes walking or out in a car and if we happen to meet on the road—well, we just happen to, that's all," Andy said defiantly. "Of course they'd have a fit—Miss Lucilla and Mrs. Hobart. But Linda knows I come from just as good a family as hers."

"Well, you can't expect a man in love to be consistent."

"We aren't—in love! I like her and— What has being consistent got to do with it?"

"I thought you'd just said there aren't any fam'lies aroun' here good as the Graydons and that they're completely above suspicion. They aren't," Rocky said. "I don't say one of that bunch out at The Stockade killed Cooper, but he certainly was there long enough to c'llect one of their towels and a sheet of their writin' paper."

"I guess you can't get around that," Andy admitted. "He must have dropped in to see them—"

"Washed his hands, swiped a guest towel an' put it in his satchel, and then dropped into a bedroom to help himself to some writin' paper?" Rocky suggested blandly. "At least, I'd guess that paper came from a guest room. What was he doin' the rest of the time since he left the city?"

"Well, even if he did stay with the Graydons for a while, that doesn't mean someone here in town didn't kill him."

"No. Only I wonder who besides myself, Clarence and whoever he'd been with before he landed in town knew that he was at the hotel. He may 've called on someone, soon as he hit town, before he met me. I had the impression he'd just got in and had come straight down the main street, where I met him, tryin' to find the hotel. He was comin' from the right direction to have walked from The Stockade."

"You don't think the Graydons would throw a guest out in a storm to walk into town, do you?" Andy said scornfully.

"No, and that makes it all the more interestin'. He was plenty burned about something. What would make a guy madder than to get thrown out on his ear to walk a mile in the rain?

"But we're wastin' time. Get those pictures developed soon as you can. I want a copy of the best one."

"I'll do it right away, unless there's something else—"

"Go over the room for fingerprints. Talk to the hotel staff. I want to make inquiries about him aroun' town right away."

"Well, I hope you find out something," Andy said. "Because if you don't . . . Well, I mean: it stands to reason somebody—besides the Graydons—must have known him."

"Are you trying, from the depths of your worldly wisdom, to tell me that to claim the Graydons are involved in a murder case is apt to be dang'rous—for me?"

Andy tugged at the lobe of one large red ear. It was a habit he had, when embarrassed or baffled, and just now he was both. Something in Rocky's tone made him feel his last remark had been a mistake. And the way Rocky had phrased his question—well, it wasn't quite the way he usually talked.

"I—I didn't mean . . . Well, of course you can't find out anything that isn't there to find out," he stammered. "And of course the Graydons are subject to the law, just like anybody else."

"You might remember that," Rocky said gravely. "Are you goin' along with me on this or not?"

"You mean . . . Why, of course I am! Just because I don't see how they could have anything
to do with this—anything criminal—and I think
Linda's a swell girl and I'd hate to see her mixed
up in—"

"When did you see her last? No, never mind,"
Rocky said hastily. "If you'd known about Cooper
from her you wouldn't have been so anxious to get
over here to investigate."

"Gosh, I never thought about that! But I hav-
en't seen her for a week. I—well, I don't like this
sort of—of sneaking. And neither does she. Not
that—"

"All right. I'm goin' on now. Look over this
room a little more thoroughly and lock it up. I
may not get to the inquest so you'd better go and
see what happens. Nothin' will. If we don't con-
nect before, I'll see you tonight."

Rocky meditated, walking through the hotel
lobby and out toward the main street of town,
upon the peculiar attitude of any small town toward its aristocracy. Brookdale resented the Graydons, the Hadleys and Dewey Stinson. They said:
"Too stuck up ever to come to any town doings.
Send the servants in to do their shopping—what

they buy here. Dress for dinner every night . . . Wouldn't it make you laugh?"

But they also said, to out-of-town people: "You've heard of the Graydons, haven't you? Oh yes, they live here." And if Miss Lucilla Graydon's cook telephoned that she would like to have a cake of yeast at once, the delivery boy jumped into his truck and headed for The Stockade at full speed.

It wasn't, Rocky admitted, going to be an easy job to question the Graydons. He remembered Jake Thompson, whom he'd succeeded as sheriff, saying: "I've never had any dealings with that outfit. They'd be a tough proposition to handle. They're like in a book; all cooped up out there together. You'd think they'd get on each other's nerves.

"Old Graydon," Jake added, "was a good guy—when he wanted to be. It wouldn't do to ask how he made his money, but he had guts. More 'n the younger generation has. I'd hate to ever 've had to buck old Josh. But the bunch that's left kind of overestimates their importance."

Rocky was inclined to agree with Jake. The Graydons might be Brookdale's most prized and peculiar appendage but they really did not count for much in the town and certainly not in the county. Their mill was small and the average mill-hand is a transient worker. Joshua Graydon very

probably had been able to make county officials
roll over and play dead but it was doubtful if his
son even knew their names.

Still, remembering Earl Graydon's supercilious
air and Dewey Stinson's more pleasant condescen-
sion, Rocky shook his head. It was not going to
be easy to talk to them. And the women would be
harder to deal with than the men. Women always
were.

He had reached the end of the long business
street and the so-called roundhouse where the
Graydon Southern's one engine rested between
trips to the Junction. Harry Carpenter, senior
and only conductor on the road, was sitting on
the steps of the barnlike building, chewing at his
pipe. Rocky lighted a cigarette and sat down beside him.

"How's the passenger business?" he asked.

"Passengers are a nuisance," Mr. Carpenter stated. "Always in a hurry. One the other morning that
kept bellyaching about the way the train ran."

"What mornin' was that?"

"Thursday."

"I s'pose you'd remember him? He was likely
the first you've had in three months."

"The first pay passenger in God knows how
long," Carpenter said. "The hotel car's stopped
meetin' the train now, so—"

"What'd this fellow look like?"

"Small, with a mustache and white teeth."

"Mind steppin' over to Lorenzo Sloane's about four and takin' a look at him?"

"He at Lorenzo's? Sure, I'll go," Carpenter said stolidly. "Did he die natural? . . . No? Well, I didn't like his looks. Reminded me of a guy tried to sell me a dollar diamond ring in the city once. Said it was worth five hundred."

Rocky grinned. "Was it?"

"No: it was just plain glass."

"Well—did you talk to this fellow?"

"I asked him was he visitin' friends. He says: no, not exactly. I told him we had a good hotel here. He says he knew that but he wasn't stayin' there."

"See where he went after you got in?"

"Straight toward town. Oh yes, he asked what was the nearest rest'rant. I told him Pete's Place."

Rocky stood up. "All right: you tell Lorenzo, if he asks you, why I sent you over but that your evidence don't need to be taken at the inquest."

Pete, a pimply youth surrounded by an odor of burning grease, leaned over his counter and said: sure, he remembered that guy. He ate his breakfast and didn't have anything to say except to ask where there was a garage or a taxi in town. He—Pete—told him to try Jim Robbins.

"What time was he in here?" Rocky asked.

"Well—about nine-thirty. I noticed his satchel and thought he must be off the train. He acted like he was in a hurry. No, I never saw him before—or again."

Rocky went on, drew blank at the newsstand opposite the courthouse where, so far as anyone remembered, no dark, mustached stranger had stopped to buy cigarettes or a newspaper. Farther down the street Jim Robbins was putting air into a tire in front of his garage.

"That fellow?" he said in answer to Rocky's question. "Sure, he was here. I've wondered about him."

"Why?"

"He wanted to go to The Stockade and he had a satchel but he certainly didn't look like the kind of person who ever visits the Graydons, even if they didn't meet all their guests at the Junction."

"What time was he in?"

Robbins frowned. "Let's see . . . It was after ten; say about ten-fifteen. I'd promised Bill Elkins his car by noon so I looked at the clock to see if I had time to take this guy to The Stockade. Well, I did—"

"What'd you talk about?"

"We didn't. I'm not much of a talker. I was curious, though, and I asked if they were expecting him. He laughed and said they weren't—like it amused him. When we got there he paid me off and said he wouldn't need me any more."

"Did you see if he went toward the houses or just into the mill office?"

"He told me to let him out at The Stockade gate. Then he seemed to be waiting for me to leave so I did. He could have gone into The Stockade to any of the houses or across the road to the mill."

"Will you go over to Lorenzo's and take a look at him? . . . Yes, he's dead. And I'd be obliged if you'd keep still about this. I'd rather no one knew, for a while, that he went out there."

"I get you," Robbins said. "And I can keep my mouth shut. Your car's all right if you want to use it."

Rocky was frowning as he got into the car and for an instant he sat still, without starting it. Nine-thirty to ten-fifteen was three quarters of an hour and that was considerably more time than Walter Cooper had needed to eat breakfast and walk on to Robbins' garage. Particularly if, as Pete said, he had been in a hurry. Pete could put a plate of ham and eggs before you in five minutes flat.

He must ask Pete what time Cooper had left the lunchroom. The man hadn't bought anything at the newsstand and it wasn't likely he had stopped at any other store on his way to the garage. It should be possible, eventually, to find out if he had gone

to see someone in Brookdale before starting for
The Stockade.

Well—Rocky put his foot on the starter—it was
an unimportant point. Yet a little bell in the back
of his brain rang the warning that it was not. He
thought uneasily: I'll clear it up this afternoon.

He would have been spared an unpleasant time
of groping in the dark if he had known then, or
in twenty-four hours, where Walter Cooper had
gone when he left Pete's Place. But the one man
who could tell him that seldom talked to his fellow townsmen because he was almost totally deaf.

IV

Linda stood at a window with her back to the room
and looked out at the gray afternoon. Miss Lucilla
poured herself a fourth cup of tea and wondered
what was keeping Earl and Ellis at the mill.

"Dad said he had a lot of work to do and probably wouldn't get over today," Rose Hadley said.

Linda remarked, without turning: "I don't know
why they should come over for tea. This isn't England. Of course Earl and Dewey never do enough
work to prevent their coming."

Dewey whistled and helped himself to cake.
"Our little Linda seems to be in a very bad humor.
Tell Uncle Dewey all about it, darling."

"I'm not your little Linda and you aren't my uncle—thank goodness. I am suffocated with relatives as it is. And tea is an absolutely unnecessary meal. We all eat too much and don't take enough exercise."

"I'm sure you do, dear," Anette said. "As long as you go on walking so religiously you needn't worry about your figure."

Linda looked at her Uncle Earl's wife with open dislike. Anette dealt in maliciously suggestive remarks that made you wonder how much she really knew. It wouldn't work this time, Linda thought, because she didn't particularly care how much Anette did know. But Aunt Bertha was saying:

"It's very dull for Linda here, Anette. She's not used to it."

"*She* doesn't have to stay here, so I refuse to waste pity on her," Anette said coolly. "She could have accepted any one of a dozen invitations—"

"I'm tired of visiting people. . . . Aunt Bertha, it isn't going to rain."

"I think it is," Bertha Hobart said. "And if you should be caught in a downpour like we had last night—"

"Oh, so that's it," Dewey said. "Linda is 'suffering from enn-ui.' That's what you used to say when you were about thirteen."

Linda smiled at him reluctantly. It was very difficult to be angry with Dewey, even when his look at her said: "I know something but I won't tell." You couldn't be angry for very long with a person who ignored petulance and sarcasm. Of course Dewey must have had to learn, a long time ago, how to get along pleasantly with a community of women.

"I don't see," she said, "why I should be expected to die of pneumonia if I get my feet wet. Other people don't. Or is royalty formed of more delicate clay than the common herd?"

Miss Lucilla chuckled.

"Sometimes," Mrs. Hobart said, "I think it was a mistake to send Linda to Miss Bannister's. She seems to have picked up the most extraordinary ideas and ways of talking. Why do you, lately, refer to us as the 'royal family', Linda?"

"I thought you knew. That's what Mrs. Allan called us."

"And who," Anette said, "is Mrs. Allan?"

Linda laughed. "That tone of devastating indifference doesn't affect me, Anette. And I doubt if it would Mrs. Allan. She's the sheriff's wife; the new sheriff—"

"Have we a new sheriff?"

"You should borrow Clara's Brookdale *Sun* sometimes. Yes, there is. He wasn't officially elected until this month but he's been acting sheriff for more than a year. He was a railroader once, and he's not old, like Mr. Thompson was. And his wife is the prettiest thing. She has gorgeous red hair and she seems," Linda said wistfully, "so—so alive and happy. A girl at Miss Bannister's had an older sister who'd gone to school with her. Mrs. Allan's father was quite well to do but when he died she had to earn her own living and she was a nurse when she married Mr. Allan. I'd like to be a nurse."

"So would most girls—till they try it," Miss Lucilla said briefly.

"But why the crack about the royal family?" Dewey asked.

"That was funny. Aunt Lucilla decided we should go to the Ladies' Aid bazaar because Miss Jewett is president. We swept in, bought a few pieces of hideous fancywork, and swept out again. I was at the tail end of the procession and I heard Mrs. Allan whisper: 'Having opened the garden party, the Royal Family made an impressive exit, loyally cheered by the villagers.'"

Dewey snorted and put his plate down hastily. Rose Hadley echoed his laugh rather uncertainly and Miss Lucilla chuckled again.

"She sounds," Mrs. Hobart said impersonally, "quite typical. That sort of cheap wit—"

"It wasn't cheap," Linda said. "And not a bit the kind of thing Brookdale people usually say about us. We were ridiculous and she knew it. As a matter of fact, her husband is a lot more important person than any of us."

"I've seen him," Rose said unexpectedly. "He's very good looking."

"Better looking than I am?" Dewey said, putting one hand lightly over hers.

Rose blushed. She always did when Dewey touched her. Linda supposed Rose couldn't help doing it, but if she was going to marry Dewey in the spring it was time she stopped acting like the almost obsolete "shy schoolgirl." Still, she probably couldn't help that, either.

"N-no, of course not," Rose said quickly. "Or— in a different way, though you're both blond . . ."

Dewey laughed. "In a very different way," he said. "Mr. Allan is a handsome barbarian with a Texas drawl and his own ideas regarding the king's English."

"I'll grant you the drawl," Linda said. "But he can speak the king's English when he wants to. I heard him."

"You heard him?" Bertha Hobart said.

It was Linda's turn to flush. "There happened to be a very interesting murder trial here not long ago. I was there twice."

She thought: there, that's one in the eye for Anette if she thought she was going to have the pleasure of telling that.

"I was there twice," she repeated. "And I wouldn't like, from my observation of Mr. Allan, to have him investigate any murder I'd committed."

There were times when the words you spoke were like stones dropped one by one into a still pond. You heard them—plunk! plunk!—and the water stirred into widening circles and after that there was silence again.

As a child, when she'd said something that was considered "unladylike" she'd been made to feel as she did now. But this time, Linda thought, she hadn't said anything that should be met with that sort of silence. They had to talk about something: heaven knew there were few enough fresh topics of conversation among them.

"Since we're discussing village characters," Anette asked sweetly, "who is the gawky redhead-ed boy who bowed to you with such Chesterfield-ian grace the other night when we rode through town?"

Before she answered, Linda raked Anette with the merciless glance of nineteen for thirty-six. There was too much of Anette, she decided; too many soft curves, too much lipstick on a beauti-fully shaped mouth, too much softly curling black hair, too many ruffles and insets of lace on her clinging lavender gown. She was still what Aunt Bertha had called her when Earl married her: "just a trifle common—"

"That was a friend of mine," Linda said deliberately. "Andrew Duncan. You may remember the Duncan box factory."

"I remember," Miss Lucilla said. "Duncan was a fine man. His father, I suppose?"

"Nevertheless, I do think," Anette said with her brittle high-pitched laugh, "that Linda chooses queer friends."

"It must run in the family then. I never chose anything like the last specimen Earl produced. Or was it you who was responsible for him, Dewey? You do talk to people when you get away from the family estate, but whatever led Earl to exchange two words with him . . ."

Linda stopped. Did Dewey suppose she wouldn't catch the quick glance he and Aunt Bertha exchanged: a look that was, on his part, a queer mixture of amusement and embarrassment. And now Anette was trying to catch his eye but he wouldn't look at her. There had been something very odd about their late house guest and Linda intended to find out what it was.

"I wasn't here when he arrived but, if he was Earl's friend, why stay here, when Aunt Lucilla wasn't well?"

"But I still have only one maid, my dear," Anette said. "Besides, he was Dewey's friend too."

"I've seen worse than Cooper," Dewey said quickly. "He really isn't a bad fellow when you get to know him—"

"Perhaps—if he's the kind you want to get to know. I don't like knee-patters, myself."

"Linda!"

"Well, he did, Aunt Bertha. Or tried to."

Miss Lucilla stirred restlessly in her high-backed chair. "You should have told me."

"I was quite able to handle him. But Clara says he was wandering around downstairs Thursday night and I'd like to know why."

Linda stopped again. They were all interested; queerly interested, it seemed to her. After all, what she was telling them could not be very important.

"Clara wanted a bite to eat," she went on. "You know Clara. Then she came into the dining room to get a little brandy 'to settle her stomach' and heard Mr. Cooper in the hall. He told her he'd been looking for a book but he didn't have one with him, Clara says. Perhaps Grandfather's library was too much for him. But he asked me if I'd been here when Grandfather died. Did they know each other?"

"No, he didn't know your grandfather," Miss Lucilla said.

"Well, I thought Clara must have complained to you. That would account for his leaving so suddenly." No one made any answer to this. "Well, why did he leave?" Linda said impatiently.

"He remembered," Dewey said, "that he had important business in town."

It was his suavest tone and it made Linda feel very, very young. She turned her back on the room once more, muttering: "*Very* important business, to take him out in that storm."

Again, no one spoke. She stared out at the frost-seared side lawns; at the hard, beaten path that led to Earl Graydon's house. Her grandfather had built for himself a smaller house than this one but, like it, a replica of a pioneer blockhouse.

The Hadleys' house was the twin of Earl's; they had been built at the same time, when Earl and Anette married and Ellis Hadley became manager of the Graydon Lumber Company. And then Joshua Graydon built the log wall, higher than a tall man's head, shutting them off from road and surrounding pines.

Linda hated the high wall. Perhaps her father had, too, and her mother had never been inside it. That might be why she had spent half her childhood running away from nurse or governess into the cool green woods . . .

She drummed on the windowpane until Anette said:

"Oh, for pity's sake, Linda! You set my nerves on edge."

"Everyone's nerves seem to be a little on edge."

"It's the weather," Bertha Hobart said. Then: "Yes, Moody—what is it?"

Lucilla Graydon had let the butler go after her father's death, remarking that she was tired of looking at his wooden face. But Moody had stayed on and Linda often thought that no one could possibly have been more wooden faced than Moody.

She had a habit, exasperating to Linda, of folding her hands over a bulky white-aproned waist and staring at a point just over your head while she was talking to you. She seemed to be looking fixedly at a large dark portrait of Joshua Graydon as she announced:

"There's a Mr. Allan to see you."

"Whom does he wish to see, Moody? And why?" Mrs. Hobart said.

"Any of you. He asked if Mr. Earl was in. I told him I didn't know. I think," Moody said expressionlessly, "that he intends to see somebody."

Dewey rose quickly. "I'll talk to the fellow, Bertha. I can't imagine—"

"No," Miss Lucilla said. "Bring him in here. He probably wouldn't be satisfied with you, Dewey. Well, Moody—what are you standing there for?"

Moody glanced uncertainly at Mrs. Hobart and then went out with heavy and unhurried tread. In an instant she said: "Mr. Allan, ma'am," and shut the door sharply. It was unreasonable, Linda realized, to be suddenly so anxious that this tall backwoods sheriff should hold his own against Graydons and near Graydons. Perhaps it was disloyal and, as Earl had once charged, she wasn't a "true Graydon." But she'd suffered, too, from their "grand manner." It was only lately that she had begun to feel their disapproval wasn't important and that they were sometimes a little ridiculous.

Rocky Allan's nostrils had widened a little as if he were faintly conscious of a bad odor. He would be, coming in from outside into this stifling hot room with its smells of smoking coal, rich food, Anette's heavy gardenia perfume.

And Anette was—well, she was funny. And disgusting. Linda knew that slow, speculative narrowing of Anette's eyes. She'd seen her glance at so many men in just that way. The French chauffeur Earl had discharged last summer . . .

Abruptly, Lucilla Graydon got out of her chair, seized the tongs and broke a lump of smoking coal into small pieces. "Well?" she said. "What can we do for you, Mr. Allan?"

There had been time, in the silence that followed his entrance, for Rocky to look about the room and at every person there. Linda wondered if he had deliberately forced one of them to speak first. She rather thought he had, though he said:

"It's hard to see you all in here after comin' in from outside. You're Miss Graydon?"

"Yes. You wanted to see me?"

"Any of you. I want to ask you about a man named Walter Cooper who was visitin' you."

"Cooper? What's he been doing?" Dewey said easily. "He isn't in trouble, is he?"

"He's *a* trouble," Rocky said. "He got himself killed last night at the hotel. We know he'd been out here, so it looks like you're the only ones who can tell us about him."

"Oh, but he had friends in town," Anette said. "Who were they, Dewey? I'm so stupid about names."

"I'm sure I don't know."

Anette reddened but she said meekly: "I must have been mistaken then." Her original lie might have been very stupid but she didn't ignore the warning of Dewey's discourteous answer. "After all, I hardly spoke to the man."

"He said he didn't know anyone in Brookdale . . ." Rose stopped, twisting her fingers together nervously. "I—I just remembered I'd asked him that . . ."

Dewey smiled at her reassuringly. "I really hadn't given it any thought, Mr. Allan, but if Cooper told Miss Hadley he didn't know anyone in Brookdale, that settles it. Is it important?"

"Don't you think it might be?"

"Sit down," Miss Lucilla said. "Well, stand up if you prefer. I'll tell you what we know about Cooper which is very little. He was a very casual acquaintance of my brother Earl. Where did you meet him, Dewey?"

"In San Francisco this summer. We were staying at the Palace and we—well, we got into a poker game, Bertha." His smile at her was a charming plea for tolerance. "Earl didn't want to tell you that."

Linda heard her own voice saying: "I didn't know . . ." She stopped but it was too late; Rocky's eyes shifted to her instantly.

"Didn't know what?"

"That—that Earl plays poker."

"I've confessed it isn't generally known," Dewey said. "But we played with Cooper, among others. I'll have to admit, too, that we'd all had two or three over the limit and we were ready to swear undying friendship with almost anyone. Earl told

Cooper he must visit us and I seem to remember seconding the invitation very enthusiastically."

"I'd like," Linda murmured, "to see Earl when he has that many drinks in him then."

"Of course Earl forgot about it the next morning, as I did. So we were definitely embarrassed when he showed up here Thursday. He didn't seem at all the same sort we'd thought him that night. But there was nothing for it but to take him in."

"And since we have more room here than my brother has, he stayed in this house," Miss Lucilla said. "He wasn't a welcome visitor but we didn't have to put up with him very long."

"I was goin' to ask," Rocky said, "if he didn't leave rather hurriedly."

"Hurriedly? He decided he wanted to take the early morning stage to Reno, so it was more convenient for him to stay at the hotel last night," Dewey said. "So the chauffeur—Lovett—drove him in—"

"Where'd he leave him?"

"At the hotel, of course. Where else would he?"

"I happened to meet Mr. Cooper on his way to the hotel. He was walkin' and he'd been walkin' quite a ways. He was mud to his knees. I've plenty of evidence to prove that. So you didn't send him into town in a car, Mr. Stinson."

V

Dewey continued, for an instant, to lean graceful-
ly against the back of Rose Hadley's chair. Then
he stood erect and smiled engagingly.

"Well, that's very inconvenient," he said. "So
you talked to him? Did he—"

"He didn't tell me why he was walkin'. But I
don't think he was feeling very kindly towards you
all."

"N-no, I don't suppose he was. The fact is—"
Rocky's lips twitched. "Well," Dewey said quickly,
"does something amuse you?"

"I was rememberin' an old lady in a play who
says that whenever anyone starts out with 'the fact
is', it's usually the beginning of a lie."

Dewey grinned. "Has that been your experience?"

"Mostly. Go on: you were sayin' . . ."

"That the—the truth is that there was a little
unpleasantness connected with Mr. Cooper's departure from these halls. He—well, he—"

"What Dewey is trying to say, Mr. Allan, is that
the man insulted me," Anette said. "My husband
overheard him and reacted in the usual manner."

"What is the usual manner? I wouldn't know."

"How fortunate you've been, Mr. Allan." That
was Bertha Hobart. "Earl ordered the man to leave
the place instantly. If he hadn't been our guest
Earl would have thrown him out."

"Since when has Earl turned cave man?" Linda murmured.

Rocky looked at her thoughtfully and turned back to Mrs. Hobart. "If he was, as you say, your guest, didn't your hospitality extend to givin' him a ride into town?"

Mrs. Hobart's lips thinned to a straight line. "Certainly. But Lovett was having his dinner and we didn't feel—"

"We didn't feel like disturbing him simply to accommodate Cooper," Dewey said. "And Cooper refused to wait. He packed his things and rushed out into the storm without telling us what he was doing. Otherwise, I would have driven him in."

Rocky looked at Mr. Stinson with something like admiration. The man was probably the fastest liar unhung but he was so plausible that it was almost a pleasure to listen to him. Under ordinary circumstances, he thought he might have liked Stinson.

You shouldn't, he admitted, let the slim elegance of a man's tailoring, the broadness of his "a's" or even the fact that women would always call him "charming" prejudice you against him. And Dewey, at least, if he resented this questioning, was taking pains to hide the fact.

Mrs. Hobart was not. One small narrow foot beat a steady rat-tat-tat! on the carpet and her slender shoulders were wonderfully expressive of well-bred impatience. She was younger than Rocky had supposed, or did not look her age. He knew, from the Brookdale *Sun*, that Miss Lucilla had recently celebrated her fiftieth birthday. Earl Graydon was the youngest of the family and he was in his forties.

But Bertha Hobart looked a scant thirty-five. Rocky had heard her called the "beauty of the family." She had fine, delicate features, soft black hair and smooth, beautiful hands. Anette Graydon wore three glittering rings; Mrs. Hobart not one. Even to Rocky, her dull black dress, trimmed with sheer immaculate white, appeared to be what Eleanor called a "creation."

He had expected Lucilla Graydon would resemble Queen Mary for no better reason than that his one glimpse of her had showed him only a preposterously hatted figure sitting in a parked car. But not even stiff black silk, net-and-lace fichu and band of black velvet about her thick throat could make Lucilla Graydon look a *grande dame*.

She must resemble old Joshua: stocky, dark and beetle browed. Shimmering square-cut amethysts were absurd on her pudgy short-fingered hands. Her voice was gruff and deep as a man's She said:

"That's what happened. I don't claim we weren't glad to get rid of the fellow."

"What time did Cooper leave?" Rocky asked.

"Why, it must have been about eight o'clock. No, later than that," Dewey said, "because we have dinner at seven-thirty."

"And Lovett waits till you're done before he eats? It seems to me a little late—for a working man."

Dewey crushed his cigarette out with almost loving care. He needed to consider his answer carefully, Rocky thought. If he had lied about the lateness of Lovett's dinner hour, then there had been nothing to prevent the chauffeur's taking Cooper into town. But if Dewey put the time of Cooper's departure from The Stockade too early, he still was proved a liar. Because Cooper had not reached town before nine o'clock and under no circumstances should it have taken him more than half an hour to walk into Brookdale.

There was a faint gleam in Dewey's slate-gray eyes that said he recognized his dilemma and couldn't help being a little amused by it.

"Lovett does have his dinner earlier than we do," he said. "About—what time, Lucilla?"

"The servants eat at six. That's the way the cook—Clara—wants it." Miss Lucilla selected a chocolate from the large box on a table beside her. "Lovett was through his dinner by seven. But all this hullabaloo took place before that."

"You see," Dewey said, "none of the ladies except Anette knew anything about this row until it was all over. Anette had gone to speak to Earl at the office—"

"I wanted to know if he couldn't take me to Reno today. He wasn't there but Mr. Cooper was, waiting for him. So then he began to—to talk. And Earl came back . . . But we've been over all that," Anette said. "And he sent me away, so I don't know what else he said to Mr. Cooper."

"Plenty. I happened in just as he was threatening to kick Cooper out—literally. That was just before six," Dewey said, "and I knew Lovett would soon be at his dinner."

"Your reluctance to inconvenience your servants is cert'nly very commendable," Rocky said blandly.

"It isn't easy to keep servants here. Besides, I thought it would be less embarrassing for everyone for Cooper to dine with us and make his excuses afterward. Earl finally agreed and so did Cooper."

"What changed his mind? I take it he did suffer a change of heart?"

"Uh—yes. Well, Earl wasn't here and I suppose the longer Cooper thought it over, the more it rankled—having been told to leave. And I think he had a drink or two before dinner. Soon after dinner he informed me he wouldn't be beholden to us for anything and went upstairs. Linda had already gone to her room then.

"I supposed he'd gone to pack and I told the others that he was leaving. He didn't come downstairs again and when I went up to his room I found he'd cleared out. Then I told Bertha and Lucilla the whole story. Of course the storm had just started and he probably didn't realize how bad it was. He must," Dewey said regretfully, "have had two or three more drinks."

"If he did, the rain washed away the effects. He wasn't drunk when I talked to him. What was his business?"

"Oh—insurance, I think. But I suspect he wasn't employed at present. I rather expected him to borrow money from me. If he was short of funds he probably hoped to stay here for some time."

"Maybe. Only the railroad fare up here isn't exactly cheap. When'd you first meet him?"

"This summer. Well, in September, to be exact. Either the thirteenth or fourteenth. We were at the Palace those two days."

"And he was stayin' there too?"

"We supposed so. Of course he may not have been."

"And he was here most of two days without tellin' you anything about himself?"

"I'm afraid we didn't discuss personal affairs."

"What did you talk about then? What did he do with himself while he was here?"

Bertha Hobart said: "Mr. Allan, my sister has told you he was not a welcome guest. He had the freedom of the house and if he could not entertain himself . . ."

"In other words," Rocky said, "you put up with him but didn't waste any time on him. And he calmly camped down on you but didn't tell you anything about himself?"

"He told me he had no living relatives he'd ever met," Linda said. "He spoke of having an unhappy childhood. He said his father remarried and his stepmother didn't like him—and so on and so forth. He spoke of a half sister he'd been fond of but said she was dead. And he said that, until he came back recently, he hadn't been in San Francisco for years."

This girl, Rocky thought, would tell the truth, now, so far as she knew it. Later on, when she understood the full implications of his questions, she might not. She was puzzled and uneasy—and perhaps a little resentful. Whatever the others knew or were trying to hide, they had not taken her into their confidence. Perhaps they were afraid to do that and had thought she wouldn't dare tell what little she did know.

But though she looked so very young, with her silver-gilt hair and small slim body, the tilt of her chin and direct gaze of her wide-set blue eyes suggested she might have an inherent dislike for evasion. After all, she was Joshua Graydon's granddaughter.

"I thought, too," she went on, looking only at Rocky, "that he might have been an actor."

"That's funny. I had the same notion myself."

"Why?"

"His accent sounded stagy to me. Of course that was just a thought in passin': the same as his looking like most of us think actors should look. At least, a certain type that plays in English drawin'-room comedy."

"You're right," Linda said. "I think I had the same feeling about him. Just the way he balanced a teacup on his knee. Well, he'd traveled a good deal. I gathered he'd been in Mexico and the Orient. And he spoke once of 'doing one-night stands' in the Midwest. But I didn't want to interrupt to ask if he'd been an actor."

"He seems quite to have confided in you, dear," Anette said.

"He was here and—unfortunately—so was I. That was yesterday afternoon. Rose and I were in Reno until late Thursday and I stayed all night

with her. I'm afraid I didn't pay very close attention to all Mr. Cooper said."

"Did you think he knew anyone in Brookdale?"
Rocky asked.

"N-no. I don't think we even talked about
Brookdale."

Rocky turned to Rose Hadley. "When you spoke
to him about Brookdale did you ask if he'd ever
been here before?"

Rose looked appealingly at Dewey. Rocky had
been wondering, since he had first seen her, why
she wasn't pretty. She should have been; she had
small, regular features and really beautiful brown
eyes. But her mouth looked a little wilted and
her heavy weight of hair was pulled unbecomingly
straight back from ears and forehead. She fingered the clip of brilliants at the throat of her
dark straight dress until Dewey said:

"Tell him, my dear—if you know."

"I did ask him, just to be polite. He said he
hadn't ever been here before. But I wondered . . .
Later on, he said he saw they had a new theater in
Brookdale. But—but the theater there isn't so new
that you'd know it was, just by looking at it."

"It cert'nly don't glisten with newness," Rocky
agreed.

"And he asked me," Rose said conscientiously,
"if I was here when Mr. Joshua Graydon died. I
wasn't—"

"Why—that's funny! He asked me the same thing," Linda said. "But you didn't tell me when I said—"

"I started to, Linda, but I didn't want to interrupt Miss Lucilla."

Rocky turned to Miss Lucilla. "How long have your servants been with you?"

"Really, Mr. Allan, I don't see—"

Lucilla Graydon cut short her sister's protest. "Clara and Moody for about four and five years. Lovett—he's really man of all work—came in September."

Rocky frowned. Lovett was his best bet but he very probably had already been told exactly what to say. The women had been here too long not to have learned to keep their mouths shut.

He couldn't ask the really important questions and hope to be answered. He couldn't ask each of them what he was doing between nine-thirty and midnight last night. If he asked—as he wanted to do—for a detailed account of their movements during the two days Cooper had been with them, they would tell him to mind his own business. Because he had to accept, for a time, their story that Cooper had been only a very casual acquaintance.

"Do you mind if I talk to Lovett?" he said.

"I do mind! There's no reason—"

"Nonsense! Don't be silly, Bertha. Talk to Lovett," Miss Lucilla said. "Cooper may have talked to him. However, Lovett was never notified Cooper was leaving."

"Here's Earl now," Dewey said quickly. "You know Mr. Allan? He came to tell us that Cooper was killed at the hotel last night. Since he was staying with us—"

"Of course, of course. What surprising—and distressing—news. I can hardly believe it," Earl Graydon said unconvincingly. "Well, I suppose you have told Mr. Allan what little we know? What a pity we let him go to the hotel."

"You think he'd still be alive if he'd stayed here?" Rocky said. "I might as well save your time and mine, Mr. Graydon, an' tell you Mr. Stinson's already had to discard your first story. So let's hear *your* second version."

"I don't like your tone," Graydon said. "Cooper insulted my wife and I told him to leave. I'm sorry to embarrass you, Anette."

Rocky thought he had never seen anyone appear less embarrassed than Anette did. They were an odd couple; she with her look of a Follies girl who has done well for herself; Graydon with his down-at-the-corners mouth and an indescribable primness of face and manner that always seemed to Rocky to call for sideburns and muttonchop whiskers.

"Of course I am sorry to hear about Cooper," Graydon went on hastily. "It's very regrettable. Is it quite certain he didn't kill himself?"

"Because Anette repulsed him?" Linda said sweetly.

"Melinda! Don't be—vulgar. We don't know enough about him to know what his circumstances were."

"If he killed himself, he was a mighty lively corpse," Rocky said. "Because he managed to dispose of the weapon."

"Oh, in that case . . . But men have shot themselves before now and managed—"

Dewey Stinson said softly: "You damned fool!" and Rocky drawled:

"I didn't say he was shot. Funny how often people trip up on a thing like that. When'd you find out Cooper was dead?"

"I—Hadley was in town early this afternoon and he heard some details. Someone on the streets knew the man's name. Is it," Graydon said, recovering something of his usual harshly precise tone, "particularly important?"

"What do you think? I'm not surprised you did know, since news like that gets aroun' so quick. I am a little surprised you were foolish enough to try to make me think you hadn't heard about it."

"Foolish?"

"Mr. Stinson knows you were, if you don't. Because," Rocky said, "it looks like you were very
anxious for me to think your stories were told on
the spur of the moment an' that you didn't have
time to rehearse them."

Bertha Hobart rose quickly and put her hand
on an old-fashioned red bell rope. "I think we
needn't listen to any more of this," she said. "I'll
ring for Moody to show you out."

"Thanks: I can find my way out—when I go.
My mother," Rocky said mildly, "came from Virginia. Her folks were dirt poor but they all had a
very high and mighty way with them."

Miss Lucilla chuckled and bit into another
chocolate. "Sit down, Bertha. I don't think the
young man is impressed. You and Earl are acting
like damned fools. As Dewey has remarked. It's
true we did know before you got here—all of us
but Rose and Linda—that Cooper was dead. If I'd
had my way, we'd have told the truth at once. But
Earl didn't want to embarrass Anette and we did
all want to avoid publicity. Besides, we'd no way
of guessing you'd just happened to run into Cooper last night.

"But of course he might have talked at the hotel and you were fairly certain, anyway, to trace
him back to us. If you found out about Cooper's

sudden departure we would have to tell you the whole story. Earl said: 'They won't believe it.' Then he had the bright idea that you'd be more apt to if you thought we hadn't had time to concoct a story before you arrived.

"Well, we did tell you the truth." She showed strong white teeth in a sudden grin. "Finally, I should say. But think of Earl's dignity. He wouldn't fancy admitting he'd been in a casual poker game and got slightly plastered. As to the rest of it— that's not so good, either, is it? From our standpoint it's not pleasant to admit we had to show the man the door so that he went to the hotel and got himself killed."

Rocky hesitated; then shrugged resignedly. "Oh, all right," he said. "Let it go at that. We'll find out who Cooper was and what he's been doing lately."

"Is that a threat?" Earl Graydon said stiffly.

"You know better 'n I could. You needn't worry about publicity, though. I don't want to broadcast any of this for a while. I don't want reporters flockin' up here, and when it's just a strange man who got killed in a hotel, that's not worth three lines in a city paper. One of you had better come in and take a private look at Cooper, though. It'd be kind of funny if he wasn't the same man. Of course he is—"

"You may be sure none of us will talk," Earl Graydon said. "But may I inquire in what way you think we are involved in his death?"

"You're the only ones I've found who knew the man at all. He wasn't robbed and I haven't yet located any homicidal maniacs aroun' here."

"You haven't yet had time for any thorough investigation."

"Lookin' for maniacs or someone who knew Cooper? I'll do both. But even if he did know someone in town—he didn't know, himself, that he would be stayin' at the hotel last night. And there are other points. Which," Rocky said politely, "I won't bother you with today."

VI

It was good to be outside again. He carried with him the jumbled picture of a dimly-lighted, high-ceilinged room, overheated, crowded with furniture. He closed his eyes and counted tables: small tables, large tables, round tables, square tables, gilt tables, carved tables—eight of them altogether.

Eight tables, he considered, were too many for even a very large room. He doubted if one piece of the house's original furnishings had ever been retired from use. What Miss Lucilla and Mrs.

Hobart had added were just so many layers superimposed on the original foundation created by their father.

Rocky frowned at the ancient rusted cannon that for thirty-five years had guarded the square house. It wasn't right when the dead refused to die. Old Joshua had built a wall about the Graydons, willed them a way of living —and taken his own enormous vitality with him.

That wall—Rocky looked about him and drew a neat mental map. There were big double gates opening onto the county road and from there a driveway made a circle in front of the house and then ran along its left side to the garage in back.

The one building—it had originally been the stable—must serve everyone, for there were no garages back of the other two houses in the enclosure. They were to the left of the older house, separated by several hundred feet of hard earth. Each had its small lawn, brown and dying now, and its own driveway.

A stocky man with a bunch face was sitting on a bench in front of the garage. Rocky had seen Charles Lovett often enough; at the post office or in the stores. He smiled at him affably.

"They said, over at the house, that it was all right for me to talk to you. Want to confirm that?"

"I guess not. What d'you want?" Lovett said.

"How many cars have you got?"

"Four. The big sedan, Mr. Graydon's coupé, Mr. Hadley's coupé and Mr. Stinson's roadster. Miss Linda uses that as much as he does. I use one of the coupés to go after the mail and for groceries."

"I'd like to look at 'em if you don't mind."

"Well—no." Lovett got up slowly, knocked the ash from his pipe, and opened the garage doors. "There they are."

"And very clean and polished too. How often do you do that?"

"They expect me to keep them looking good. The older ladies, especially. But they don't use their car so much. I washed Mr. Hadley's car this afternoon. He was out in it this morning before it stopped raining. Left before I came out to the garage. He got stuck somewheres, he said."

"You mean he was out in it before he went to Brookdale?"

Lovett nodded. "I think he drove to Spanish River." There was a small lumber mill at Spanish River that had once been owned by Joshua Graydon and still kept connections with the Graydon Lumber Company. "I didn't know for certain he went into Brookdale later on," Lovett added. "But he came in after noon and said he was through with the car for the day."

"So none of the other cars had been out in the rain?"

"Not that I could tell. What's it matter?"

"The rain started about eight last night. Were any of the cars out in it?" Rocky persisted.

"No one stirred out of here after the rain begun. Or yesterday afternoon, either. Mr. Graydon went into town by himself about noon but that's all."

"And we hadn't had any rain for at least two weeks. . . . Where was Hadley's car parked last night?"

"Behind the sedan. I used it to go to town—but before it rained. It was easiest to get out, if that's what you mean, because there ain't room for the four of 'em in a row. Though Mr. Graydon's car would've been just as easy to get at. It was behind the roadster."

"Do they have you keep a record of mileage on the cars?"

"Just in a general way," Lovett said. "So I know when to change the oil."

"That's nice. Do all the women know how to drive? And have keys to the garage?"

"I suppose they've all got keys. I don't know. Mrs. Graydon and Mrs. Hobart know how to drive. I don't know about old Miss Graydon. I always drive the ladies everywhere."

"Where do you sleep?"

"There's what they call a guest cabin on the other side of the big house. You see—over there in them trees?"

"Um-hum. That's quite a ways from here."

"The women—Clara and Moody—didn't want a man sleepin' in the house near 'em." Mr. Lovett smiled unpleasantly. "They needn't worry, but it's dames like them is always afraid a guy might proposition them. They don't use the cabin any more and it suits me."

"It's a long ways from the driveway and the garage," Rocky said. "But anyway, it's no use askin' if you heard a car drive out late last night."

"How'd I hear anything—but thunder?"

"That's it. And you couldn't see car lights from that cabin. And even if you do have to drive pretty close to the big house to get out those gates . . . They're the only exit, aren't they?"

"Sure they are. And no one could hear a car last night. . . . Not that I know what this is all about."

"Oh, of course not," Rocky agreed. "Did you know that the fellow who was stayin' here was murdered last night?"

"We-el—when he come back the last time with the car Mr. Hadley told me. I says I didn't even know he'd left and Mr. Hadley says: 'Neither did I until this morning.'"

"You like Hadley?"

"Sure: *he's* human. I don't know anything about this Cooper," Lovett said. "We ain't encouraged to talk to the guests. . . . Here comes Mr. Hadley if you wanted to talk to him."

Rocky looked at his watch. "Five-thirty. He must keep pretty busy over at the mill."

"*He* works," Lovett said significantly. "The others lay off regular for their tea." He added hastily: "Not that it's any of my business. You got to keep your mouth shut on this job. Only a guy don't want to get in bad with the law, either."

Rocky ignored the man's virtuous smirk, watching Hadley walk toward the older house, hesitate, and then turn toward his own. "You think things over," he said, "and if you remember anything worth tellin', of course you'll let me know."

There was a distinct tinge of cynicism to this last remark that made Lovett look after him uneasily as he walked away. Hadley, a stooped, graying man with kind, burned-out eyes, stood still and waited for him.

"Mr. Allan, isn't it? Then it is true the man killed at the hotel was the same Cooper who was here?"

"He was. But I take it you didn't see much of him?"

"Very little. Come into the house," Hadley said courteously. "It's chilly out here and I must admit I'm rather tired. Will you have a drink?" he asked in the square dark living room. "No? Well, I will, if you don't mind. What can I do for you?"

"Well, you said you hardly saw Cooper."

"My daughter and I didn't happen to be at the big house while he was there. We always," Hadley said, smiling, "call it the big house, though Linda says that's one name for a jail. Rose and Linda were in Reno all day Thursday—the day he arrived. Rose is buying her trousseau—I suppose you know she and Dewey Stinson are to be married this spring?"

"No, I didn't." Those two, Rocky thought, would make as oddly assorted a couple as Anette and Earl Graydon. He wondered why Dewey, who was the sort you'd expect to have a nice taste in women, was marrying Rose Hadley.

"Well, that has nothing to do with your question. Cooper did ask to be taken through the mill but Dewey acted as guide. He brought Cooper into my office and we talked for a few minutes. Except at a distance, I didn't see him again."

"Weren't you in your office when he and Graydon had their row?"

"Yes, but Dewey's office is between Earl's and mine."

"What's Mr. Stinson's position at the mill?" Rocky said curiously.

"Second vice-president and chief accountant." Hadley's tired eyes twinkled briefly. "It sounds very impressive. . . . Well, I didn't know what had happened yesterday until I came back from Brookdale and told them—"

"I got all that. What time does Graydon usually quit work?"

"Is that—necessary to your inquiry? Well, if it is . . . He and Dewey almost always stop work for a while at about three-thirty for tea. I do too—sometimes. If Earl doesn't go over to tea or goes back to his office afterward he almost always leaves by five o'clock."

"And goes home?"

"Yes, unless he stops to talk to his sisters."

"But he and Stinson were late at the mill yesterday?"

"I—I don't know. I didn't see them leave, but—"

"Mrs. Graydon says she went over there to ask her husband to take her to Reno today," Rocky explained. "That must have been about five-thirty. But it seems he'd usually be home before then."

"Oh. Well, perhaps she was anxious to get the matter settled. I don't know," Hadley said uncertainly. "I didn't ask too many questions as it was an embarrassing episode."

"It must've been," Rocky said with a marked lack of sympathy. "Well—when you got your car out this morning, did you think anyone had used it since you last did?"

"Lovett had. You mean: after he did? That idea never occurred to me."

"It rained all night, beginnin' about eight, and this mornin' till about eleven. The road between here and Brookdale is pretty muddy, since it isn't paved. If your car 'd been out in the night you couldn't have helped knowin' it."

Hadley walked slowly over to a table and added more soda to the whisky in his glass. "It hadn't been out in the rain then. I would have noticed if it had."

"You're prepared to swear to that?" Rocky said.

Hadley turned and faced him again. He said: "I will swear to that," with no resentment but an odd suggestion of weariness. "Why is it my car you're concerned with?"

"Lovett washed it this afternoon. The others are clean but they don't look freshly washed, so I don't think he lied about yours being the only one he just washed. You took your car out in this morning's rain."

"I had to drive to Spanish River. I went before Lovett had unlocked the garage. So I was the first to see the car this morning. And I am prepared to swear it hadn't been taken out in the rain."

"That is beginning to dawn on me."

"I don't blame you if . . . Of course you won't take my advice," Hadley said with his slow, almost shy smile, "because you're too young and impatient. But you're wasting your time. I've lived fifteen years here and I know the Graydons. Also, I owe them a good deal, so I'd rather not discuss any matters in which I'm not directly concerned."

"I suspected that. Have you got a phone?"

"In the hall. You ring once to get Brookdale. If you've nothing more to ask me and don't mind letting yourself out, I'll go upstairs," Hadley said. "I should be dressing for dinner. So if you don't mind . . ."

"Not a bit." Rocky watched Hadley go up the narrow stairway and then called his own office in Brookdale.

"Sheriff's office. . . . Oh, I was wondering about you," Andy said. "I've got a picture for you that's a pip. Looks just like him."

"That's good. Mail one and that snapshot from Cooper's watch to Pat McCarthy. You'll find his address in the files: he's done some work for us before. Take the letter out to the Junction so it'll get picked up by the westbound train tonight and put enough stamps on it for special delivery."

"O.K. Want me to write a letter with it?"

"A note sayin' they're the pictures mentioned in my telegram. I'll wire soon as I get back to town. What about the inquest?"

"Cut and dried. Doc thinks the bullets are from a 25 automatic but he doesn't really know. I've got them. They brought in an open verdict but of course some people were curious, wondering why Cooper was in town—"

"No one came forward to tell anything about him?"

"No," Andy said regretfully. "But I—well, I found a pretty fair lot of fingerprints in that room and—"

"Tell me about 'em later on," Rocky said ungratefully. "Come over to the house about eight. I've got to call Eleanor now.

"Oh, it's you," Eleanor said. "I was wondering—"

"Honey, I don't know what time I'll be home."

"Don't be so apologetic. Dinner is stew, anyway. It will keep."

"That's fine. I want you to go to the library and look through the files of the Brookdale *Sun*."

"How far back?"

"Begin with old Mr. Graydon's death. That was about five years ago. There ought to be a lot about that."

"Reams. Anything else?"

"Anything else you can pick up about this bunch out here. And find out when the present theater was built. Less than five and more'n three years ago, I think. I wasn't aroun' here that long ago. And see if they had any vaudeville or plays in the old theater. Don't work too long at it: I ought to be home in two hours."

PART TWO
"A PERSON OF NO IMPORTANCE"

I

After protesting politely that he "couldn't eat a thing", Andy Duncan accepted a large piece of lemon pie, though his eager: "Well, what's happened, Rocky?" suggested that for once he preferred facts to food.

"Nothing's really happened. Well, I talked to Harry Carpenter at the roundhouse . . ."

Andy's long face looked increasingly longer as he listened to the pleasant, drawling voice. He scraped the meringue from his pie, then ate it hastily, as if he felt he needed something to sweeten Rocky's unimpassioned recital of his afternoon's investigations.

"Well, I guess you had the right idea," he said at last. "It does look like there's something the Graydons don't want you to find out about. But murder . . . And you know they really would hate publicity."

"The wrong kind," Rocky said. "They've never minded havin' their doings plastered all over the local or city papers."

"N-no. Was Linda . . . How did she . . ."

Rocky grinned. "Pretty as a picture and she's evidently got a lot more backbone than you'd think when you first look at her. She made one or two cracks that . . . Well, I told you she was willing to talk. Would it be a breach of confidence on your part to tell me how she gets along with the fam'ly?"

"She'd tell you herself. She says they bore her. She'd like to know people like—well, like you, Eleanor. You know, her father was dared to— well—to defy the old man. He cleared out when he was of age. Linda said he never set the world on fire but he did manage to get along without asking for help. He married, and Linda's mother—well, she . . ."

"All well-conducted royal families have these little matrimonial difficulties," Eleanor said. "Look at Mrs. Simpson. Did Jeffrey Graydon marry beneath him?"

"Maybe they thought so. Her mother was a stenographer, but what of it? They both died of flu in 1920. So then, of course, Mr. Graydon brought Linda up here. Of course, while Linda talks a lot, if anyone—like me—criticized the family she probably wouldn't like it."

"I wouldn't try it. There's a lot of Graydon in her. I think she'd be loyal to them in a pinch but not unless they give her good reasons why she should be," Rocky said. "And right now she don't know what it's all about. Either that or she's the best actress unhung."

"Please, Andy, don't hit my husband! You want to be a detective," Eleanor said, "so you might as well learn now that a trustful and trusting faith in human nature is *not* part of a detective's stock in trade."

Rocky laughed. "I trust Linda Graydon, Andy— so far. And I don't think Rose Hadley knows any more than she does. They were both gone when Cooper arrived. But the Hadley girl— Or is she a girl? What do you think, honey? You've seen her."

"She's about twenty-eight or twenty-nine," Eleanor said promptly. "Though that's just an opinion. Dewey Stinson can't be much older than she is."

"He don't look it, but any man named Dewey has to be somewheres between thirty-six and thirty-eight. I reckon they didn't name babies Dewey much later 'n 1900. What's Linda Graydon say about that engagement, Andy?"

"That's the kind of thing she doesn't say any-thing about."

"Which probably means she thinks it's a funny match. Well, I was going to say that I imagine Rose Hadley would do as she was told, without arguin'. Linda wouldn't. But right now she don't know anything to tell."

"Well, Mr. Graydon was right when he said you really haven't had time to investigate here in town."

Rocky looked at his deputy in mild exasperation. He pointed to the clock. "That says eight-thirty and I just finished eating before you came. Of course, we'll keep at it—"

"'We?'"

"*I* have somethin' better to do than run to ever' house in town, askin' if they ever saw Cooper be-fore or durin' his last visit here. I've already seen the most likely people."

"But how . . ."

There are, Rocky said didactically, always a certain number of people in every small town who have time on their hands and nothing in their minds but a busy curiosity regarding their fel-low citizens. He knew, from a year's residence in Brookdale, who were the men who spent most of the day leaning against stores on Main Street and what women always sat at a front window with the curtains pulled back so that they could see every person and car that passed their house.

He had interviewed these fountains of knowledge but unfortunately—most of them seemed to feel—they either had not seen Cooper at all or only during his walk from Pete's place to Robbins' garage. At least half-a-dozen persons were now certain they had seen him then.

But none of them could give any detailed account of Cooper's movements to fill in that bothersome gap between the time he left Pete's place and his arrival at the garage. Pete was certain Cooper had left the lunchroom not later than nine-fifty. He had arrived at the garage at ten-fifteen: what had he done during those twenty-five minutes?

It was possible he had visited someone in Brookdale before going on to The Stockade—but who? His nearest way into the residential district from Pete's Place would lead him past Mrs. McCune's corner house. Mrs. McCune, a crippled, fearsome septuagenarian, had sat all morning in a front window and she had not seen Cooper.

Of course, Rocky admitted, the average bystander is not a reliable witness. But Brookdale people, on a quiet November morning, did look several times at a stranger.

That fact was an argument against Cooper's having spent those twenty-five minutes loitering along the street.

"He would have," Eleanor said flippantly, "to be the world's prize loiterer to do that on Brookdale's main street. There's nothing to look at but the courthouse."

"Yes," Rocky said inattentively. "Wherever he went, he must've made sure first that no one was watchin' him."

"Well, if he did go to see someone here in town, his visit would have to be a short one. And I simply cannot single out any person or family here and imagine any connection—certainly none that would lead to murder—between them and Walter Cooper. There simply aren't any family secrets in Brookdale. But go on. Because I have a few bits of information I'm dying to broadcast."

"Well, I stumbled on one thing that isn't negative evidence. If Malcolm Burd isn't mistaken, and I don't think he is, it don't matter whether or not Cooper saw someone in Brookdale before he went out to The Stockade."

Burd had a small farm near Spanish River and a fiancée living on the outskirts of Brookdale. Ordinarily he would have arrived at her house by eight o'clock on Friday night, but he went out to his car to find one tire dismally flat. By the time he had put the spare on, it was raining so hard that he had to drive very slowly.

Because he was late, he kept looking at his watch. So he knew that it was ten minutes of nine when he saw a man ploughing laboriously through rain and mud at the side of the road, slowed the car and shouted to him "Jump in. I can't take you all the way into town," Burd added. "I'm late and my girl will be worrying. But I can take you almost there."

Cooper—Burd's description of the man left no doubt that it had been Cooper—answered with a surly mutter of which Burd heard only the word "hospitality!" Then he thanked him, with the ungracious remark that a short lift was "better than none at all." Burd let him out, telling him that the beginning of the paved street was only a few hundred yards away.

Then he turned off the main road and left Cooper standing in the rain. But this afternoon, hearing in the post office of a stranger who had been killed at the hotel, Malcolm Burd had remembered the man walking along the road.

"It would take Cooper just about five minutes to walk from where Burd left him to where I met him at nine o'clock," Rocky said. "And fairly fast walking too. So now we know Cooper didn't see anyone before he met me. Or are pretty sure of it.

So no one but the Graydon bunch knew he was going to be at the hotel last night."

"Burd's happening along like that is a lucky break. But I'm afraid it's going to occur to him that The Stockade was the last place he passed before he picked Cooper up. And he probably won't keep his mouth shut."

"Well, I suppose people will talk," Eleanor said. "But how much of the Graydons' story do you believe?"

"First, I want Pat McCarthy to find out if Cooper was in San Francisco as long ago as September; the dates Stinson said he and Earl Graydon met the fellow at the Palace."

"What makes you think Cooper might not have been in the city then?" Andy asked.

"I don't think: I wonder. He told Linda Graydon he hadn't been in San Francisco for years. Well, McCarthy should be able to trace him through the Warren Hotel—if it's in the city—and that picture in his watch. And he may 've been an actor, in spite of Stinson's sayin' he sold insurance. That would make him easier to check on. As to the rest of their story—I can believe Cooper might 've made a pass at Anette Graydon."

"After due encouragement," Eleanor said. "They had a French chauffeur who was too good looking.

. . . Oh, I have my sources of information. Go on."

"Well, what I can't down," Rocky said, "is their explanation of why they took Cooper in. They didn't have to, even if Graydon ever was drunk enough to invite him. There's a dozen excuses they could've made to get rid of him and, if I know them, they'd make 'em in a way to penetrate the thickest hide."

Eleanor nodded. "'Sorry, my good man, but we aren't receiving guests just now. You will find the hotel at Brookdale quite comfortable.'"

Rocky chuckled. "Earl Graydon or Mrs. Hobart to the life. They admit he wasn't a welcome guest and the reasons they give for puttin' up with him aren't good enough."

"Y-yes. You can't get around that," Andy said. "But when it comes to his being killed, what motive—"

"That's the stickin' point. I can only guess why he might have been killed. And I can only suspect them collectively right now."

"Of course," Andy said slowly, "Earl Graydon must have been pretty sore at Cooper."

"*If* that incident involvin' his wife ever occurred. Even if it did, that's hardly motive enough for murder, as it stands. And Linda said something like: 'Since when has Earl turned cave man?'

No: we've got to find out why Cooper came here, why they took him in—and maybe why they threw him out."

"And what about Mr. Hadley's story?" Eleanor said.

"In one way, Stinson and Hadley seem to be two of a kind—they lie like gentlemen. Only Hadley's efforts ain't quite as artistic as Stinson's. I think Hadley was lying about the condition he found his car in this mornin' and that he knows I know he is."

"But, look here: If he knew, the minute he saw his car, that it had been out in the storm, and he took it out right away in the rain to cover that up . . . I'm getting all mixed up," Andy said, "but if he did that, he must have known, early in the morning, that Cooper was dead. And how could he? If he'd been out in it himself, he'd have had sense enough to clean the car. Wouldn't he?"

"If he could make a decent job of it late at night. It'd be safer to get to the garage early an' take the car out in the rain. Which he did. But the fact he got out so early does look like he must've at least been uneasy about somethin', even if he did tell Lovett he didn't know Cooper was gone. Of course no one could've heard a car last night."

"But the driver might put on the lights. For a minute or two at least. And," Eleanor said, "Mr. Hadley suffers from insomnia."

Rocky looked at her admiringly. "That may turn out to be a very useful fact, honey. Well, about this trip to Spanish River—I know the bookkeeper there pretty well. Hadley was at the mill, all right. They have just one big office, so Dearborn knows Hadley came in, talked to the manager about nothin' special, and then left. After he'd told me that, Dearborn began to get uneasy, so I told him to forget it. Of course Hadley could depend on the manager at Spanish River to say he had a real reason for a trip down there. What did you do after I left you, Andy?"

"I talked to the servants but they'd got a peek at Cooper on his way out and were sure they'd never seen him before. No one heard any shooting. Ella was the last one to clean Cooper's room. I took their fingerprints. There were some of Ella's in the room. And prints all over the doorknob, of course," Andy said disgustedly. "Cooper's all over the place and some old ones, badly blurred. I don't think Ella dusted very well."

"That all?"

Well, Andy said, Rocky hadn't told him to talk to Arney or Cronin, the two men who lived at the hotel. But he ran into Arney in the lobby and asked him if he'd heard any shots during the night.

Samuel Arney said he hadn't heard anything but the storm and not much of that. Then he suggested, with benevolent amusement, that Andy take his fingerprints. "Just to prove to you that I'm a public-spirited citizen," he said in his dryly legal voice. "And why not take Cronin's too?"

Cronin, who came into the hotel just then, said ungraciously that he didn't care if Andy did. But he thought Rocky Allan might notify the Press when some real news broke. It was a hell of a note when the editor of the Brookdale *Sun* didn't know, until he heard it on the streets, that a man had been murdered in his own hotel. He'd left the place early and he hadn't heard any shots and he'd never seen Cooper before.

"I'll smooth Ernie down tomorrow," Rocky promised. "All right, honey: it's your turn."

"I didn't spend much time over the newspapers," Eleanor said, "because I happened to remember Miss Jewett, and, you know, newspapers never print the really interesting facts. So I talked to her, instead."

Miss Hazel Jewett was a coy lady of uncertain age, the current president of the Ladies' Aid and the one person in Brookdale who had ever been on terms of intimacy with one of the Graydons. Although—she said—she was "quite a bit younger than Lucilla", they had been girlhood friends.

Miss Jewett talked of the Graydons with a laughable mixture of malice, respect and complacency for her own connection with them. And with constant reference to the fact that her own father had been a judge and that Lucilla Graydon had lived in town until she was fifteen and "really had no more pocket money and not any nicer clothes than I did, my dear.

"Because it wasn't until dear Lucilla was fifteen that Mr. Graydon made a lot of money and built The Stockade and sent Lucilla away to school. Bertha," Miss Jewett said brazenly, "is nearer my age—forty-four—but I never knew her very well. Or Earl, who is the youngest. Jeffrey I did know. He was next to Lucilla and the most fascinating person. But so headstrong, and he married . . . Well, one often wonders, doesn't one, why men marry as they do?"

Miss Jewett liked to talk about the half-dozen times each year when she was called for and driven in state out to The Stockade for tea. "Lucilla," she said, "confides in me." Whether or not that was true, Eleanor judged that Miss Jewett kept eyes and ears open to advantage whenever she was at The Stockade.

Anette Graydon, Miss Jewett said, was a "hussy", even if she had come from a very good old Sacramento family. She'd married Earl for his money and then found she couldn't spend it as she wished, living at The Stockade. They'd all expected her to produce a son and heir but Anette hadn't. In fact, she had even announced she had no intention of doing so.

Old Mr. Graydon, who wasn't always as "delicate" as one would wish, had told Earl his wife was a "bad bargain. 'You should have picked one with less looks, who wasn't so set on keeping them.'" Anette was afraid not to behave while her father-in-law was alive because he controlled the purse strings.

But even then she was always "flirting", Miss Jewett said with a disapproving click of her false teeth. "They always tried to keep it from old Mr. Graydon. I know that in the last year or two Earl has discharged a bookkeeper and a very nice chauffeur because of her. And he won't let her go to the city alone. But I think he's still—well, in love with her. Some women—it is dreadful the attraction they have for men, isn't it? Not really nice."

II

Eleanor stopped and reached for a cigarette. "Am I boring you?"

"On the contrary. I never thought about that old girl," Rocky said. "What'd she say about her contemporary, Mrs. Hobart?"

Miss Jewett said that Bertha had married young and the marriage hadn't turned out well. Of course she was a little spoiled and Mr. Hobart was very jealous. They were happy enough for ten years but then he lost his very good position.

People whispered he'd taken the firm's money. From then on, Bertha stayed a great deal with her father. He hadn't made her a marriage settlement and he was willing to support her—but not Mr. Hobart. However, Mr. Graydon was born a Catholic and, though he certainly wasn't a religious man, he didn't approve of divorce and neither did Bertha, who had been educated in a convent.

Mr. Hobart took to drinking—and maybe worse things—but Bertha kept going back to him. Only then he would always start drinking again and lose another job his friends in San Francisco had found for him. Finally Mr. Graydon sent for him just before he died and put him to work in the mill.

And he seemed to do quite well. He had impressed Miss Jewett as quite the gentleman and very handsome the one time she met him. But he died of pneumonia not very many months after Mr. Graydon passed away.

Lucilla was very like her father and, while he said she, and not Earl, should have been the boy, they quarreled a good deal. They both had terrible tempers. And Mr. Graydon had wanted his daughters to be "real ladies." But Lucilla . . . Well! However, she was the real head of the family now.

Earl had always been afraid of his father; so afraid that he couldn't seem to help lying to him at times. And two things Mr. Graydon couldn't bear were liars and people who didn't pay their debts. As Anette was extravagant and not too truthful and Earl was very much under her influence, even after he was married he was always in difficulties with his father.

Lucilla had had a great many advantages but she had never been pretty so it wasn't strange she hadn't married. When she was younger she was always going up to the logging camps and she liked to hunt and fish. She was quite rheumatic now, poor dear. She ate too much candy: bought a dozen boxes at a time and always had one beside her.

Mr. Hadley was a charming man and it was too bad he suffered from insomnia. He and Dewey Stinson were distantly related to the Graydons: Dewey to Mrs. Graydon, while Mr. Hadley was Joshua Graydon's third or fourth cousin.

People had thought it rather odd when Mr. Graydon brought Mr. Hadley in to be general manager of the mill when he had a son to take over the business. But Lucilla said that Ellis knew his business and had more brains than Earl ever would.

Mr. Graydon even sold Mr. Hadley quite a bit of stock in the mill so that when he died Earl and

Mr. Hadley would have the controlling interest. There had been a Mrs. Hadley but she died when Rose was a baby. Her father had done everything he could to make that up to her, though.

Rose was well educated and really quite clever, but the poor girl was dreadfully shy. Mr. Hadley had wanted her to be with young people and kept sending her away to visit relatives but it didn't do any good, as far as her marrying was concerned. "And then," said Miss Jewett, suddenly colloquial, "of all things! She landed Dewey Stinson!"

Eleanor inquired soberly if Mr. Stinson was considered a hard fish to land and hadn't Anette ever cast flirtatious eyes on him? Miss Jewett said Anette probably had but he evidently hadn't given her any encouragement because he and Earl were good friends. And of course they wouldn't be if Dewey and Anette had—well, *had* . . .

It didn't seem quite the thing for him to live with Lucilla but she said she thought she and Bertha were old enough to risk gossip. And that she didn't care a "d-damn" for gossip, anyway, and a cook always served up better meals when there was a man in the house.

And Dewey certainly had managed to remain a bachelor for a long time. Even though he spent a lot of time in the summer with the people who stayed at the very expensive Pluma Blanca Inn.

Lucilla said that women were always chasing him. And then he'd chosen to marry Rose, and after knowing her for six or seven years.

It was about seven years since Mr. Graydon had given him a position, for Mrs. Graydon's sake, though she'd been dead some time. But Dewey got along very well with the men at the mill. And he really deserved credit for making good when he hadn't been brought up to earn his own living, only his mother had run through all the money his father left.

Of course, Dewey said that he didn't earn his salary since the Depression. He said they could get along without him and Earl if they had Ellis Hadley. She rather imagined, Miss Jewett said shrewdly, that the mill wasn't making too much money for them. Anette had only one maid now and hadn't entertained as much as usual this last summer.

Bertha and Lucilla didn't draw their incomes from the mill and they should have good ones. But Lucilla had played the stock market—she was a gambler—and Bertha had expensive tastes. She'd taken Linda to Honolulu after she graduated—but of course Mrs. Allan knew all the details from the Brookdale *Sun?* It had been a graduation present and before they left she gave Linda that dance at the Fairmont.

And while Earl had had a little money from his father, Anette must soon have run through that. He had inherited the stock in the lumber company and with business what it was . . . Well! The rest was divided between Lucilla, Bertha and Melinda. Melinda had gotten her father's share because old Mr. Graydon adored her. And he'd deeded the houses to Lucilla, Earl and Mr. Hadley before he died. Because Lucilla would always live here but Bertha didn't care so much about it, though she did spend winters here lately.

Of course, Miss Jewett said, somewhat tardily, the Graydons were really a wonderful pioneer family, only you had to understand them. And she was glad to see that Mrs. Allan was interested in local history. As her father, the judge, always said . . .

Rocky continued to stare at the fire through half closed lids. Andy thought he had looked half asleep for the past fifteen minutes but Eleanor knew he was letting what she had told him "soak in."

And perhaps some fact mixed in with Miss Jewett's trivialities would be important. Eleanor knew one woman who would spend half her life in prison because of an unconsidered reference to yellow roses. So it wasn't wise to skip lightly over trivialities: one might point the way to a murderer.

"Well, I went on to the library," she said. "The present theater opened to the public four years ago this last spring. The old one, it seems, was something of an eyesore. It might have made an impression on Mr. Cooper, if he ever saw it."

"Well, that's something. What about their programs?"

"As far back as I could go, they didn't have any stage acts in the old theater, except for Marveloso the Mind Reader."

Andy grinned. "That wasn't Cooper. He read minds so well he had half-a-dozen people glaring at each other and not speaking for a while. But he's the only act I ever remember them having."

"It was just an idea," Rocky said cheerfully. "What else, honey?"

Eleanor took a sheet of paper scribbled over with notes from her sweater pocket. "Mr. Graydon's death, which occurred in July of '31; that is, a little over five years ago."

Joshua Graydon was seventy-five that July and, as the Brookdale *Sun* put it, "had been failing in health for some time." But he was well enough to ride out every afternoon, driven by his chauffeur and usually accompanied by a Miss Maud Evans.

The road between Brookdale and Merton was not paved then, and on a still summer day dust clouds hugged the ground long after a car had passed. Driving home toward Brookdale, the chauffeur had the late afternoon glare of the sun in his eyes. That, and the dust, must have blinded him, for there was a headlong collision with another car that swung around a corner toward them.

No one lived to say exactly what had happened. The chauffeur, Thomas Elsey, Miss Evans and the driver of the other car were dead when their bodies were taken from the wrecks. Joshua Graydon died at The Stockade at ten that night, without regaining consciousness.

"I could have told you all that if you'd asked me," Andy said. "But I don't see why—"

"Who was Miss Maud Evans?"

"Apparently a person of no importance," Eleanor said. "She was spoken of as companion and nurse."

"She was a little of both," Andy said. "Mr. Graydon was too stubborn to have a real nurse but he told someone he wasn't going to let his daughters look after him till they'd get to wishing he was dead. I guess Miss Evans was a sort of practical nurse, but she was more a companion."

"Well, Miss Jewett didn't know her," Eleanor said. "Because she visited a cousin in Santa Cruz that summer and missed out on all the fun. At least, I gathered she felt a little defrauded at not being here for the funeral."

"She would. I saw Miss Evans once or twice but I can't remember what she looked like," Andy said.

"Didn't the papers say if she had any relatives?"

"They practically ignored her, Rocky. They did say: 'It is not known that Miss Evans had any surviving relatives,'" Eleanor said.

"Well, does it matter?" Andy asked.

"Why did Cooper ask both Rose Hadley and Linda Graydon if they were at home when the old man died?"

"Well, that is kind of funny."

"Damn funny. And the circumstances of Graydon's death don't make it any less so."

"But there was nothing peculiar about his death!"

"That's what's peculiar." Rocky laughed. "Me 'n Sherlock Holmes: the dog that didn't bark. Graydon died in a commonplace enough way—except that his death was unexpected an' he was never able to talk again. Still, Cooper's question is pretty hard to account for. Unless . . ."

Eleanor waited patiently and Andy jerked at one ear, opened his mouth and closed it without saying anything.

"Well, Steve Brodie took a chance. Hand me the phone, sugar. Six-nine, please. That's right.

. . . Clarence? This is Rocky. Listen: do you still think you've seen Cooper somewheres before?"

Clarence said he knew he had but he didn't know where he could have seen the fellow. Cooper hadn't registered at the hotel: not in the last seven years. He'd found time to go over the records for that far back.

"And is my face red? Oh well, I'm glad you went ahead an' did that? Well, can you remember five years back, Clarence?"

"Fifteen—or twenty-five. A hotel clerk's got to remember things. Faces, especially. That'd be '31. Any special month?"

"July—well, make it June and July."

Andy squirmed impatiently. "Why don't you ask him—"

"Shut up," Rocky told him pleasantly. "No, not you, Clarence. You go on an' think. . . . I don't like that kind of suggested evidence, Andy. Let him remember for himself." But he obligingly took the telephone away from his chest and held it so that Andy and Eleanor, leaning forward, could hear Clarence's voice.

"Well, that's the year the Pluma Blanca Inn didn't open up because people were too broke to go weekending with other people's husbands and wives. It was awful hot and dusty . . . Oh yes, Mr. Graydon was killed in July. The dust—"

"I've read about that accident. Four people killed."

"That's right. Four—I got it!" Clarence yelled. "Why didn't you mention Miss Evans to me right away?"

"I just heard of her, Clarence. What about her?"

"Why, she was kind of a nurse to Mr. Graydon. I saw her sometimes. When he took a ride he usually parked a while on the main street and talked to people. Not like his son. So I saw her enough to know her.

"Though I couldn't," Clarence admitted in a rather puzzled tone, "begin to describe her. She was so—so ordinary looking. Anyway, one day—around the last of June—this fellow, Cooper, walked into the hotel and asked if his sister—"

"Sister!"

"What's that?"

"That was only Andy explodin'," Rocky said. "Go on."

"He asked for his sister—Miss Evans. Said she was supposed to meet him here. In a minute or two she drove up in one of the Graydon cars. They acted real glad to see each other: she did, especially. They had lunch here and sat and talked in the lobby an hour or two and finally the car came back and they got in it and drove off."

"Of course you've no idea where they went?"

"No, but he came in on the Reno stage and had a suitcase. Maybe she took him to the train to go to San Francisco. It came through in the late afternoon then. I was in the dining room when they were," Clarence added. "I sat with my back to 'em. She said—I remember because she sounded like crying—something about seeing him for such a short time when he was going so far away for so long."

"That was a long time ago, Clarence."

"I've got a good memory. And I was interested, not having much to do because business was bad that year and her being connected with the Graydons. I even remember her saying she was sorry she couldn't ask him to The Stockade but that Mr. Graydon had been nice, letting her have the car and time off."

"You win, Clarence. I'll be over to talk to you soon. Meanwhile," Rocky said, "keep your mouth shut."

"Sure. But if I was you, I'd certainly see the Graydons. They may have heard her talk about Cooper."

"That's a very good idea," Rocky said solemnly. He put down the telephone and looked at Eleanor and Andy. "Well?"

"Don't smirk," Eleanor said. "*Very* well. She was his half-sister, of course; the one he spoke to

Linda Graydon about. He must have wanted to find out how much she did or didn't know."

"B-but—look here," Andy said, "if she was his half-sister, then he had a perfectly good reason for coming up here. To get her things, maybe, or ask them about her. And they had a perfectly good reason for taking him in."

"Exactly." Rocky stood up, yawning. "Such a very good reason that you wonder why they were so very unwillin' to mention it."

III

It was no use; the thousandth sheep leaped as briskly over the stile as the first had done. Linda murmured: "Oh well, I never did like sheep. And who ever considered them worth counting?"

Her grandfather, she remembered, had once said to her: "Fool other people all you want to, or can, baby. But don't fool yourself about yourself or other people, just because you love them or think you owe them something."

Adult advice to a child who now began to understand what he had meant. She wanted, Linda admitted, to be considered "grownup." She resented the "run away and play, dear" attitude the others were taking toward her and Rose. But tonight she had been almost ready to take advantage of that protective attitude by telling herself: "It doesn't matter; it's not important. I'll just forget it."

But it wasn't grownup to ignore murder, even if you could. Well, then . . .

For an instant after Rocky Allan left them no one spoke. Then Dewey said thoughtfully:

"That man is dangerous."

"Nonsense. He—well, he can't be," Earl said. "He's only going through a few routine gestures."

"He managed to trip you up," Dewey said dryly. "Neither did I fare too well—and I'm a fairly accomplished liar. As to the routine gestures . . ." He shrugged.

"Dewey's right," Miss Lucilla said. "He's got eyes like a cat's when it smells a mouse. And I should judge he was incorruptible. So don't make a damned fool of yourself, Earl."

"Must you talk like that. And I'm not the only one. After all, you—"

"I know. Well, we all have our faults—and make mistakes. If it's the damn you object to—someone has to do the swearing for this family. I said, all along, that we'd better tell the truth."

"I understood you to say that you had—finally," Linda said.

Earl scowled at her. "Please don't try to be witty."

Linda stamped her foot. "Then tell me what it's all about! Why shouldn't I tell what little I do know when you don't give me any reason why I shouldn't?"

"You should trust those older and wiser—"

"Fiddle-faddle!" Miss Lucilla said. "She's too old to take things on trust. If I had my way . . . However, least said, soonest mended. Come here, child."

Linda obeyed sulkily.

"I'll have to ask you to trust me, after all. Do you?"

Linda looked into the small black eyes with their fleshy brows; shrewd, almost fierce eyes that could still be very kind. "Y-yes; I suppose I do," she said slowly.

"Then I'll admit Cooper's connection with this family is something we aren't anxious to have known."

"But—"

"It's nothing that can concern you, dear," Bertha Hobart said. "We want to save you from being questioned, if—"

"If the whole thing comes out," Miss Lucilla said grimly. "What we're keeping back is—well, say, our well-known family pride has run away with our common sense. Now, are you satisfied?"

"Oh, I guess so."

"I must go home," Rose said abruptly. "Dad will be there by now. Linda, have you any cold cream to spare? I forgot to get it, Thursday . . .

"That was the first thing I could think of," she whispered in the hall. "I know they wanted to get rid of us. And I wanted to ask—do you know any more than you've told?"

"No. I'm as much in the dark as you—or are you?"

"Oh yes. We'd better go upstairs for a few minutes. . . . I only saw Mr. Cooper once. Yesterday at teatime. You remember he drank just one cup and then left. I suppose because none of the men were here."

Linda frowned. "I'd forgotten that. He must have gone over to Earl's office then. Wanted to see him—I wonder why? And Anette left early."

"Linda"—Rose rearranged bottles on the bureau—"I don't like Anette!"

"That's two of us. I'm glad you have that much spunk."

"I don't speak out as you do. 'Dear Rose is so quiet.' But dear Rose is not a half-wit, even if she can keep her mouth shut. After all, I'm ten years older than you, though one wouldn't think so, the way they treat both of us."

Rose laughed and Linda realized suddenly how seldom one heard that sound from Rose and how very attractive it was. Not at all like Anette's horrid little tinkle.

"I know people are always going to look at Dewey and me and say: 'Well, *why* did he marry *her?*'"

Rose went on. "I'm resigned to that. But I'm not resigned to Dewey's lying for Anette."

"Oh—do you think he did?"

"She may have been Mr. Cooper's connection with this family. You heard what Miss Lucilla said. And we don't really know what happened over at the mill yesterday. It may all have been more serious than they said. So far as Earl is concerned—he's putty in Anette's hands."

"They quarrel all the time."

"She does. And she doesn't bother—well, she would probably call it 'being nice' to him," Rose said contemptuously. "But that's all she has to do to make him willing to forgive her anything and do anything she wants."

Linda said: "Oh!" rather blankly. "I hadn't thought about that. But of course she doesn't find him very attractive."

"That's obvious. But Dewey virtually admitted it's been left to him to do most of the lying."

"Oh, don't worry about your boy friend."

"And Dad's worried," Rose said. "I could tell he was at lunch time. Even if Dewey didn't say so, I'm sure Dad must know what happened at the mill. Well, I must go home. It's too bad we were asked to dinner here tonight."

"Oh, we must keep up our form," Linda said disrespectfully. "We dined with Earl and Anette last week."

"My turn next. And I can't teach that girl how to cook."

"Your dinners couldn't possibly be any less festive than tonight's little gathering will be. But we'll talk—oh yes, we'll talk—of everything except what we're thinking about."

The men chose politics and worried the subject like determined dogs with a stale bone until Linda said maliciously:

"Why talk of the election since November third has passed? Especially when it's a painful subject for you, Uncle Earl. Let's discuss *Gone with the Wind* or the Duke of Windsor and Mrs. Simpson."

Dewey smiled at her reproachfully. "Is that kind? Name your subject and I'll find something to say. The less I know about it, the more I'll have to say."

"Oysters!"

"The oyster is a slippery bivalve considered by some deluded persons edible in its raw state. The fact that oysters are not in season during those months spelled without the letter 'r' is not due, as many ignorant persons suppose, to a mysterious affinity with said letter. It is simply a matter of birth control. The oyster is celebrated in literature, as witness that well-known epic, *The Walrus and the Carpenter* . . ."

Because Dewey was willing to talk nonsense and Mrs. Hobart discussed Rose's trousseau with her, there was at least an illusion of conversation. Miss Lucilla always gave her first attention to food. Ellis Hadley never talked a great deal and tonight Linda thought he kept looking from one to another of them with queer intentness. As if he were trying to make up his mind about something.

And Anette was sulky. It was she who made the evening's one reference to Walter Cooper. Bertha Hobart, picking up the needle-point footstool cover she was working, said regretfully:

"If you'd only remembered to get that wool for me when you were in Reno, Anette."

"I had too much else to do."

"But I wrote down the colors for you, dear."

"I forgot. Why didn't Linda get it Thursday? I'm always to blame for everything in this family," Anette said. "And I think I've been damned obliging. I hope you won't forget that when you think about the late Mr. Cooper."

Miss Lucilla smiled bleakly. "We aren't given to forgetting. . . . Linda, will you put up the card tables?"

Miss Lucilla loved cards and there was a long rivalry between her and Dewey. Often, with Mrs. Hobart and Earl Graydon as partners, they played until midnight. But at the other table, after four hands, Ellis Hadley suddenly admitted to a headache.

"If you don't mind, Anette . . ."

"Oh, of course not!" Anette threw her cards onto the table. "The best hand I've had! No, I don't care!"

"I'm sorry. But I think I'll go home. You don't need to come, Rose. Dewey will . . ."

But Rose insisted on going with her father and refused to let Dewey break up Miss Lucilla's table. Anette sat down by the fire but Linda did not intend to risk a tête-à-tête with her in her present mood.

"I'm going to bed, too, if you don't mind," she said. "My head aches a little too."

Knowing that what she meant to do would be called "sneaking" by Earl or Anette did not keep Linda from doing it. After all, Clara and Moody liked to have her drop into the kitchen to talk to them. Moody might be very exasperating but she was fond of Linda. That, in fact, was what made her exasperating: when she considered Linda "un-ladylike" she sniffed loud disapproval.

In the hour before bedtime, when she and Clara sat in comfortable rockers close to the enormous wood range and drank innumerable cups of tea, Moody relaxed slightly. She liked to tell Linda stories about the very rich and very stingy old lady she had worked for before coming to The Stockade. But tonight Linda, sitting on a kitchen chair with her heels hooked over its rungs, gave Moody no time for reminiscence. She said:

"Moody, you know the sheriff was here, asking questions about Mr. Cooper, and I don't want to say the wrong thing when he talks to us again. But I hate to bother Aunt Lucilla or Aunt Bertha because it's very embarrassing for them."

"Indeed it was! Never, since I've been here, have we had a guest like that."

"He was pretty bad, wasn't he?"

Moody put the tip of her tongue between her lips and then compressed them until neither lips nor tongue were visible. This mannerism was indicative of a degree of indignation that could not quite be relieved by sniffing.

"The idea! Making a fuss because his door didn't lock. I told him our guests didn't need to worry about that. But Mrs. Hobart said to find him a key. There should've been one in the lock, but keys do get lost. And then he muttered about it not being much protection and we'd ought to have Yale locks on the bedroom doors too."

"He certainly was a very odd person."

"Odd! He followed me right into the parlor where Mrs. Hobart was with Mrs. Earl. Well, when he done that I thought they'd soon settle him. But he stayed to lunch and later on I heard Mrs. Hobart tell Miss Lucilla they'd have to keep him overnight. They tell me he was a friend of Mr. Earl's and Mr. Dewey's, but they oughtn't to invite men like that here and embarrass Mrs. Hobart. At least Mr. Dewey did take him over to the mill after lunch. And after that, they tell me, he went and was disrespectful to Mrs. Earl!"

"You never saw him before, did you, Moody?"

"I certainly did not, Miss Linda—"

"Well, I can't imagine why he asked both Rose and me if we were here when Grandfather died. You were here then, weren't you?"

"I'd just come that spring," Moody said. "But I can tell you Cooper wasn't ever around. Probably he'd just heard a lot about Mr. Graydon and was curious."

"You weren't here then, were you, Clara?"

"Me? No," said Clara, who was round and fat, with a vaguely sweet and persistent smile. "I didn't come till the next summer. Your old cook got me the job when she seen she wasn't long for this world, poor thing. Moody says you used to have a butler but I'm glad he's gone. A butler is an awful nuisance to have around."

"He went back to England and England can have him. There was more of us when I first came," Moody said, "but we get along all right now. That Molly Harris was never worth her wages. I wonder they didn't let her go sooner."

"Molly Harris—I was trying to remember her name. She was the little woman with eyes like buttons, wasn't she? And she sewed beautifully."

"She did do that," Moody admitted. "But she was too curious."

"Is that why they let her go?"

"Oh, they didn't exactly make her leave. But she thought it was lonely here and she got to thinking she heard ghosts."

"Ghosts? Whose ghost? Where? I always did think we needed a ghost."

"Don't you talk like that, Miss Linda. She tried to tell me about hearing funny noises she couldn't have heard unless a ghost was making them. But I wouldn't listen to her. And naturally, it was a nuisance at a time like that."

"Oh—then it was right after Grandfather died?"

"Yes. I guess that's what got her to thinking things like that," Moody said. "She was pretty thick with that Miss Evans, who was another curious one—and she was killed in the wreck too. But you didn't know her at all and I hardly did. Did I ever tell you how the lady I worked for before I came here believed in what she called transmigration of souls? Well, maybe you couldn't blame her, because her husband had suicided and that's a terribly disgraceful thing to happen to a family. But she used to make my blood run cold . . ."

And that, Linda thought, turning her pillow for the third time, was that. Why had Anette said she was being "damned obliging?" Was Aunt Lucilla lying still? She never did, but . . . Well, why had Walter Cooper been wandering about the house late Thursday night? And why had he been so anxious to lock his door, and why was he interested in Grandfather's death?

She decided: this hasn't done any good, after all. I might as well read. She pressed the switch of her bedside lamp and heard its tiny click but no light followed it. The bulb was probably burned out: she would have to get up and put on the center lights.

She got out of bed, shivering, stumbled barefoot across the room and found the light switch near the door. She snapped it on and, with a foolish sensation of surprise, realized that there was still no light.

IV

An instant before she had not greatly cared whether or not she read the book on her bedside table. Now she had a sudden frantic desire for light. There was something vaguely terrifying in the idea that she could not see if she wanted to.

A fuse had blown out, of course. She knew where the fuse box was at the end of the hall near the kitchen. And there were extra fuses in a drawer of the kitchen worktable.

Linda found her padded robe, put it on and thrust her feet into wool-lined slippers. She should have a flashlight—or matches, to light the candle she'd used Friday night. She had told Moody, time and again, to fill the little container on the table every morning. But Moody didn't approve of even an occasional cigarette and that was her way of saying so.

Well, she didn't need a light to find her way about this house. But, briefly, she hesitated. It was as if the old walls had whispered a warning: stay where you are! Then she straightened her slim shoulders and slipped silently into the hall.

Her light footsteps were swallowed up by the thick carpet as she felt along the paneled walls until the stair railing curved under her fingers. She counted steps carefully; she had learned to count that way, toiling up and down on fat five-year-old legs. She'd never forgotten just how many steps there were. This was the last one.

Linda stopped. Her hand tightened on the stair rail's knobbed newel post. That noise . . . It wasn't a sound that could be born of tense nerves; it was too definite in character. And now she heard it again, muffled by a closed door but still brassy; brassy and clanging, with the clatter and ring that came from a pair of fire tongs or a poker dropped against the bars of a grate.

She thrust her hands deep into the pockets of her robe and felt them close into small hard fists. There was a fireplace in the living room, of course. And one in the library. That dark book-lined room was almost never used now. Joshua Graydon had bought his books by weight; because they were matching sets and had substantial leather bindings. They weren't the sort of books that many people read nowadays. But Walter Cooper had told Clara—and perhaps been surprised into telling the truth—that he had been looking for a book.

Linda went forward slowly, hands outstretched. Not so much because she did not want to blunder against a wall or table as to thrust back the darkness that seemed pressing, thick and impenetrable, against her. It was like swimming beneath stagnant black water. But at last she touched the sharp edge of a table. She identified it by its carved, twisted leg; it was the one that stood so close to the library door.

In the blackness beyond, inside the library, someone whispered suddenly: "You wouldn't dare." Linda felt her palms grow wet. But she pressed an ear close to the door, steadying herself with a hand on its knob.

It was not quite closed, after all: it had, she remembered, a way of sticking when you pulled it shut. Did she dare try to enlarge that tiny space through which she heard the toneless whisper of voices? Not yet. If she waited . . .

She thought she heard the word "dare" repeated and then two single words: "witness" and "regretted." It was not the words that were terrifying but the whispering voices that inhumanly lacked color or sex. They were accentless and characterless. "Murder," spoken in those tones, was a word more frightening than when screamed aloud. "Murder"—"again" and, finally, "armed."

Linda put both hands on the doorknob. No use standing here listening when she caught only a word now and then. If she could slip into the room and slam the door shut before anyone could move to stop her . . .

The door grated harshly against warped wood. She stood still, shaking. Inside the library another door closed gently: the one she'd forgotten because no one but her grandfather had ever used it. The side door he'd had put there so that he could slip quietly out of the library. But it was too late now to think of that.

Even if she had matches or a flashlight there was probably, nothing to see in the library. Unless . . . She sniffed inquiringly. There was a faintly acrid smell of smoke in the room now that the door was open. If a fire had been lighted in the disused grate there, perhaps it could be stirred up from a few lingering sparks.

She was uncertain about the location of furniture in this room. But there were bookshelves that reached to the ceiling, a solid, almost immovable oak table and an old-fashioned roll-top desk. There were half-a-dozen leather chairs with seats and high backs upholstered in red leather and . . .

Something round and hard pressed suddenly against the small of her back. A strong hand gripped her shoulder: she felt the bite of strong fingers through her thick robe. The pressure increased with her stifled cry and she bit her lip, understanding that her life depended on silence. For an instant the blackness swirled giddily about her. Then, dumbly, she obeyed the hand that forced her toward the wall.

She stopped finally, feeling the bookshelves against her breast. Ruthless fingers yanked at the heavy cord of her robe, pulled it free and twisted it about her ankles—twisted it painfully tight. But though there was no gun against her back now,

Linda had a clear vision of where it would be. Lying on the floor in close reach of swift, relentless hands. And if she dared turn . . .

She shivered and stood still. If he—or she—would only speak! But there was no need for speech; the grip on her shoulder had been eloquent enough. And the cord about her ankles. Her wrists would be next.

But her wrists were miraculously left unbound. A hand against her back pushed her closer against the bookshelves. The gesture said: Stay there; as you are! Linda stayed, trembling—still with fear but now, and increasingly, with anger. Why, if she wasn't to be killed and her hands were left free . . .

Then, with the clang of a poker against the grate, she understood. Whoever had built that fire wanted to be certain it was dead. And as long as her ankles were bound he could take his time about that. She couldn't play hide-and-seek with him in the dark and he didn't have to stand guard over her. Two big tears slipped down Linda's cheeks. Very clever! Damned clever! She'd pay someone back for this!

A key rasped in its lock. There was a tinkling sound as if it had fallen against a hard surface and then the outside door to the library closed. Linda tried to take a step forward, lost her balance and fell to her knees. She broke two fingernails loosening the cord about her ankles, bruising her fingers on the hard knots.

A tiny light flared unexpectedly from the fireplace.

She ran to it, caught the paper up recklessly and beat out the flame. She saw what had happened: one charred fragment had fallen through the bars of the grate and a lingering spark had ignited it. So he hadn't been so clever, after all! She couldn't see, now, what it was she'd kept from destruction, but it was something

She sat down on the floor, shivering again, her anger swept away by an unnerving wave of fear. For she realized suddenly that it was someone she knew who had threatened her so silently. She could still feel the hard circle of a gun pressed against her back. And Walter Cooper had been shot.

Anyone could get in here, of course. Earl had a key to the front door: so did Ellis Hadley. When they were all away one summer he had been given a key that he still had.

There had been two people. Perhaps one had searched the library and the other had surprised him before he left but hadn't raised any alarm. Or perhaps they had come together. And she had given them some clue—one she couldn't read the meaning of—when she had mentioned Clara's account of Walter Cooper's midnight ramblings.

Linda got up wearily. The hall door was locked and the key was gone. But was it? She wouldn't have heard that tinkling sound if it had been thrown onto a thick carpet. It must have struck wood. The table, perhaps.

She felt over the table's polished surface. Two tall cut-glass decanters, a hammered copper inkwell, a pad of paper, the cold clay of a small bust of Napoleon—all reminders of Joshua Graydon's tenancy of the room. And finally the key, lying near an edge of the table.

Linda unlocked the door. She was unutterably weary but, for some reason, no longer afraid of the dark. Perhaps because she no longer needed to imagine its dangers: she knew what they might be. When she saw the faint light at the end of the hall she went toward it, unafraid.

And of course there was nothing to be afraid of. It was only Dewey—Linda's mouth twisted into an ugly smile. It might have been "only Dewey" who had left her in the library. And here he was, investigating the fuse box with the aid of a flashlight, whistling softly between his teeth as if something puzzled him.

"Did someone disconnect the lights?" Linda said politely.

Dewey's thin muscular shoulders stiffened. "You shouldn't sneak up on me like that, Linda.

Consider my weak heart. No; I think a fuse has blown out."

"Don't bother to lie about it. I thought that too. I don't now. Someone pulled the switch. Isn't that it?"

"Well—yes. Though how you guessed . . . Would it be impertinent to inquire what you're doing down here at this hour?"

"You tell me, first."

"I couldn't sleep."

"That's two of us," Linda said. "And you found there were no lights? So did I. And came down to fix them? So did I. Only I didn't have a flashlight or even a match."

"And not much sense!" Dewey stopped; added quickly: "You might fall downstairs and break your neck."

"You couldn't possibly have been going to say that it's dangerous to wander around this house in the dark?"

"I just said so, didn't I? Let's stop sparring, my dear. Have you just come downstairs?"

"No."

"Then what have you been doing to occupy your time?"

Linda hesitated; then: "Don't you wish you knew?" she said. "Well, I had a sudden desire for a book from Grandfather's library. I—got locked in and I just got out."

"Did you break down the door?" Dewey said casually.

"No; I found the key. I suppose a key was provided so I wouldn't have to pound on the door and rouse everyone."

Dewey closed the fuse box and addressed the ceiling. "And this female with the nasty glint in her eye is the tomboy I used to take fishing with me!"

"You did, didn't you? But I'm trying to forget things like that," Linda said gravely. "How good you all were to me when I was a little girl. Because I'm not now. Anyway, if I told you and everyone else that someone was in the library not long ago, looking for something, what would they say to that story? Honestly now!"

"Honestly? Well, probably that you had a nightmare. At best, that some burglar—"

"Wanted to steal Grandfather's inkwell or Napoleon. You're right, though: that's about what they'd say."

"But, Linda, if—"

"No. I'm sorry, Dewey, but you won't tell me anything, so I'm—"

"Not telling me? I don't know that I blame you. But I can't tell, Linda, because—"

"Because you aren't responsible for this situation? Well, that's what Rose is worrying about."

"She is?" Dewey said eagerly. Then he laughed. "I don't want her to worry. But it's nice to think she does—about me."

Linda's candid face too faithfully mirrored her surprise. Dewey smiled wryly. "Does it never occur to any of you that I may love Rose?"

"Well, you—you asked her to marry you. After all, that's—that's something."

"A great deal. I've reached thirty-seven without marrying, you know."

"But not without opportunities," Linda said mischievously.

Dewey shrugged. "As you say. One of these men who 'just never grows up.' Hell!" He managed, with his ordinarily sleek fair hair falling untidily over one eye, to look even younger than usual. "I never had any ambition to be Peter Pan."

"It's the mother in them," Linda said solemnly. "The women, I mean. Well, I don't think Rose feels at all maternal."

"I suppose," Dewey said almost shyly, "you'd be surprised to know how often I wonder if Rose will really love me."

"Why, Dewey—she does. She doesn't even see your faults, and *that* degree of blindness must be love."

Dewey laughed, but: "Oh, that," he said. "I didn't mean that—but never mind."

"Oh, you mean *love*," Linda said intelligently. "Well, that will be more or less up to you, won't it? After all, you must have had plenty of experience."

"Out of the mouths of babes! Is this what they taught you at Miss Bannister's, Linda?"

"Girls do talk things over. That's the only time I ever made you blush, Dewey. And, you know, I think Rose could be rather—wonderful to someone who made her love him. I realized, after a talk we had today, that—well, that maybe still waters do run deep."

"I know that. She's never had a chance," Dewey said, scowling. "She is shy—and no one here ever did anything to help her gain self-confidence. Lucilla couldn't, Anette wouldn't, and, while Bertha's been kind to her, the contrast between them was never to Rose's advantage. I didn't do anything to help. But she seemed like a schoolgirl to me, long after she was. It's taken me these last three years, since she's been home all the time, to get to know her—halfway."

"I've been a self-centered little prig myself, ignoring her as a possible friend," Linda said. "But, Dewey—when you're married I do hope you'll help her choose her clothes."

Dewey grinned. "I have plans." He looked at her closely. "How about a drink? You look rather as if you'd been drawn through a knothole."

He led the way into the dining room, switched on the lights and poured her a small glass of brandy. They touched glasses.

"Health—and happiness," Dewey said. "And—Linda, promise me you won't roam around in the dark. Not outside, at least. And—why don't you get out of here? Pay someone a visit. Believe me, it would be the best thing for you to do."

"Would it? Well, I'm not going."

"I didn't suppose you would. You are beginning to remind me—sometimes not too pleasantly—of your grandfather. Well, since you're staying—don't meddle."

"Is it . . ." Linda stopped and smiled sweetly at Bertha Hobart. "Did we wake you? I'm sorry. You see, we couldn't sleep, so—"

"So we sought the consolation of strong drink," Dewey said. "The lights went out, Bertha, and we both had the same idea—which was to fix them."

"Yes, I knew they were off and because I couldn't see what time it was, I couldn't sleep."

"What—what time is it?" Linda was suddenly conscious of her bare ankles and short robe. Aunt Bertha could make you feel such a nitwit with just one affectionately reproving glance. And she looked like something out of a movie, with her hair braided down her back and the heavy folds of a red house coat sweeping the floor.

"It's past two o'clock. Time children were in bed."

"Does that mean me?"

"That means you, Dewey. Put the glasses in the kitchen and please be quiet and don't wake Lucilla. Come, dear."

"We—we didn't frighten you?" Linda said uncertainly as they went up the stairs together.

"A little. You see, your door is open and the lights are on now. So of course I wondered where you were. And I admit I was—nervous. It was foolish, not to be able to sleep just because I couldn't see the time. As if time meant anything. . . . Moody must learn to see that there are matches in our rooms."

"You tell her and she will. She doesn't pay any attention to me."

"She is rather—independent. Jump into bed. You're sure you're not chilled?"

"I'm cold," Linda admitted. "You aren't going to scold? Why shouldn't I stop to have a drink with Dewey? He's practically old enough to be my father."

Mrs. Hobart smiled. "Perhaps—in actual years. But perhaps Lucilla is right. You're growing up—grown up, as you're always saying. I realized suddenly that I was married at your age."

"Were you? Nineteen? That was—"

"Twenty-five years ago. I was very prewar. I was thinking about that too," Mrs. Hobart said. "Don't marry too young, Linda."

"I'm not going to. And if you mean Andy Duncan— don't worry."

"You know Anette," Mrs. Hobart said. "She likes to strike at us through you when she can. And don't . . ."

"Don't what?"

"Do—anything you may regret."

"Oh—Aunt Bertha! I'm sorry, but that's so indefinite and—and exasperating. You really mean: don't meddle. That's what Dewey said. But wouldn't you rather know the truth about things?"

"Things?"

"You know what I mean. Who killed Mr. Cooper—"

"Even if it was one of us, Linda?"

"Yes! Knowing would be better than suspecting everyone."

"That is, you decidedly do not think that ignorance is bliss. But when you've lived longer," Mrs. Hobart said slowly, "you may find it's preferable to knowledge. Because what a person may do doesn't always kill your love for him as quickly as you suppose. No: let's not talk any longer. You'll have to make your own decision. Good night, dear."

When her aunt had gone, Linda turned on the bedside lamp again and studied the scrap of paper she had put in a pocket of her pajamas. At first sight it was disappointing: a fragment not more than an inch and a half across at its greatest width. It was almost triangular in shape, its base badly charred but the two sides only a little scorched.

Then, making out a printed JU— and the printed numbers 19—, followed by a written 31, she realized that this had been a page from a diary. Only five whole words of writing were left: "Well, I cer—", then: "today, Mr. Gr—" and finally: "to—"

She was certain she had never seen the neat backhand before and the words were entirely commonplace. To her, at least. They might not be—to Mr. Allan.

V

Sunday morning breakfast—Anette wanted it called brunch, but Miss Lucilla said: "Fiddle-faddle!"—was at ten o'clock. Everyone would be there, as they had every Sunday morning for the past fifteen years. But Miss Lucilla, who woke early, had rolls and coffee in her room at eight o'clock.

It was seven-thirty now. Linda sat down, scribbled a few lines on a sheet of paper, slipped downstairs and into the kitchen.

"Take this to Aunt Lucilla with her tray, Moody. I'm going for a ride. No, I won't stop for coffee."

Lovett already had the garage doors open and was cleaning car cushions. At least, they were piled high on a bench with a small vacuum cleaner lying beside them. But as Linda came up to him he was standing still, staring at something in his hand.

He closed his fingers quickly and thrust the hand into his pocket before she could see what he had been looking at. He said quickly:

"I'll get the cushions back in Mr. Stinson's car. Too bad you haven't one of your own."

"Mr. Stinson's does very well." Linda thought Lovett was inclined to be impertinent—to her. He said now:

"Kind of early for a ride, isn't it?" his eyes on her slim legs as she got into the car.

"Quite early. Be sure to return anything you find slipped down behind the cushions, won't you, Lovett?"

Lovett reddened. "I always do, miss. Did you lose something?"

"Not that I know of. Did you find something?"

"Just Miss Hadley's hairpins, miss. She does shed a lot of them. . . . You've got plenty of gas." Lovett was suddenly and satisfyingly deferential. "I'll ride along and open the gates for you."

Before she had time to shift into high after driving through the gates, Linda saw a stooped blue-overalled figure just emerging from the mill offices across the road. She recognized old Hanson, night watchman at the mill when they were not running a night shift, and stopped the car.

"Jump in," she called. "I'll take you home."

Hanson bobbed gratefully, wiped his feet on the running board and perched on the extreme edge of the seat. "That's real nice of you, Miss Linda. I ain't as young as once. I'm pretty tired when morning comes. Especially with such goings on as on T'ursday night."

"What goings on? I thought you slept most of the night."

Hanson smiled politely. "You have your little joke, Miss Linda. You know I don't sleep. I been here long time; they trust me. I don't sleep T'ursday night and I see things."

"What kind of things? Tell me about it."

Hanson's story, in spite of peculiarities of idiom and a scanty vocabulary, carried a certain stark ring of reality. It was when he was making his second rounds, after midnight, that "it happened", he said. He had been through the mill proper and was coming back across the strip of ground that separated it from the offices. He had a good flashlight but of course its light carried only so far.

Well, Miss Linda knew how dark the nights were lately. There were funny shadows in the mill yard. If you looked at them long enough you thought you saw them move. You had to make certain they weren't people because someone with a grudge against the mill owners might be up to mischief. He'd had his job long enough that he didn't imagine things that weren't there.

And he certainly saw someone move away from the side entrance to the offices. The door that opened onto the yard; not the main door on the road. But by the time he got close enough that his light did any good, the person who had been in the shadows was gone.

There were stacks of lumber in the yard, piled so high you couldn't see over them. Leif had stood still and listened. Sometimes sounds echoed at night. He thought he heard running footsteps and someone panting a little. On the other side of the stacked lumber, that was. So then he had run around the end of it: run as fast as he could.

But it didn't do any good. Whoever it was had a head start on him And his view of the mill gates and the road was cut off while he was behind the lumber. When he was out in the clear again, he couldn't see anyone, though he'd gone all the way to the gates and outside of them. But he had seen it, just the same: someone dressed in something dark, he thought. And tall, though he might be mistaken about that.

Midway of Hanson's recital they had stopped in front of his weathered log shack. Linda, elbows on the steering wheel, said:

"I suppose the doors were all locked?"

"Them doors lock themselves, Miss Linda."

"And everybody has keys."

"Sure they do. But it wasn't one of you, so no one got into the offices even if it did look like somebody coming out. It must have been just one of these no-accounts we got working for us sneaking around. Mr. Hadley says he will keep lookout on one or two he ain't trust too much. So do Mr. Stinson."

"Did they? Would you . . ." No, she couldn't ask Hanson to talk to Mr. Allan. He wouldn't understand why he should and he'd been too long with the Graydons to talk without their permission. "Never mind," Linda said. "You'd better run on to your breakfast."

She knew where Andy lived—at Mrs. Telefer's boarding house. She marched into the shabby red house, head high.

"Will you kindly tell Mr. Duncan that Miss Graydon would like to speak to him?"

The Graydon manner was effective. Mrs. Telefer waddled hastily up the stairs instead of shouting from the foot of them. In a few minutes Andy came down, red hair shining with water, his very clean and starched shirt buttoned crooked. And looking, but trying not to, a little embarrassed.

"I'm sorry," Linda said, "but it was the choice of two evils—coming here or marching into the sheriff's office."

"The—do you want to—"

"Let's go outside where there's no one to listen to us." Linda did not bother to lower her voice. Mrs. Telefer's bedraggled skirt vanished around a corner as they went through the hall. "Yes, I want to talk to Mr. Allan and I don't want anyone to see me going into his office. So I've sacrificed your reputation—"

"Don't be silly! I was thinking about you. I'll take you to Rocky's house: that's the best way. Gives you an excuse of some kind, like saying Eleanor asked you to breakfast."

Eleanor was making waffles and Rocky had just concluded two telephone conversations that he pronounced "interestin'." One, with the manager of the local telephone company, had elicited the information that there had been no calls from The Stockade or mill into Brookdale after six o'clock on Friday evening.

It occurred to Rocky to ask what sort of service they had at The Stockade. The answer made him smile sheepishly when he remembered that he had used Hadley's telephone in the lower hall while Hadley was upstairs. Because "they've got phones every place", the manager said. "They ring once to get us for outside calls but they can ring each other without calling us. Like a rural line with a lot of different rings for each house. Old fashioned, but they've had it twenty-five years. The mill's on a separate line, though. They have to call here to get that. It's a wonder—"

"That means they can all listen in on each other? Has Hadley got an upstairs extension?"

There were upstairs extensions in all three houses. And a telephone in the garage, too, and in the guest cabin where the chauffeur slept.

Rocky's other inquiry was addressed to Dr. Bradley, who answered it explosively because he objected to being wakened at eight o'clock.

"Anything fishy about Joshua Graydon's death? What put that into your head? I was there. . . . What? . . . No, I'm not their doctor unless they have a bellyache at two in the morning and can't wait to get to a city specialist. Joshua Graydon never had a doctor, though. . . . Oh, he did see someone in the city before he died. Fellow told him his parts were wearing out. I could have told him the same thing for a tenth the money. Same thing I tell Hadley. But old Josh died of—if you want details—fractured leg, crushed chest, fractured skull. Good thing he never came to."

"And the others? Miss Evans and the chauffeur?"

"They were dead when I got there. The same as Josh, only more so, far 's details go."

"How old was Miss Evans? Did you know her at all?"

"Oh, about thirty. Why should I know her? She had about as much personality as a rabbit. Pink nose that twitched. Can't stand women with pink noses. That all? . . . Well, for God's sake, call a little later in the day after this."

Eleanor put the waffle iron on the table and invited Rocky to "plug it in. The coffee pot too. You mustn't," she said, returning with a pitcher of batter, "neglect these little courtesies that make marriages last, even if your mind is occupied with far more important things."

"Um-hum," Rocky said absently. "I wish people wouldn't get killed on Friday. By the time you get started it's Sunday. God knows when I'll hear from Pat McCarthy. And I've got to send him another wire."

"Concerning what?"

"That fellow Hobart. It's just possible he might've known Cooper. It's safer to— Oh Lord! Somebody at the door. And I'm hungry."

"I think," Eleanor said, after looking out the window, "that you won't mind waiting a while in this case. It's Andy, with Linda Graydon. He's bringing her to the side door, now."

Linda looked flushed and defiant and very young. She refused breakfast; began: "I've decided to—that is . . ." and then slammed a scrap of paper down on the table. "There! There it is and I—"

"You'd better have something to eat," Eleanor said. "Confidences come more easily over food."

"Well, I am hungry. And I love waffles. I—I don't know where to begin," Linda said. "I thought I did."

"Begin at the beginnin', go straight through to the end an' then stop," Rocky drawled. "Or can you?"

Linda looked at him gratefully. "I'm glad you see that perhaps I can't. But I'm afraid. Someone else may be killed if you can't do something about it. Isn't it true that after any murder there's apt to be someone who knows too much about it—for the murderer's peace of mind? Or that sometimes someone doesn't even know he knows anything but there's the danger he might realize he did sometime, so he has to be removed?"

"Yes, that's quite often the way it works out."

"Well—even if someone knows too much and *knows* he does, being an accessory isn't as bad as being killed for knowing, is it?"

"Most people would say nothin' was quite as bad as bein' killed," Rocky said. "Sirup? Andy? Well, make up your mind what you're entitled to tell me. And then tell all of it and not just what you think is important."

Linda frowned at her plate. She would tell—well, she wouldn't tell what Rose had said to her about Dewey or Dewey about Rose. Or her conversation with Aunt Bertha or even Anette's remark about having been "damned obliging."

She would tell him that Dewey had been in the hall when she came out of the library and that Aunt Bertha had come downstairs to find them. And she would repeat Moody's conversation as faithfully as possible and Hanson's story, and describe her own experience in and out of the library.

"I'll be talking forever," she sighed. "Well, here goes."

Rocky heard her through without interruption, mechanically consuming an extraordinary number of waffles as he listened.

"There," Linda said finally. "Is any of that any good?"

"As the small boy said to his teacher: 'Good? Hell, it's perfect!'" Rocky pushed his plate aside. "When you told about Cooper wandering aroun' the house everyone heard you but Graydon and Hadley?"

"Yes. But what I said could have been passed on to them by Anette and Rose. You know that, of course."

"What did you think when you met Cooper?"

"I wondered why they let him stay. Aunt Lucilla wasn't well and was in bed most of Thursday and Friday. If he was a friend of Dewey's and Earl's, I didn't think much of their taste."

"What do you know about his movements while he was there?"

"I stayed all night with Rose Thursday because we got home late. And I was with her most of Friday morning, looking over the things we'd bought. I met Mr. Cooper at lunch time. That was a perfectly pleasant meal: so was dinner that night—I thought. I told you about talking to him in the early afternoon. Then Rose and Anette came over for tea but Aunt Lucilla didn't come downstairs until dinnertime. And none of the men were there except Mr. Cooper. He didn't stay long and Anette left early too.

"Well, I don't know what he was doing the rest of the time. I went upstairs right after dinner Friday night. I was bored. I didn't hear Mr. Cooper come upstairs but I was reading and his room was across the hall from mine. I'm afraid that's all I can tell you."

"Now: about these words you heard outside the library. Have I got them right? 'You wouldn't dare'—'dare'—'witness'—'regretted'—'murder'—'again' and then 'armed'?"

"I think that's the correct order. I said them over and over. And there were long pauses between all but the first three and the last two. I mean: intervals when I couldn't hear anything at all."

"And you've no idea who was talkin'?"

"It seems impossible, but I found out a whisper hasn't any personality. I suppose you're thinking about Dewey and Aunt Bertha."

"No," Rocky said, "their wakin' up isn't anything to get excited about, any more than Miss Lucilla's not wakin'. And you're right about a whisper bein' hard to identify. This hand on your shoulder. You said it was strong but you wouldn't know if it was—man's or woman's?"

"No. My robe was too thick for that. Though I could feel fingers digging into me."

Andy muttered incoherently and Linda smiled at him. "I don't think I was in any danger. I was just inconvenient for a few minutes, like any nosy woman is. Mr. Allan—what about that scrap of paper?"

"It looks like it came from a small diary. The words that 're left don't do us any good, but as a lead it can't be beat."

"Why?"

"Well, the writer put down something about Mr. Graydon—your grandfather. I'll guess that even if we've only a *Gr* to go on. If it referred to your uncle—well, who would call him Mr. Graydon?"

"But I never saw the writing before and I know everyone's. Even Mr. Hadley's."

"O.K. But I was goin' to say that only someone who didn't know either Earl or Joshua Graydon well would refer to either of 'em so formally in a diary. There bein' two Mr. Graydons in '31, Earl would probably be designated by his first name too. The important thing is that probably only an employee would say 'Mr. Graydon' in a diary."

"Yes—but who?"

"Mr. Cooper's half-sister, Maud Evans."

VI

Eleanor smiled, thinking that Rocky wasn't above striving for dramatic effects. And it wasn't quite fair to startle Linda, as she so obviously was startled.

"But—they must have known! Why didn't they tell me?"

"That," Rocky said, "is what I want to know." But Linda raced on:

"Now I see why some of the things I told you are 'perfect.' That scrap of diary and Moody's saying Miss Evans was curious. If she was and kept a diary . . ." Linda stopped, one hand going to her mouth in a dismayed gesture.

"Yes," Rocky said, "you see where it's leadin' you. But it was there all along."

Linda drew a deep breath. "What?" she said steadily.

"Blackmail. I always suspected that. Everything Cooper said and the way he came up here suggested that. Now we find out he was Maud Evans' half-brother. And she died when he was—probably—a long ways from here. If he finally came up to ask about her, common courtesy might call for you to extend him some hospitality. So why do everything to hide his connection with Maud Evans; the one good excuse you had for toleratin' him at all?"

"Because—because there is something connected with her that they—we don't want known."

"It looks that way. Of course we've got to prove that piece of diary was hers."

"You will. I know you will. But how did Mr. Cooper get it? If he had it?"

"He must have. If one of you had it, it would've been burned long ago. But we'll have to find out what became of Miss Evans' things after she died.

They should've been sent to him but I don't think he was in the state then. He told you he hadn't been in the city for years."

"So that was why he didn't come up here before? Because he didn't have a chance to look over her things until recently?"

"Maybe. He didn't seem to be very prosp'rous but he put out money for the railroad fare up here."

Linda pounded the table with a clenched fist. "Oh—and they talk about the younger generation! Old people haven't any sense! Suppose he did know something discreditable to us through his sister? Why lie about it when it would have been so simple if they'd told the truth?"

"It would have been simple if he hadn't been killed," Rocky corrected. "Blackmail's a good motive for murder, you know."

"Yes—but why did he hide papers in the library? If he did?"

"He showed he was uneasy, wanting a key to his room. It's hard to see how he could be robbed, but a blackmailer can't complain if he is. He must have had some documents—the good old documents!— to get very far with his game. He probably had the most important ones on him, because he'd have to hand 'em over to get paid. But he may've figured on holdin' out a few."

"Then—why didn't they just pay him and turn him out?"

"I'd like to know," Rocky said unsatisfactorily. "That's arguin' everyone was concerned."

"Oh! Yes—but do they *all* have to be—in it?"

"No. It seems if they had been, they'd have paid him and thrown him out. Or just thrown him out at once."

Rocky was thinking: someone didn't dare turn him away. For someone, Cooper had a secret and dangerous message; one that couldn't be confided to other members of the family. Acting as a group, they could have disposed very quickly of Cooper. And between them, if they wanted to pay, they could surely have raised the money.

There were no facts to prove his theory but he was going to accept it as proven and go on—to look for the one person or persons Cooper had come to The Stockade to deal with. He'd had opportunity to talk privately to anyone there. No use saying that because Mrs. Hobart and Anette Graydon were first to see him, his threat was necessarily to either of them. They had probably received him as Maud Evans' half-brother. But afterward . . . He said abruptly:

"Did you see Mrs. Graydon Thursday night or at all Friday until teatime?"

"No," Linda said. "I didn't."

"Did you talk to her much then?"

"No. I told you she didn't stay long."

"And Miss Lucilla didn't come down for tea?"

"No. I don't think she met Mr. Cooper until dinnertime Thursday or saw him again until Friday night. I don't know, of course."

"When you got home Friday did you talk to her?"

"I went in to ask how she was," Linda said. "That was after lunch. But she was asleep."

"That's fine. Gives me an idea," Rocky said provokingly. "I can use one. Well, I guess that's all."

"All! Why—"

"All you can tell me. I've got some questions to ask your aunts. And I want Molly Harris' address. Do you think they have it?"

"I don't . . . Yes, Aunt Lucilla has. I addressed Christmas cards for her last year and I sent one to a Miss Harris."

Andy, perhaps weary of the role of silent listener, ventured: "You don't think she's important?"

"Moody said she was friendly with Maud Evans. Also, she got fired."

"Because she got to hearing ghosts," Andy jeered.

Rocky looked at him thoughtfully. "She heard something she couldn't have heard unless she accounted for it like that," he said finally. "I've known two or three people who thought they saw ghosts. They didn't—but they saw *something*."

"What about old Hanson's story?" Linda asked. "Could the person he saw have been Mr. Cooper? But that doesn't make sense."

"Probably Hadley is right and it was just one of the mill hands," Rocky said absently. "It don't seem important."

In less than thirty-six hours he was to remember that remark, standing at a hotel, watching the fog creep slowly over the city and thinking of death that did not creep but struck swiftly as a snake.

Just now he was too much obsessed with Maud Evans to give Hanson's story the attention it deserved. His question to Linda: "Is that all you can think of to tell me?" was more or less automatic. And when she shook her head and answered: "I think so. I'm so mixed up that I can't be certain of anything," he did not try to recall by suggestion anything she might have forgotten.

He said instead:

"Will it be easier if I go out to see your folks right now or shall I come a little later on?"

"Oh, I have to face the music, with or without your sustaining presence," Linda said forlornly. It was very evident that her youthful conviction that she was chosen to lead the Graydon tribe out of the wilderness was beginning to waver. Eleanor said quickly:

"Common sense is on your side, my dear. Family loyalty can be dangerous in situations like this."

"That's what I thought last night. Now—well, I didn't know what you were going to tell me, of course."

Rocky wondered if she really knew how dangerous the Graydon family feeling might be. It was easy enough to guess that, as a group, they had lied. But who had told the original lie that convinced them they must deny their real connection with Cooper? Or had Cooper really tried to blackmail them as a group?

Rocky shook his head impatiently. If they'd taken Cooper's presumptive attempt at blackmail seriously, why suddenly throw him out and risk his enmity? That action seemed to mean that not everyone there feared Cooper—alive.

But someone had, and for that someone all the others were lying, perhaps innocently, perhaps half suspecting the truth. And, in the latter case, blind to danger or choosing to risk it.

"I think I might as well drive along behind you," Rocky said, rising. "But you'll have to wait till I shave."

"I'll wait," Linda said. "But must you?"

Rocky grinned. "I draw the line at dressin' up in my best Sunday-go-to-meetin' suit but I couldn't stand up to either of your aunts with yesterday's whiskers on my chin."

"Y-yes, they do make you feel— Or Aunt Bertha does. She wasn't very nice to you," Linda admitted. "But she's really sweet."

"To her equals?" Rocky said blandly. "Don't get mad. I've heard Mamma talk the same way to c—s as your aunt did to me. It's a gift. I'll be with you in a minute."

He wasn't, he thought, as he followed Linda into the big living room, going to waste time asking them if they wanted to change their stories. Let that wait until he knew more than he did now. You had to have something better than theories to deal with accomplished liars.

Everyone was there: they probably had just finished breakfast. He wondered idly if they didn't ever get tired of sitting in this room and looking at each other. Then Miss Lucilla said harshly:

"So you brought her back, eh?"

"He didn't ask me to talk to him," Linda said. "I went—"

"Of your own accord? Oh, I got your note. Well, it's done now. And no doubt you meant well," Miss Lucilla conceded.

Earl Graydon cleared his throat; a sound of disagreement that drew a stony glare from Miss Lucilla. Earl blinked, pursed his lips and said nothing, but Rose Hadley got up quickly and went to Linda.

"She was worried," she said. "I have been too." She colored painfully as Anette laughed, and said with an unlooked-for flash of temper: "Well, why shouldn't we be? You don't tell us anything but expect us to lie just the same!"

Rocky decided that she was pretty, after all. Dewey looked as if he thought so too. His air of ironic detachment had vanished when she sprang to Linda's defense. He said:

"Sit down, you two. Children should be seen and not heard."

"I hope," Mrs. Hobart said, "that you'll remember Linda is—is impulsive. She seems to feel, according to the note she left us, that there is some danger we don't understand."

"When she tells you what she told me, you'll see she'd be a fool not to think that," Rocky said bluntly. "Everything she told me she learned for herself. One thing she didn't tell me, that I already knew, is that Cooper was Maud Evans' half-brother."

After an instant Earl Graydon said: "Maud Evans? Who—"

"You must believe a lie well stuck to is better 'n the truth half told, Mr. Graydon. Don't bother," Rocky said impatiently. "I'm not even goin' to ask you all why you didn't tell me. Although"—he grinned suddenly—"it bein' Sunday, I might give you a text for a sermon."

"What's that?" Dewey said, ignoring Graydon's portentous frown.

"'That which is crooked cannot be made straight: and that which is wanting cannot be numbered.'" Dewey laughed. "Well," Rocky went on, "what I do want to know is what become of Miss Evans' things after she died."

"How do I know?" Earl snapped. "I hardly knew the woman. Bertha—"

"I don't know. We had our own—trouble then, you know. The servants . . . But Moody is the only one who was here at that time."

"Well, you didn't just donate her things to the annual rummage sale, did you?" Rocky said tactlessly.

That the remark was tactless he gathered from Miss Lucilla's reaction to it. She leaned forward, gripping the arms of her chair with her broad ringed hands.

"You impertinent young whippersnapper!" she said. "Why, you . . ."

Her remarks for a full minute were mainly un-
printable. Rocky looked uneasily from her hands
to the table beside her, saw nothing there she could
conveniently throw at him, and felt it was safe to
give his full attention to her words. They were
worth attention: there was no doubt she had spent
her time in the logging camps to some advantage.
He wished, remembering Andy's insistence that
the Graydons were "cultured" persons, that he
might have been there to hear Miss Lucilla.

She paused at last for want of breath. Mrs.
Hobart had been wringing her hands and saying:
"Lucilla! Please!" Anette was tittering unpleasantly
while her husband said—not too loudly—"Lucilla, control yourself!" and Dewey appeared frankly
and openly diverted.

"You'll—you'll have to pardon my sister," Mrs.
Hobart said when she could make herself heard.
"She hasn't been well."

"Don't worry, ma'am. I've been cussed by ex-
perts," Rocky said amiably. "She's just one more
of 'em."

Miss Lucilla laughed. "I stick to what I said:
you have the nerve of a brass monkey. Sorry I lost
my temper, though. It happens now and then."

"And," Mrs. Hobart said frostily, "your suggestion that we were careless in our disposal of Miss
Evans' property—"

"I'm sorry. But I have a lot of work to do and it's gettin' late—if that clock's right."

Dewey smiled. "Now you're treading on Moody's toes. The clocks are always right; she sees to that. She's a human time clock herself, never a minute off."

"This is no time to be conversational, Dewey," Miss Lucilla said impatiently. "We were talking about the Evans woman. We buried her: you can find her grave if you're curious. Then a maid, Molly Harris, told me her one relative was Cooper and found an address in her things. I had Ellis wire—"

"It was to a hotel in San Francisco," Hadley said. "The return wire said Cooper was out of the city and asked if we could arrange funeral services here."

"Which was a cool proposition, but we did. Then we wired again, asking what to do with her things. What money she had was in a San Francisco savings bank. It was up to Cooper to straighten that out. A wire came back, signed with his name, saying to send her belongings there. I told Molly Harris to pack up every scrap that belonged to her. Every last scrap," Miss Lucilla said majestically. "She did and we sent them away. That, I considered, ended our responsibility."

"Of course. You've got Molly Harris' address?" Rocky asked.

"I suppose I have to give it to you, though why you should bother a harmless soul . . . Oh, all right," Miss Lucilla said. "Linda, run upstairs and bring down my address book."

PART THREE
"IT COULDN'T HAVE BEEN MISS EVANS—"

I

The telephone operator said: "Sheriff's office? Mr. Allan? Will you accept a collect call from Mr. McCarthy of San Francisco?"

"Will I! Put him on."

"O.K. collect, San Francisco. Here's your party. Go ahead."

"Allan? Wait a minute." Faint sounds indicated that Mr. McCarthy was settling himself for a comfortable chat. "You were in a hurry so I thought I'd phone."

"I was afraid you couldn't do much on a Sunday."

"Oh, I had the afternoon. I got your pictures then. But before that I went to the Warren. I know that dump, see? Cooper had been there, all right, and checked out Wednesday night. He'd been there since the Saturday before. Said he'd just got back from Japan. He talked to the manager—or clerk. They're one and the same.

"Cooper said he'd been working clubs and theaters all over the Orient. Some of those gangs make good money, but he probably wouldn't have been staying at the Warren if he brought back much dough. I can check up with the agencies."

"No; I don't think that's important—now," Rocky said. "But what about 'Yours Forever, Pearl.'"

McCarthy chuckled. "I saw her coming out of the hotel and when I got your picture I hotfooted it back to talk to her. Well, did I have my hands full! She's known Cooper a long time and she pulled an act when I told her the news. At that, I think she felt kind of bad. The manager says they were pretty thick: rooms adjoining and all that.

"She couldn't tell me any more about him than I'd already found out. Only she said he'd been away five years or more. She knew him before that. But she's got no idea who could have killed him."

"Is there any chance she has any of his things? He only carried a satchel up here. Were you in her room?"

"Yes, and you said to find out if he left anything at the hotel. He didn't, in the room he had. She flared right up when I asked her, but my bet is he left what he didn't take up there with her. How much is it worth to you to get hold of his things, if she's got any of them?"

"A lot—maybe. How long's she been at the Warren?"

"Seven years. Cooper used to stay there, but the place keeps changing hands, so the guy that runs it now didn't know him—"

"Seven years . . . That's fine. Well, what about the other angle? Did they treat you so well at the Palace?"

"Oh, I have connections," McCarthy said complacently. "Stinson and Graydon were there September thirteenth and fourteenth, all right, but Cooper wasn't even in the city then. But say, what about little Pearlie?"

"I'm comin' down myself. There's someone else I've got to see—pers'nally. I can take off by seven tomorrow and meet you by ten, allowin' time to get across the bridge if I land at Alameda."

"So long as it's you and not me that does the flying," McCarthy said. "Where'll I meet you?"

"Oh—I suppose my wife will be with me and she likes to stay at the Clift. That's as good as any place."

"I'll be waiting for you. We'll have to see Pearl before four. She works at one of these all-night lunch joints. With probably," McCarthy remarked, "other activities on the side. Not been bothered with reporters?"

"Why should we be? A few lines in today's paper sayin' a man was killed in a hotel."

"Oh, sure. Never mind, I won't tell. If I did, some of the boys would pull out on tonight's train."

"No, thanks. I've got to go over an' pacify the local press now. Another blessin' I'm counting is that our D.A. won't get back from his usual weekend trip till tomorrow mornin'; him and the hotel owner. Well, I'll be seein' you."

Andy came in as he pushed the telephone aside. "I've had supper and I thought maybe you'd want me here, as long as you've been working."

"I want to clear ever'thing up. I've talked to Clarence. He sticks to his story. Hadley came in to 'view the remains.' Just a formality. I'm goin' to the city tomorrow to talk to Molly Harris. That," Rocky said, grinning, "leaves you in charge."

"Gosh!" Andy hesitated between gratification and apprehension. "Well, if you have to go . . . Only I can't handle that bunch out at The Stockade."

"I haven't done so well with 'em myself! Let them stew in their own juice for a while. I'll be back the middle of Tuesday mornin'."

"Well, then—I'm not to do anything at all?"

"Go ahead and solve the case if you want to," Rocky said unkindly. "You'd better stay in town, though, whatever happens in the rest of the county. I'm going over to the newspaper office. Ernie Cronin called up a while ago and, from what he said, I'll have to do some artistic lyin' to satisfy him—"

"I'll stay here for a while. I'd like to use the typewriter," Andy said. "I thought I might make kind of an outline. Questions, you know."

"And answers, I hope," Rocky said not too sympathetically. "Go right ahead."

He went out, passing Oscar Finch in the hall, but Oscar was not wearing his earphone, which meant he didn't care to talk or be talked to. Rocky nodded, wondering if Oscar ever left the county clerk's office, except to sleep, and went on down the courthouse steps.

Andy sat down to the typewriter, reflecting, not for the first time, that what Rocky lacked was system. He had found out a lot of interesting facts, but anyone could do that. And then Linda's being so frightened last night—poor kid!—was a lucky break.

Of course Rocky had already guessed Cooper's game had been blackmail but he couldn't really prove it, even if it was about the only reasonable explanation for his coming here. And where did that get you? Nowhere, apparently. And now Rocky was dashing off to talk to a maid who thought she'd seen ghosts. A person like that might very easily think she did, at The Stockade, and after a thing like that automobile accident.

Anyway, Andy reiterated, being systematic was a great help, no matter what you were doing. He made three neat headings: MEANS, MOTIVE AND OPPORTUNITY, and looked at them approvingly.

MEANS—well, that was the gun and they didn't have it. Someone had it—or some gun—from what Linda said. But none of that was really worth writing down. Andy pulled at his ear, considering MOTIVE.

If that was the fear of blackmail, what had any of the Graydons done that they could be black-mailed for? Everyone knew all the unsavory spots in the old man's career. Well, suppose that, as Rocky had hinted, Cooper's supposed information wasn't something that affected the Graydons just as a family. What on earth could any one—or two—of them have done that they didn't dare have known?

Andy took the paper out of the typewriter and threw it in the wastepaper basket with a shame-faced grin. Well, he thought, there was all that stuff Eleanor had repeated, that Miss Jewett had told her. But there'd been no system to the way she repeated that. Rocky had listened to all of it instead of cutting her short. As if it mattered how much candy Miss Lucilla ate. Or . . . The telephone rang. Andy said: "Sheriff's office. . . . No, this is Duncan. What can I—"

The voice at the other end of the wire was hoarse and a little breathless. "Well, listen. This is Lovett. The Graydon's chauffeur. Listen, is Allan there?"

"No, he isn't."

"Well, I got to talk to him. He said if I remembered . . . Well, I don't think I'd better drive in. Can you get in touch with him in a hurry or should I call his house?"

"He may not be home. You can call the newspaper office."

"I don't want to do that. Maybe I'd better not call from here any more at all. I'm in my room. I'll stay till he gets here. You tell him that. I . . . ."

"Hello!" Andy said finally. "Are you still there?"

"Yes. Yes, I was just listening. You do what I said, buddy. Right away."

Andy hung up, then snatched the receiver from the hook again. "Operator! Get me the Brookdale *Sun* right away."

Ernest Cronin said: "Rocky just left to go home. Is there anything I—"

"Not a thing, Ernie. It isn't important. . . . Operator! Ring Mrs. Allan, please. . . . Eleanor? Is Rocky there?"

"Not yet. I've been expecting him."

Andy said: "Hell!" which was, for him, extreme profanity. "Excuse me, Eleanor. He must be almost home now. Tell him Lovett wants to talk to him; wants him to come out there. And he sounded excited—or scared—about something. I wish Rocky 'd pick me up here," Andy said wistfully. "Is his car there? Well, maybe he will."

He looked at the clock. Just eight. If Rocky did stop by for him he should be here in five minutes. Well, ten at the most. When ten minutes had passed he thought hopefully: "Maybe fifteen, if he got held up going home. I'll go out and see if I can find him."

He had gone half a block when car lights swept across his eyes, blinding him momentarily. Then Rocky called: "If that's you, come on," hardly stopping the car. "I wasn't going to come after you," he said grimly. "One of these pests that want to tell you how to do your own work better button-holed me on the way home, so I just got started."

"I figured that. What do you suppose Lovett has to tell?"

"How do I know? I'd be glad just to know he'll have a chance to tell it. Why the devil," Rocky said with a greater degree of irritation than Andy had ever encountered in him, "didn't you jump in a car yourself and go out there hell-bent?"

"Why, I didn't think of it."

"Well, that's my fault. I haven't encouraged you to go ahead on your own. And I suppose you don't know that anyone at The Stockade could hear what Lovett was sayin' to you just by listenin' in?"

Andy said: "Good Lord! He thought someone might be doing that." And Rocky put his foot down, hard, on the accelerator.

Lovett hung up the receiver and wiped his moist palms on his trousers. He was acting like an old woman, getting in such a sweat over this business. Maybe, after all, no one had been listening in. But anyone could who wanted to.

He supposed they'd say they never did, and that might be true for most times but things were different now. And when he rang Brookdale they could hear that ring in all three houses.

Well, he was safe here—wasn't he? The door was locked and he'd closed the windows. Maybe he'd better put out all the lights except the one by his bed.

He rubbed his hands together; they didn't seem to stop sweating. But why the hell hadn't they cleared some of the trees away from this place? When there was any wind, like tonight, the funny sighing noise it made kept you awake hours, once you got to listening to it.

Lovett sat on the bed and stared at his grimy fingers. He might be a fool, anyway, passing up a chance to make a little easy money. But that stuck-up snip . . . Lovett spat thoughtfully. Pretty legs she had. He could go for her. But she'd seen he was cleaning out the cars and she'd been too quick with her: "Be sure to return anything you find."

Just as good as calling a man a thief. All he'd ever kept was cigarettes and a little loose change. But he'd heard old Sourpuss whispering to Clara that Miss Linda had gone in to see the sheriff this morning. So it was even money she'd told him and a wonder Allan hadn't already been out to see him.

And he wasn't anxious to get mixed up with that long-legged bastard. Maybe they didn't have a third degree up here in the sticks but that guy could take you apart if he got mad enough. Throw you in jail and let you rot there.

Lovett took a drink: not his first. That steadied his hands. Hell, he was safe here and he was doing the safest thing too. Because if he collected a nice little wad of hush money, his chances of ever spending it might not be very good. Not unless he could lam out of here, and if he did that they'd probably say he must have killed that guy Cooper.

Anyway, he couldn't be sure—a look wasn't much to go on. But Lovett shivered and reached for the bottle of whisky again. Still, that kind of a look, when he'd just muttered: "I found your cigarette lighter in Mr. Hadley's car today . . ."

There was something funny going on here, any-way. Not just that business about Hadley's car. Saturday night's mail . . . . He always took that out to the Junction when there had been any let-ters written in the afternoon. Something about the trains and post office in this hick town. But last night . . .

The doorknob rattled a little as someone turned it. Lovett grinned unpleasantly. Maybe they thought he'd open the door? Fat chance! He was too smart for that.

Still, he wouldn't get anything out of Allan and it might be safe, after all, to just . . . Well, no harm in talking it over. If it was worth his while, he still had time to think up some cock-and-bull story to tell Allan. He walked unsteadily toward the door. He'd talk a little, without unlocking it.

II

"But you're not," Andy said disbelievingly, "going to the city after this!"

Rocky went on writing. "I can't raise the dead," he said inattentively. "You can clear up odds and ends tomorrow." He reached for a blotter; then handed Andy what he had written. "For your in-formation. If you can shake those stories, you have my blessing."

Andy reddened sensitively, taking the sheets of paper. He had been left in Lovett's cabin to call the doctor and coroner, while Rocky went on to announce Lovett's death to the Graydons. And, he said, "get their stories before they have a chance to get together."

Lovett had called the office at about five minutes of eight. Rocky and Andy had arrived at his cabin at eight-twenty-five. Dinner had been at the old-fashioned Sunday hour of four; the evening, it seemed, was spent mainly in digesting it and listening to the radio. Andy read the neat statement:

"*Lucilla Graydon:* upstairs in bed; says she didn't feel well. Heard no shots. Telephone in upstairs hall but says she didn't hear it ring as had radio going in her room.

"*Bertha Hobart:* in her bedroom though not in bed. Heard no shots. Verifies Miss L.'s statement regarding radio. Could have listened in on upstairs phone or sneaked down to lower hall to phone there. So could Miss Lucilla.

"*Linda Graydon:* was with Rose Hadley. Left here about seven-forty-five. Heard telephone ring at Hadley's; paid no attention to it. Heard no shots; Hadley's house farthest from Lovett's cabin.

"*Rose Hadley:* see above.

"*Anette Graydon:* in living room with radio turned on. Didn't hear shots or telephone. Her maid paying visit to Hadley's maid. Neither heard shots.

"*Earl Graydon:* writing letters in room across hall from living room with door closed. Says Anette playing radio too loudly and couldn't hear anything else.

"*Ellis Hadley:* went over to offices to get papers about eight—he says. No verification. I met him, coming back, about eight-forty.

"*Dewey Stinson:* had living room to himself and says he went to sleep over a book and didn't wake up till eight-thirty.

"*Clara and Moody:* Also have radio and were playing it. Clara has idea she heard a 'popping noise' during Jack Benny's program but very uncertain. (Mill hands' bunkhouse too far away for them to hear anything.)"

"Well," Andy admitted, "that only eliminates Linda and Miss Hadley. Though how anyone would dare slip out, particularly from this house—"

"Someone took that chance. Once outside, there's no lights on the grounds and it's a dark night."

"I don't see . . . Lovett had the windows locked and most of the lights out. And he sounded scared when he talked to me."

"So why did he—probably—unlock his door? The damned fool! Someone talked him into it. And he'd killed most of a quart of whisky."

"You think someone offered him money to keep still?"

"Must have. No other reason to let someone in when he'd showed he was scared. And thought when he was talkin' to you that someone might be listening in. Did you hear a radio when you were talking to him?"

Andy frowned. "I've tried to remember but I can't be sure. If he heard one playing, I should have. But you could listen in on the downstairs phone here or the upstairs phone at Earl Graydon's—or Hadley's—without Lovett hearing a radio playing in the background."

"At Hadley's, yes. At Earl Graydon's, maybe. Anette Graydon had hers goin' full force, according to Earl Graydon. Miss Lucilla says she wasn't playin' hers loud. Which means she could've heard the telephone ring. So could Mrs. Hobart, in that case. Well, that don't get us anywhere. I wondered, comin' out, why Lovett hadn't peddled his information to the person concerned. I'd have expected him to. He must have tried it first and either got scared afterwards or didn't get any results—right away."

"He was shot twice," Andy said slowly.

"And Cooper three times. Well, if Doc is right about the gun, a 25 automatic is a weak load. But a convenient gun to carry. Anyway, they weren't taking any chances."

"And what was he going to tell you? Linda says—"

"Go bring her in, will you? I haven't had time to talk to her yet."

"Well . . ." Andy went reluctantly, because the Graydons were in full force across the hall. But no one paid any attention to him and Linda was up and swiftly across the room as soon as he appeared at the door.

"I wasn't hysterical when I said it was my fault," she told Rocky. "But how did I know? I thought I'd told you everything. I hadn't thought about a car—"

"What car?"

"Whatever one was used to get from here to the hotel the night Mr. Cooper was killed. Some car must have been used. Well, Lovett takes care of the cars and if one was out in the storm—"

"He said none had been."

"Yes, but he cleaned all the car cushions this morning! Took them out and vacuumed them. You know how you lose things in a car: how they drop behind the cushions. And he had something in his hand he didn't want me to see."

"So that was it?" Rocky sighed. "I should get up and let Andy kick me where it'd do the most good."

"Why," Andy said rather smugly, "didn't you examine the car?"

"Because I figured Hadley already had done that. Which is no excuse. If he did, he missed something. It must have been something pretty small—but distinctive. You didn't see what he had in his hand, Miss Graydon?"

"No. He closed his hand and put it in his pocket. So, as you say, it must have been something small. What do people lose out of their pockets and purses? Almost anything and everything, I suppose. Oh, Mr. Allan, why didn't you say something to me about cars!"

"It's no excuse to say I didn't want to give you any more unpleasant ideas. Did you talk any to Lovett this mornin'?"

"I asked him—to—to put him in his place—to be sure to return anything he found slipped down behind the cushions. Oh! Oh—gosh! Do you suppose . . ."

"He probably thought you'd told me about that so he'd better talk to me. But don't worry. He'd evidently tried to collect hush money before he called me, and that meant his life wasn't worth much. I suppose he knew who he had to be afraid of but they talked him into openin' the door. So whatever he found in the car isn't on him now."

"Moody says he heard her tell Clara I'd been in to see you. Maybe that made him change his plans and decide to talk to you," Linda said.

"Probably. Any guns aroun' this place?"

"Guns? Grandfather's collection is right in the drawer of that table where you're sitting."

"Oh." Rocky opened the drawer. "They seem to be in good condition."

"Everything in this room is dusted religiously. And Aunt Lucilla has a gun in her room: a large one. Perhaps Dewey has one, too, in his room. You see, we used to do target shooting when Grandfather was living. Aunt Bertha and Earl and I used his guns," Linda said conscientiously. "And Mr. Hadley has his own. Rose and Anette wouldn't shoot. Anette doesn't like to and Rose is a little nearsighted."

"Oh well, if this place is an armed camp! No small automatics in this drawer. . . . Well, I reckon that's all. You run on to bed."

"I believe I'm being politely dismissed. Good night, Mr. Allan. Good night, Andy."

"You couldn't search the house?" Andy ventured.

"You wouldn't find that gun if someone still has some use for it. But I will just retire these from circulation." Rocky locked the table drawer and put the key in his pocket. "Now, you'd better go home and go to bed."

"But—"

"You need to get some sleep tonight. Tomorrow find out all you can about Lovett, here and in town. What he did yesterday and today. Apparently nothin' out of the way. Mrs. Graydon's maid is cross-eyed and the Hadley's weighs about two-fifty, but find out if either of them had much to do with Lovett."

"Aw—Rocky! I can't ask questions like that!"

"This is your practical experience," Rocky said heartlessly. "Go to the inquest too. I've already arranged that with Sloane before he and Doc left. I'll look Lovett's things over again, though all I found was some pretty rank letters from some dame in the city. I'm stayin' here tonight, in that cabin. I suppose they'll agree it's as well to have someone keep an eye on the grounds tonight. Graydon suggests Lovett had an enemy in Brookdale who sneaked in an' killed him."

"But that telephone call?"

"Coincidence, Mr. Graydon says. Well, find out if Lovett did have any enemies. Let's be thorough. Can you pull the trigger of a gun without closin' your eyes?"

"Of course I can!"

"Well, get yourself a gun and wear it tomorrow night. You'd better stay in that cabin and keep an eye on the place. You can take my car home now and tell Eleanor to be ready to leave by seven. Come back for me tomorrow about six. I can't think of anything more for you to do tomorrow, but anything else that occurs to you—"

"I can do in my spare time, I suppose? Thanks: I think what you've outlined will keep me from being bored with life."

Rocky laughed. "Well, maybe it is too much? How about getting—"

"No; if you pulled in any special deputies I'd be hours explaining things to them. I'll get along all right. But how about you, doing without sleep?"

"I'll get some sleep. I'm stayin' here more for the moral effect than anything else. You— Open the door, will you? Someone knockin'."

"We've been talking it over," Ellis Hadley said, "and wonder if one of us shouldn't appear at the inquest."

"So you're elected again?"

Hadley nodded. "It happens that I hired Lovett. Interviewed him in the city when I was there on business."

"Know much about him?"

"No. He had good enough references."

"And he wasn't at all handsome," Rocky said innocently.

Hadley looked at him sharply. "No. He'd been discharged from several positions within six months, but it isn't easy to get a man to come up here and he knew his business. Lucilla gave me his references if you—"

"I'll take 'em. About the inquest; one of you had better attend, the cor'ner thinks. And I reckon you'll make a much better impression on the jury than Mr. Graydon would."

Hadley smiled reluctantly. "Lucilla said something to that effect. But while Earl does sometimes have an unfortunate manner it's really only that he—he—"

"Suffers from an inferiority complex?"

"Why, how did you—"

"Oh, ever'thing adds up to that. His father, his older brother, Miss Lucilla, you bein' manager of the mill—an' his wife. And people like him, if they've got a fam'ly reputation that amounts to anything, are apt to wrap themselves up in it for protection."

Rocky stopped, stared thoughtfully at Joshua Graydon's clay Napoleon, and reached for a sheet of paper. He wrote: "Find out if anyone saw where Earl Graydon went when he was in town Friday. Especially if he was at the bank. You'll have to be careful how you go about it, but do the best you can."

He folded the note, handed it to Andy and said: "You'd better beat it, kid." And to Hadley: "Manners haven't any place in a murder investigation."

"That's quite all right," Hadley said automatically. "You're a rather good judge of people, aren't you, Allan?"

"Of men, maybe. Murder cases are a lib'ral education in human nature. But women—I don't even understand my own wife sometimes," Rocky complained. "She surprises me. So did your daughter."

"When she spoke out 'in meeting'? Yes; she surprises me now and then. Even Dewey, I think, and he understands women rather well."

"Maybe. I always thought, though, that the fellow who said 'I learned about women from her' was just kidding himself."

Hadley laughed. "Very likely. And it's true we often don't know anything about those we love best. And can't even do what we want for them," he added soberly. "But I—I think Dewey will make Rose very happy."

"I'm sure he will," Rocky said politely. "Will you tell me: why does Miss Lucilla dress like a—a dowager?"

"You think it doesn't suit her? She admits that but she has a rather perverse sense of humor and says that as she's been cast in the role of the old lady who rules with a hand of iron in a velvet glove, she will at least dress the part. Though, as she says, she doesn't wear the velvet glove."

"No, I wouldn't say she did." Rocky studied Hadley covertly, wondering why the man didn't go. He stood frowning at the floor, shoulders sagging.

"I was wondering," he said at last, "if we are going to have labor troubles. Frankly, we can't afford to. Linda says she told you Hanson's story."

"Does it worry you? Have you got any men workin' for you who might make trouble?"

"There are always one or two. But, no; I haven't been expecting any trouble. Still, someone wandering around the mill after midnight . . ."

"Hanson decided, I understand, that this midnight prowler couldn't have come out of the mill offices, though his first idea was that someone did. But it might not have been a man he saw or a mill hand. I wonder if you've been thinkin' about that just now?"

"I'm afraid I'm very tired," Hadley said. "It came into my head and I thought you might know."

Rocky looked at him with polite disbelief. "Yes? Well, is there anything in your offices anyone would want?"

"Only the company papers and books and a few odds and ends. No; it must have been one of the men. Time will tell. Well, I'll say good night, Mr. Allan."

Rocky, already wondering if it was safe to leave Andy to carry on alone, let Hadley go without thinking to inquire what were those "few odds and ends" kept in the company offices.

III

Rocky looked up toward Chinatown's brilliant pagodas, at the narrow red-and-green temple across the street and the tiny discouraged park with its mangy grass and rusted benches.

"Nice neighborhood," he said.

McCarthy, pink-jowled, dapper and derbied, said: "Fringe of Chinatown. Go down Kearney and you'll run into a mess of Filipinos. You'd be surprised the number of white girls . . . Well, this is it. I told you it was a dump."

The Warren Hotel announced itself to the world with a modest sign on its single door: "Permanent and Transient. Rates Reasonable." They went up a narrow stairway, dimly lighted.

"Theatrical?" Rocky asked.

"No, just a joint. Most of the theatrical hotels are over around Turk. I guess Cooper came here because of his little Pearl. Well," McCarthy said, "there don't seem to be anyone around. Let's see if Pearl is in."

There was no one on duty at the small desk in the upper hall, where an odor of stale food lingered damply. McCarthy knocked on a back door; said in a subdued roar:

"Pearl! Visitors! Are you decent?"

"Oh—it's you." Pearl was undeniably the blonde of the picture in Cooper's watch though she had discarded her curls for a dry and dusty permanent and there was a gap in her toothy smile. She said: "Oh, you got someone with you. Well, come in. I ain't dressed yet but it's all right, seeing's it's you."

"That's the baby." McCarthy pinched her arm perfunctorily. She giggled and sat down on the bed, generously displaying fat white legs.

"Sit down, boys. Throw them things off that chair, Mr. . . .?"

"Allan," McCarthy said. "He's the sheriff from the place where Cooper got killed."

"No! Him a sheriff!"

"Why not?" Rocky said absently. How long had she had that black eye? It must have been a peach when it was fresh. A little over a week . . . Yes, that would be about right for its present greenish-yellow tint.

"Why, I thought country sheriffs wore chin whiskers and straw hats," Pearl said with a certain naïveté. "Or, anyway, high boots and sombreros."

"You've been to the movies," Rocky said, grinning. "We take our boots off when we go to bed—or come to the city. McCarthy tells me you knew Cooper a long time. Did you ever meet his half-sister, Maud Evans?"

"Catch Wallie introducing me to her! She was too good for me—little chinless, washed-out"—Pearl searched for a word and finally ended—"rabbit! Oh, she was all right."

"What'd she do?"

"Oh, she had jobs with old people mostly. Reading to them and taking their dogs for walks. I guess she was kind of a practical nurse too."

"Cooper see much of her?"

"When he wanted to borrow money," Pearl said cynically. "She always gave it to him. Well, he was nice to her."

"Did you see him before he started off on this—what would you call it?—grand tour?"

"Not so grand, the way it turned out. Sure, I saw him. And I remember, now, that Wallie 'd come through some hick town to see her before he left. And get some money from her, I'll bet. He'd been somewheres over around Reno, I think."

"Well, they did write to each other, didn't they? Did he know, when he left, exactly where he'd be?"

"No, he was just starting out with this bunch to go through Mexico and maybe South America and then the Orient and maybe on to Australia. He didn't know for sure where he'd be," Pearl said unsuspiciously. "I guess he told her he'd let her know, soon as he was sure about the bookings or was going to be in one place long enough for letters to reach him. That's what he told me he'd do. She'd always wrote to this address because he was never long in one place when he wasn't here."

"Fine! So when she was killed they wired him here. And you opened the wire and answered it: said he was out of town and could they bury her in Brookdale."

"I didn't have no money, even if she was anything to me. And God knew when Wallie 'd be back. Couldn't keep her in cold storage till he got here, could I?"

"But you answered another wire," Rocky said with dangerous affability. "And signed Cooper's name to that because you thought you might as well have Maud Evans' things. So they sent the lot to you. And I suppose Cooper blacked your eye for that when he found out about it."

"Why—you—"

"Save it, sister. After what was said to me yesterday, your vocabulary would be just monotonous. What'd you do with her things?"

"Sold them," Pearl said sullenly. "No use the clothes rotting, what there was of them. That's what I told Wallie." She fingered her damaged eye reflectively. "He was pretty mad, though. But I kind of liked Wallie."

"He knew his sister was dead?"

"I wrote him that; not that I'm much on writing letters. And he wasn't mad long."

"Why not?" Rocky said quickly.

"Oh, I suppose I'd better spill my guts and get it over with."

McCarthy shifted his cigar to remark: "I told you you'd better play ball, toots."

"And who asked you? Lighting a cigar in a lady's bedroom without asking her . . . Well, Mr. Allan, he wasn't mad long because he found something in her things—"

"You said you sold 'em."

"Just her clothes and some books she had. But there was this mess of papers and a little diary. I kept them: God knows why. I never got around to getting rid of them and I thought Wallie might want them."

"Did he?"

"Said he did, but he didn't look at them till Tuesday morning. Well, I'd looked at them but didn't see anything interesting. I didn't know the people she worked for. But Waffle looked through the papers and the diary and something caught his eye and he went on reading and smiling the way he did sometimes."

"Was that all?"

"Oh no," Pearl said, pulling her filthy kimono together and finally fastening it at the top with a large safety pin. "It wasn't the diary he got so excited about. Though he was interested in it and finally said: 'There may be money in this but I'll have to do a little investigating first.'"

She didn't know what he meant but he went off and didn't get back until she was getting ready to go to work. When she asked what he'd been doing, he said: "Reading newspapers." Because he was really excited then.

He began looking through the loose papers like he was scared the ones he wanted might be gone. But finally he found two sheets and read them. Then he got out the diary again and when he'd looked it over he grinned and said:

"Well, there's something wrong with the setup. This may be bigger than I hoped. It means money if I'm right, and it's worth taking a chance to find out." Then he put the two sheets of paper in his pocket.

"What kind of papers were they?" Rocky said.

"Well—wait. I'll show you."

Pearl went down on her knees, presenting an ample posterior to their gaze as she lifted the covers and pulled a dilapidated suit box from underneath the bed.

"Everything's here but what Wallie took. See: this kind of things is what I mean."

Rocky lifted the top sheet of a thick bundle. It was the carbon copy, rather blurred now, of a letter apparently written by Joshua Graydon to some old friend in Lassen County. There was no signature, but the heading and various statements in the letter made it evident Joshua had dictated it.

"You didn't say Maud Evans typed," Rocky said.

"Oh, I guess she did a little bit of everything. She wasn't no stenographer."

"Mind if I look?" McCarthy scrutinized the sheet Rocky handed him. "Well, even without a magnifying glass, I'd say she wasn't an expert typist. Too much unevenness of pressure."

"I reckon, as Miss . . ."

"Noyes is the name."

". . . as Miss Noyes says, she probably could do a little of everything. Joshua Graydon wasn't well," Rocky said, half to himself. "He might have had her write letters for him. There's quite a few to his old friends. And the old boy seems to 've begun dictatin' the story of his life. 'When I was twelve years old my father decided to move his family to California . . .'"

He settled himself to read. Pearl sighed and began to file her nails, without, however, disturbing the rimes of black beneath them. McCarthy chewed on his cigar and finally winked meaningly at the half-empty bottle on the table.

"Oh—well. But how about bringing your own next time?"

"There won't," Mr. McCarthy said firmly, "be any next time. I'm a respectable married man with six little ones calling me Daddy. Happy days."

"Down the hatch. . . . Six! What a man! Live in Daly City, too, I'll bet. Your kind always does," Pearl said unflatteringly. "Safe place to park the little woman: too far for her to get into town often and when Papa's working late—"

"There's nothin' here," Rocky said disgustingly. "And no pages missing. What'd she keep this stuff for?"

"That's what I asked Wallie. . . . Here: have a drink. . . . Wallie just said she was always keeping things. But I told you what he said after he read them two pages a second time."

"Sure there were two? Same size as these letters?"

"Same size. And everything was carbon. At least, I'm pretty sure it was. I glanced over the stuff years ago and forgot it. Then Wallie wouldn't let me read it again. But it was two pages he put in his pocket, all right."

"And he took some pages out of this diary?"

"With a razor blade. . . . What are you making a face about?"

"Your whisky has a fine flavor of something or other."

"Oh, mouthwash, I guess. I forgot to clean the glass. . . . Yes, he took a lot of pages he cut out with him?"

"I was afraid of that. That's all he took?" Rocky asked.

"I think so. He left the rest of the diary here, you see. He says: 'There's not much left there that's important but you never can tell.' Well, I read the thing, but I don't see anything to get excited about. You can take the whole mess. That is, if—"

"Sure, we get you," McCarthy said. "Not that you've got any claim to the stuff. It never was yours."

"Well, I guess I didn't have to tell you I had it, did I? And I sure would like to get me a tooth where this one got knocked out. A panhandler comes into the place I work one night and he—"

"Oh, in that case! Not that I even noticed it," McCarthy said gallantly. "Give the lady twenty-five bucks, Allan, and call it square."

"What? Oh, it's a pleasure. . . . Then Cooper decided to leave here Wednesday night?"

"Well, he didn't tell me he was going till Wednesday morning. I guess he had to put some things in hock. He came back broke."

"Didn't Miss Evans leave him some money?"

"A little in savings. I guess he kept her pretty well cleaned out. But I just kept the bankbook for him," Pearl said virtuously, fingering three limp bills. "He said he couldn't get at that quick enough; too much red tape. He got ten out of me. When I kicked, he says it would be worth every cent he put out, going up there—maybe. But that he had to go, to do some more investigating. Well," Pearl said, suddenly tearful, "he never come back. And what about a funeral?"

"That'll be tended to."

"You can take a trip up there and lay some flowers on his grave," McCarthy said. "See some scenery."

Pearl refilled her glass. "God, no! I ain't partial to scenery. Frisco's good enough for me. Your friend seems to find that diary kind of interesting. I don't see why."

"Well, leave him to it and give us another drink—"

The diary was a small one with the month and date printed at the top of each page. Maud Evans had kept the record faithfully though often she had nothing more important to write than: "Rained today. Bought new wool stockings." Rocky turned the pages hastily. June first, June second . . .

Here it was. She had a new position; she was going to be companion to an old gentleman named Graydon. He had been seeing doctors and she had interviewed him at his hotel. He was a very interesting old man and the place where he lived sounded very romantic.

Maud Evans arrived at The Stockade on the fifth of June. She recorded her impressions of the place in her small neat backhand. "It is in the mountains in northern Calif., and very medieval. I do like Mr. Graydon. Mrs. Hobart is nice when she pays any attention to you but Miss Lucilla is rather terrifying." And, later: "I don't care for Mrs. Earl Graydon. Anette, they call her. She rolls her eyes at men."

Rocky chuckled briefly and read on. "Mr. Hadley is quiet but nice. Young Mr. Graydon is quiet but not friendly. I don't think he likes me. Mr. Stinson has nice manners. But they all treat you like you don't matter. Polite when they notice you but mostly they don't."

On June fifteenth—and this someone had underscored lightly—"Miss Lucilla had an awful quarrel with her father today. I don't know what about but it's not nice of her to upset him. Not that he hasn't a temper, too, though he's nice to me." The next page, meant for June sixteenth and seventeenth, had been neatly cut out. Maud Evans resumed, on the eighteenth:

"As I said yesterday, rich people aren't always like you think they'll be. It makes you think money isn't everything. Mr. Graydon has me write his letters now. He says I type well enough and he has rheumatism in his hands."

Following a week of commonplaces regarding weather, food and the state of Joshua Graydon's health was another gap. Two pages this time, the record of four days. On the thirtieth Maud Evans had met her half-brother at the Brookdale Hotel and her next two entries dealt mainly with him.

Then, for July third and fourth, two more underscored entries. "I think Mr. Earl wanted money from Mr. Graydon today but he wouldn't give it to him. Mr. G. said he'd have to wait for his inheritance and E. said he as good as had that. Mr. G. said it was a mistake"—the writing became smaller and very cramped—"for him to think E. could even help run the Graydon Lumber Co. when he can't even keep his own wife in order. Then Mr. G. talked to Mr. Hadley quite a while."

And: "Mrs. Hobart talked to her father and cried, which seemed queer for her to do. I guess it is her husband, who seems like a nice man but Molly tells me is a great worry. He came here a few days after I did. Molly says Anette is very extravagant besides the other things."

Whatever she had written for the next five days was gone and with it the page for July tenth, when she died. Rocky sat still, turning the book over in his hard long-fingered hands. An utterly commonplace, uninteresting woman. Very nearly all you knew about her was that she wore woolen stockings when it rained and was fond of lobster Newburg. And that she would be called "curious" by people who resented her interest in their lives without realizing that she must have that compensation for the barrenness of her own.

A small pink envelope, addressed to "Mr. Walter Cooper, Warren Hotel, S.F., Calif." fluttered from the pages of the book. But there was no stamp on it or any letter in it. Rocky put it back in the diary and got up.

"I'll take this stuff along with me," he said. "Did it come to you just like this?"

"Seems to me the papers was in big envelopes. Yes; they were. But after I took them out it was too much trouble to put them back."

"O.K. Eleanor's had a long enough time in the stores to put a dent in our bank account," Rocky said to McCarthy. "She should be back at the hotel, so we'll eat there and I'll tell you what else I want you to find out for me."

"Suits me. I like redheaded women. Yes," Mc-
Carthy told Pearl, "he's married. And *his* wife
don't live in Daly City."

IV

This day, Molly Harris thought, was the kind when
you feel like something nice is going to happen.
Perhaps because of the box of candy. Days when
there was any mail at all seemed a little different.
And it was such a big box and so very expensive.
The last thing she'd expected to get, but it was
very nice of them to think of her.

She shivered a little, standing in the doorway
of her apartment. It was cold already and there
was a white bank of fog hanging over the Mari-
na. It would creep slowly in and cover the rest of
the city by evening. It was too bad she didn't get
any sun in her apartment. The building was really
very gloomy looking, with its dark stone foundation and the slate-gray paint above that. But most
of the houses on this block of Leavenworth were
like that. The rent was cheap and she had the big
bay window where she could sit and watch people
and put her "Dressmaking and Remodeling" sign.

Well, she would go in and make a little fire of
the boxes the grocery boy had brought her and
finish Mrs. Morse's blouse. She spoke to the woolly

brown dog standing with his head thrust between her ankles. "Come on, Pettums. Time to go in. Little dogs catch cold."

Pettums, with an asthmatic sniffle, nodded his head and padded slowly back into the room with the bay window. Molly built her fire, using the wrappings of the box of candy to start it. She looked longingly at the box itself. No; she had better not take even one piece. Because she could never stop with one and she had to go to see Dr. Garner tomorrow and he would scold her if he found out about it.

She sat down in the window, pushed the curtains back and threaded her needle. Two young people were coming along the opposite side of the street. The suit the girl had on—green, that was lovely with her red hair—was very smart looking. Molly wished she could see it more closely. Mrs. Morse was going to want a suit before long and she might get some good ideas from this one.

They were crossing the street. Now she would have a chance to see how those sleeves were made. They—why, they were coming here! And that was her doorbell. Of course it would be a mistake.

It was no mistake. The tall blond man sat in front of the fire and talked about the Graydons and a man who had been murdered in Brookdale. He was actually the sheriff there: this nice man

with the slow drawl and the eyes that were so pe-
culiarly light in color. And he was saying that the
man who was killed—Walter Cooper—had been
Maud Evans' half-brother.

"Oh, I remember that. I thought his name
sounded familiar," Molly said. "Miss Evans used
to talk about him. And when she was killed, poor
girl, I sent her things to him."

"Did you just bundle up ever'thing she had and
send it off? Didn't any of the Graydons look over
her things?"

"Why—no. They were still upset, and no wonder. Miss Lucilla left it all to me. She told me to
clean out the room and I got a big packing box
and put everything in it."

"Her papers too?"

"Papers? There was a little diary— Oh, I know!
The big Manila envelopes. Oh dear, I never thought
about that," Molly said. "Maybe they weren't really hers. One day when I was cleaning her room she
was putting some carbon copies of things away.
She said Mr. Graydon didn't bother about carbons
but she thought it was better to make them.

"And since he wouldn't have them cluttering up
his desk, she put them away in her room. Because
he might want to see one sometime, after all, or
lose a page of his life she was writing for him. So I

guess I shouldn't have sent those things away, but I just never thought about it."

"You were the only one who knew her well?"

"Just about. The other maid—Moody . . . Is she still there?" Rocky nodded. "Stuck-up thing!" Molly said resentfully. "She didn't like Miss Evans. She kind of looked down on her and so did the butler, of course. No one in the house ever paid any attention to her, but Mr. Graydon liked her."

"How did the Graydons get along among themselves?"

Molly coughed embarrassedly, then, her eye caught by the box of candy in all its glory of slick white paper and gilt lettering, got up hastily and took it from the table.

"Won't you have some? I'll never eat it all."

"Well . . ." Because she seemed so glad to have something to offer them, Rocky took a chocolate wrapped in gilt foil. "Aren't you going to answer my question?" he said, smiling.

"Well, the Graydons were always pretty good to me, and you know how it is. All families have little spats that don't amount to anything. Won't you please have some candy, Mrs. Allan?"

"Well—one piece. We only just had lunch."

"Oh, but candy! I'd love to eat some but my doctor won't let me. Maybe just one piece . . ."

Molly's fingers hovered covetously over the box. "No; I guess I'd better not. Maybe later. Oh, Pettums! Did he want some too?"

Pettums caught the chocolate in mid-air, gulped gratefully and lay down again. Rocky said:

"You say the Graydons were good to you, but it seems to me they fired you for a mighty little thing."

"What—who told you that? Moody, I bet. But they didn't exactly fire me. Miss Lucilla said she thought I'd better go: I'd be better off down here. She loaned me some money to get a start in dressmaking. She said that's what I ought to do instead of being just a maid."

"But what," Rocky said impatiently, "was it you thought you heard?"

"Didn't Moody tell you? Well, she wouldn't listen. But I did hear it and I told Miss Lucilla so. It was—it was awful, really," Molly said, shivering. "It was the night Mr. Graydon died. That was about ten, you know, and finally, after that, the house settled down. But I'd stayed up: we all did. And I couldn't sleep, so I went to the dining room for—well, I don't mind admitting I went to get some sherry. And I came out into the hall to go back to the kitchen that way and I heard it."

"What?"

"Miss Evans typing in the library. Just like she did when she copied the letters Mr. Graydon had dictated to her. But it couldn't have been Miss Evans, because she was dead!"

"Why did you think just of her?"

"Who else would I think of? Nobody else used the typewriter. And it was just like she typed; slow and jerky. Because she didn't type good though she was very careful."

Rocky and Eleanor stared at each other. "What did you do?" Eleanor asked.

"Maybe I screamed a little. I don't know."

"Any light in the library?" Rocky said.

"I don't know that, either. I had the hall lights on. But the typing stopped and I put out the lights and ran to bed and shivered all night."

Rocky got up and began to walk restlessly back and forth across the room. Pettums trotted after him, sniffed at his shoes, and then sat up on his hind legs with one eye cocked toward the box of candy.

"No more now. Bad for little doggies. . . . That's what I did: shivered all night," Molly repeated. "But, with all the trouble they'd had, I wouldn't say anything. But I couldn't sleep for thinking about it and I tried to talk to Moody. She told Miss Lucilla; she was always carrying tales, though mostly to Mrs. Hobart. And then Miss Lucilla talked to me. She laughed about it but she thought I'd better go, and I was ready to."

"Did anybody but Miss Lucilla know about this?"

"Oh, she must have told them. Anyway, Moody would tell Mrs. Hobart and it was probably her that wanted me to go. She didn't like me much."

"Well, I'll be damned if I— Sorry. Typing! Have you any idea what were some of the last things Miss Evans typed for old Graydon?"

"Oh yes," Molly said placidly. "His will that he made the day before he died."

She stopped, staring at this young man who looked as if he wanted to do some kind of war dance in her neat room or smash a vase—or something to relieve his feelings.

"His will! Now," Rocky said with deep conviction, "we're getting somewheres. No one ever told me he made a will the day before he died. And Miss Evans typed it for him and made a carbon copy, same as always?"

"Well, I never knew her to fail to make copies."

"And she'd be especially careful to keep a copy of that. Well—the will was signed an' witnessed?" Rocky said anxiously.

"Oh yes. I don't know by who. I remember things about that day because of what happened the next day. I started into the library to dust and Mr. Graydon told me to go away. Miss Evans was taking down something in her own writing, the way she always did first. She'd abbreviate and he'd talk slow."

"He didn't write any of his own letters?"

"No sir. His hands were crippled with rheumatism, so—"

"Well, what did Miss Evans say to you about it?"

"The will? Well, she acted—she *did* act important about it," Molly said defensively. "That night she told me she'd typed a new will for Mr. Graydon. I said I thought lawyers made wills. But she said Mr. Graydon wanted this right away and he didn't care much for lawyers, anyway. And she said it was all signed and witnessed. And she told me: 'Mr. Graydon trusts me.' So after that I couldn't ask her much, could I?"

"I s'pose not. Do you think ever'body knew he made it?"

"I don't know. But after the funeral there was a lawyer there: a Mr. Arney. And I was dusting in the hall," Molly said guilelessly, "and I heard Mr. Earl say to him: 'Father made a new will just before he died. We found it in the library. So the one you have is' . . . I forget what."

"Void? Then the will was produced, all right. But . . ." Again Rocky looked at Eleanor. "You get the idea, don't you? Pearl was sure it was two sheets of paper Cooper was after and put in his pocket."

"I see faint glimmerings of light," Eleanor said. "No wonder someone didn't want you ever to hear the name of Maud Evans."

"She was dead and when the old man died without comin' to. Well, there's the setup."

"I don't understand what it's all about," Molly said. "But if it's helped you—"

"Helped! If I hadn't talked to you I'd never have gotten anywheres."

Rocky looked at her gratefully. He remembered Linda's description: a little woman with eyes like buttons. Her eyes were brown buttons and her mouth a small red button. There was even a row of flat black buttons down the front of the shiny serge dress that was such a poor advertisement of the dressmaker's art. Funny: it was the unimportant people who counted in this case. He said:

"Look: I want you to tell me about Mr. Graydon's death."

"Well, they brought him home because there isn't any real hospital up there and the doctor said moving him wouldn't make any difference. Well, after that we just waited."

"Was ever'body there?"

"Oh yes. They sat around, like you have to do. But that's all. He died about ten."

"Did they all go home then?"

"Oh no!" Molly was shocked. "Somebody sat up. Mr. Stinson and Mr. Hadley. Mr. Earl stayed, too, but he laid down in one of the extra bedrooms: Miss Linda's or the other one. And the ladies went to their rooms: I helped get them settled."

"Would you know if Stinson and Hadley took turns sitting up?"

"I thought they sat up together. I guess Mrs. Earl was at home. I think she went before Mr. Graydon passed away. She would."

"You didn't like her?"

"No, I did not," Molly said defiantly. "Mr. Earl may be kind of a stick but he was crazy about her, and then she'd flirt with every man she saw. But Mr. Stinson was too much for her. He never gave her so much as the flicker of an eye. If Mr. Graydon had known half her goings on . . ."

"Did you know about 'em?"

"Well, there was a young fellow that was superintendent or something at Spanish River. He got to coming up too often and then, all of a sudden, he didn't come at all."

"When was that?"

"Oh, in June, I guess. But that's all I know about it."

"And Miss Lucilla and Mrs. Hobart? They always got along well with their father?"

"Of course they did," Molly said too quickly.

"I think," Rocky said in the tone he reserved for elderly women, children and dogs, "that you're lyin' to me. Isn't it true Miss Lucilla and her father quarreled quite a bit?"

"Well, what if they did? They both had tempers. They didn't mean anything by it."

"Maybe not. But what did they find to fight about?"

"Just anything, I guess. Miss Lucilla was like him but Mrs. Hobart was his favorite. But—well," Molly admitted, "I guess they didn't see eye to eye about her husband."

"What about him?"

"He drank. In his room, I mean. I'd find the empty bottles. He was all right in the daytime. Only of course Mr. Graydon wouldn't like to have to support him, too, though he seemed to work good enough."

"How did he get along with Mr. Graydon?"

"I don't know. They hardly saw each other. After Miss Evans came she was with Mr. Graydon most. She told me he said he was tired and she was 'restful.' And he insisted, as long as she was taking care of him, the others shouldn't bother about him. He didn't like to be fussed over."

"Well," Rocky said, "you can't ask people about their movements on a night over five years ago and expect to get anything out of 'em. Even if they wanted to remember."

"It's quite a while ago," Molly said uncomprehendingly. "Of course I had reason to remember it. Won't you have some more candy? Or would you like some tea?"

"No, thanks; nothing."

"I'll take another piece," Eleanor said because Molly seemed so disappointed at Rocky's refusal. "I like these bitter chocolates, don't you? Allegretti's, aren't they?"

"Yes. That's the kind Miss Lucilla always eats. She keeps a supply on hand because she has to order them. I really must have just one," Molly said, "even if the doctor did tell me not to. Miss Lucilla eats too much candy, I know. And I used to, up there and before I got sick. . . . Well, Pettums shall have just one more. Just one! Because he mustn't spoil his dinner. There!"

Pettums missed his catch this time, growled dejectedly and chased the rolling chocolate across the floor toward Rocky's feet. Eleanor said:

"Who is your doctor? I might know him. I used to be a nurse here. I was near here at the St Francis—"

She sprang to her feet, staring at her husband; at the uneaten chocolate he had knocked from her lips with one frantic sweep of a long arm. Her hand went slowly to her bruised mouth as he shouted: "Don't eat that! Don't!"

Molly Harris was already out of her chair, the chocolate she had chosen crushed in one small fist. She went to her knees, whimpering, as she lifted the head of the woolly brown dog whose eyes were already glazing in death.

V

Andy Duncan felt, as he sat down in his desk chair, that he had done a good day's work. And a satisfactory one, because he would have a nice surprise for Rocky when he got back. Not that he could see, just now, why it was important. But it must be, and . . .

He reached for the telephone. "Sheriff's office. . . . Oh—long distance? All right."

"Got pencil and paper handy?" Rocky said without preamble. "You may want to take some notes. This is important. Go out to The Stockade, find out how much candy Miss Lucilla has around the house and if there's a box missing. And where she keeps the stuff. Then take it away."

"But, Rocky! You know she—"

"Tell her for me that someone sent Molly Harris a box of candy like she always eats with enough poison in some pieces to kill—well, it did kill a dog. None of us," Rocky said grimly, "happened to pick out the right pieces. The candy was sent from there. Miss Harris built a fire with the wrappings but she remembered where it came from. She's certain it was mailed out at the Junction."

"Holy—gee! Rocky, did Eleanor—"

"She ate one piece. Never mind. Ask Hadley if he didn't keep some cyanide in his office or in one of the offices."

"But why—"

"Hanson's midnight prowler. Which I ignored! Hadley was worried. Oh—why, you said? They use cynanide for casehardening. Ask Hadley: I think he'll tell you the truth. An' take charge of the stuff, if there is any of it. Find out if there are typewriters anywheres but in the offices. Also what became of the one Joshua Graydon used to have in his library and who can or can't type. Got that?"

"Yes. It's—it's serious, isn't it?"

"I don't like poisoners. Warn that bunch at The Stockade to be careful. I've got a special job to do when I get back and I don't want to be delayed startin' on it."

"Then you've found out something? So have I,"
Andy said triumphantly. "Where Cooper was that
twenty-five minutes you couldn't account for."

"You—where?"

"Right here in the courthouse!"

For an instant Rocky's language threatened to
wither the wires. Then he said: "No, it's nothin'
serious, honey. Just Andy pullin' a fast one. . .
. He wouldn't have happened to spend the time
looking over a copy of Joshua Graydon's will?"

Andy's jaw dropped. "How did you know? That's
what he did. It was this way . . ."

Oscar Finch had worked in the county clerk's
office for more than twenty-five years. He was
not, by nature, a social person and early deafness
had accentuated this trait. When Oscar was willing to talk or be talked to he wore an electrical
hearing device. Usually the apparatus reposed in
a drawer of his desk and anyone who had business
in the office wrote out his request and handed it
to Oscar.

But Oscar did read the Brookdale *Sun,* which
had made its weekly appearance that morning,
adorned with a small picture of Walter Cooper.
Meeting Andy in the hall, Oscar had accosted him
indignantly.

"People never tell me anything. This fellow was
in here Thursday morning. He wanted a copy of

the Graydon will. He read it and made notes and looked like he was laughing to himself. But no one asks me anything. Living alone and all, how would I know he's been killed and you want to know about him?" He went off, muttering to himself.

"Well, that's a necesary link," Rocky said. "Cooper had to see that will. Look, Andy: I wanted to fly back to Reno tonight and get a car to bring me over there, since our field isn't lighted. But I had to get in touch with McCarthy again. I wanted that box of choc'lates analyzed and gone over for fingerprints."

"What about the city police?" Andy said disapprovingly.

"I can't bother with them—now. Incident'lly, Lovett must've taken that box out to the Junction. I reckon he wasn't meant to live long for more than one reason. But I was sayin'—the weather report isn't so good. I don't want to make a forced landin' between here and Reno or bail out in the wilderness. It should be all right in the mornin', so I'll play safe."

"You'd better. If you got yourself killed that would probably be the end of this case. Because no one else—"

"Listen, fella—I haven't time to tell you now. I'm tired as hell even if nothin' happened at The

Stockade last night and I break out in a cold sweat ever' time I think what would've happened if we'd been real fond of candy. Or if Molly Harris didn't have diabetes or something and don't eat it like she used to. Tell me what you've done."

"Well—wait a minute."

Andy reached for his notes. Lovett, he reported, though well enough known in town, was generally disliked and had no friends there. He had been in the stores and post office on Saturday and Sunday. Moody said he had gone to the Junction Saturday with the mail. The afternoon letters, mainly from the mill, were almost always taken out there.

"I know. Well, ask the agent at the Junction about that box of candy. And find out where the mail was put for Lovett to c'llect or who gave it to him. Go on."

Neither the Hadleys' or the Earl Graydons' maid had liked Lovett. At least, so they said. One of the girls, Andy said resentfully, had giggled and the other said he insulted her. But Clara, who was good natured and willing to talk, was certain Lovett had never had anything to do with either of them.

And the inquest was the usual Brookdale inquest. Hadley had made a good impression testifying. There was no telling what people in general thought about things but Andy hadn't time to listen to them to find out. Dr. Bradley thought Lovett and Cooper might have been killed by the same gun. Why didn't Rocky find out from an expert?

"I brought the Cooper bullets with me. They're from a 25 automatic," Rocky said. "Doc hadn't finished with Lovett when I left. We'll check on that later."

"Oh. Well, I pacified the D.A. and Mr. Derby for you. You may be glad to know the D.A.'s got a bad cold. He can hardly talk."

"That," Rocky said callously, "is just fine! I hope he stays that way. I suppose he thinks, though, that we should've protected the Graydons' chauffeur? I was afraid of that. What else?"

"Earl Graydon was here Friday about noon. People on Main Street noticed him. How did they miss seeing Cooper?"

"He may've watched to see if anyone was lookin' at him. Or they may've thought he was just lookin' at the courthouse. Most strangers do. When Eleanor suggested that I let it slip by—like a fool. And I thought my name meant somethin' to him. 'Vanity of vanities,' saith the preacher. . . . How could he have known who I was unless he'd seen my name on the office door in the courthouse? Oh well—what about Graydon?"

"He drove straight to the bank, went in, came out and drove home—I suppose. I asked Mrs. Gray if he was in and she said he was. But she looked at me kind of suspiciously. I didn't dare ask her anything more. She wouldn't have told me why he came in."

"Did she look—well . . ."

"Maybe it was just my imagination," Andy said, "but she did seem to me to look like something about his coming in had made an impression on her."

"Fine! Well, I reckon that's all. Have someone meet us at the landin' field. An' you get hell-bent out to The Stockade."

Andy took one of the rugs from near the bed and put it on the bare floor close to the door. If you looked at the faint stain there long enough it began to crawl and seemed to be spreading slowly toward you.

He turned on all the lights and sat down at the small table before the fire. If Rocky had something to do tomorrow morning that he was so anxious to get at, he should appreciate a brief statement in writing. He must think that time was important. Perhaps to prevent another death?

Andy looked at the square jar with its label: "Poison—Cyanide," and shivered. Suppose Rocky had been fond of candy? Or Eleanor? That was worse, because you expected Rocky to take risks. Suppose Linda wasn't always worrying about getting fat and one of those half-dozen boxes over there on the bed had been doctored and she . . . Andy shook his head, licked his pencil and began to write.

CANDY: six boxes on hand. Moody thinks there should be seven. Miss Lucilla doesn't keep track: Moody tells her when supply is getting low. Is kept in hall closet except for opened boxes in Miss Lucilla's bedroom and living room. If anyone could get into house (this fact more or less established?), could get at candy.

Andy stopped writing. Yes, that was enough. Later on he could tell Rocky how they acted and what they said. Mrs. Hobart had been white as a sheet before he'd finished talking to them. Then she got up and took the box of candy from the table at Miss Lucilla's elbow and threw it into the fire.

Miss Lucilla—to Andy's horrified surprise—said: "Damn it, Bertha, did you have to do that?" But her square hands were shaking a little.

Linda said: "You'll just have to get along with candy from the Brookdale drugstore. You can't tell about those other boxes." Her voice went a little high and shaky.

Dewey said quickly: "She's right, Lucilla. You might not have happened to—what was it Mr. Allan said?—pick out the right pieces."

"I don't pick. So Molly doesn't eat candy any more. She was always snitching it here. Earl wanted me to fire her for that. Well, this is one time when poor health seems to have been a blessing."

In spite of this remark Andy was inclined to admire her. All of them, for that matter. Because Miss Lucilla said they all dipped into her candy now and then. And the box Mrs. Hobart threw in the fire was nearly empty, so Moody would have been bringing out another tomorrow.

He didn't admire Anette Graydon's way of receiving his news, though. She had had hysteria. At least, she had laughed and cried, and screamed that she wouldn't stay in this place another day: she'd never wanted to live here and it was all Earl's fault for keeping her here when he should know by now that any of his precious family was perfectly capable of killing half-a-dozen people if they thought they could get away with it.

And Earl Graydon had kept saying: "Anette! Anette!" And finally: "Darling, you don't have to stay here. But you're simply overwrought." And then he had asked Andy to go and the maid had come running with smelling salts. Well! Andy moistened his pencil again.

POISON: Hadley kept cyanide in office for safety. After heard Hanson's story happened to notice someone had moved jar recently. Could tell by mark in the dust. Stinson and Graydon denied touching it. Hadley couldn't tell if any had been taken. Also thought cover on his typewriter not as he'd put it Thursday afternoon. (They haven't a stenographer right now but write their own letters.)

TYPEWRITERS: Joshua Graydon's machine taken over to mill. Linda used it when she was a kid. Mrs. Hobart wrote a few letters for him on it before Miss Evans came. Miss Lucilla and Anette Graydon never did any typing. Hadley and Graydon aren't expert. Stinson is a fairly good touch typist and Rose Hadley quite good. She has the only typewriter outside of offices.

MAIL: always put on table in hall near kitchen. Lovett took it to post office in mornings, out to Junction evenings if there were any letters they wanted to get off. Usually are, as Hadley writes most of his in afternoon. Lovett hardly ever went out on Sundays. Besides . . .

Andy hesitated. Rocky would know that, of course, but he might as well put it down.

Besides, if Molly Harris got that candy before late afternoon Monday, it must have caught Saturday night's train. If Sunday night's, it wouldn't get to the city in time to be delivered till late afternoon. Moody insists there was no package on table Saturday night. Lovett usually went out to the Junction right after dinner: about seven. He did Saturday. Didn't go at all Sunday.

But he gave a package to the station agent and asked him to see it got off with the mailbags from the post office. Agent didn't pay any attention to it, except he noticed it was plastered with stamps.

Well, that seemed to be everything. When there was time, he could tell Rocky that Mr. Hadley had insisted on his having dinner with them when he discovered Andy hadn't eaten before leaving Brookdale. And that he'd said, about the cyanide:

"It didn't worry me, at first, though I did wonder who might have been meddling with it. But lately I've been very uneasy. I very nearly warned Allan. But I've heard a poisoner doesn't very often use any other method."

"Molly Harris couldn't be reached with a gun, Dad. If it was important she be killed before she could talk, how else could it be done? Besides," Rose said, as if she were discussing the weather, "whoever took that cynanide may not originally have intended it for Molly. Perhaps for himself, if necessary. Or for someone who couldn't be shot conveniently—or quickly enough."

Andy decided that was straight enough thinking. And one thing struck him with force: they had all given up trying to explain these murders by dragging in an outsider. Even Earl Graydon hadn't said it must all be a mistake about the candy.

Well, he was supposed to see that nothing happened tonight—as if it would do any good for him to patrol the grounds if anyone was up to any deviltry inside. But he couldn't divide himself into three parts and guard all three houses from the inside, if they would let him.

Andy picked his gun up from the bed. It looked formidable enough but he couldn't find a convenient place to carry it. Rocky strapped his on his hip but he could draw and shoot like lightning. He had picked off that fellow who held up the Indian Valley Bank running. Well, a little practice might be a good thing, Andy thought. If he stuck the gun inside the band of his trousers . . .

He turned a brilliant red as Linda laughed. "Don't shoot, Davy Crockett. I'll come down." She stepped into the cabin. Andy looked at her severely.

"You shouldn't be out alone in the dark."

"I have a flashlight and a gun. Dewey gave it to me."

"What—"

"Automatic—32. He has another." Linda sat down on the bed. "Earl came over to suggest we empty all the liquor out of the decanters. Nice, isn't it? I had no appetite for dinner."

"Just the same, you shouldn't be wandering around," Andy persisted. "I'll take you back to the house. Besides, it's nine-thirty and your being here isn't very—conventional."

"Oh!" Linda snapped her fingers. "This is a fine time to be thinking of that. Aunt Lucilla's gone to bed and Aunt Bertha went over to see Rose. Dewey is there and he can bring her back. You wouldn't expect me to sit there alone?"

"You should have gone to bed too."

"Don't be fatherly. We keep going to bed because we don't want to sit around and look at each other."

"Sure, I know. It isn't any fun."

"Only you don't. They're just people to you. That box of candy: that's the worst. Because it might have killed anyone. And Mr. Allan might never have thought of talking to Molly Harris and it would have killed her just the same."

Andy put off his official demeanor and sat down beside her. She leaned against him gratefully. "I can't imagine anyone doing a thing like that. Can you, Andy?"

"Well, I've tried to pick out someone but I can't."

"Then—if you were I . . . And I thought I was so darned smart! Trying to straighten things out!"

Linda blinked angrily and finally dashed her hand across her eyes. Her thick golden-brown lashes stuck wetly together in little points, and her small fair head drooped. Andy kissed her shyly and then very competently. She gasped a little, smiled and put her head against his shoulder.

"That's very comforting," she murmured. "And surprising."

"Didn't it ever occur to you," Andy said stiffly, "that I may have kissed a girl before? I was in college three years."

Linda giggled. "I like you, Andy. And mostly because you don't try to act like a man of the world—at twenty-one."

"I can't help it if I haven't any—any savoir-faire. Some people are born with it."

"Well, who wants to be? Yes, I'd like to be kissed again. . . . But *that*—is enough!" Linda sprang to her feet, smoothing back her hair. "I do hope you aren't going to spoil everything by wanting to get married, Andy?"

"How can I, for a good many years? And anything might happen before that. No," Andy said honestly, "it would be swell to be married to you. I mean: I'd like to be married to you because—oh well . . ."

"I know what you mean," Linda said gravely. "But we're pretty young to take a chance just for *that*."

Andy reddened again but he looked at her unwaveringly. "That's it. I want to *be* someone. Well, I won't let you support me. And I don't want to stop right here all my life. But—wait for me if you can, Linda."

"You are nice, Andy. No promises, but . . ." She caught his hand "Let's make a reconnaissance in force."

"Well, if nothing else will satisfy you. We'll cut over to the garage and make a circle of the grounds. Go in back of the other two houses from the garage."

"It is dark," Linda whispered. "But I've always been glad Grandfather left the pines around this cabin and on both sides of the garage. It was the barn, then. Listen, Andy!"

They stood still, Linda's soft fingers holding tightly to Andy's hard palm. He said: "It's the wind in the trees. No, it's the garage door creaking. Someone forgot to lock it. We'll fix that."

"Oh!" Linda laughed. "Aren't we silly? Because I was sure I heard— Andy!"

They both heard it now; the choked, wordless moaning from somewhere inside the garage. Andy thrust Linda's hand aside; said:

"You stay where you are! Put on your light. But don't move!"

He jerked the garage door open and stepped inside. His foot struck something soft and inert before the light from his torch showed him Bertha Hobart's white face and bruised white throat.

PART FOUR
WALK INTO MY PARLOR

I

Everything in the bedroom was either soft gray or clear, warm yellow. The crystal bottles on the bureau sparkled a little and the heavy lustrous silk of hangings and pillows shimmered softly in the subdued light.

Andy had never been in a bedroom like this. He felt all hands and feet and large red ears. But he stuck doggedly to his questioning because he knew Rocky would expect him to.

"I hate to bother you now—and I do think you ought to call the doctor."

"No. Moody fixed me up quite nicely. My throat is sore but my skin bruises so easily. If I hadn't hit my head on a running board when I fell—"

"Did you fall? I mean: did someone throw you so you fell?"

"I think so."

Mrs. Hobart moved her head restlessly against the pillow. Andy flushed at Linda's indignant look. She wasn't very reasonable. Well, women weren't. He couldn't wait until tomorrow to find out what had happened. That is, if Mrs. Hobart knew.

"Can you hear me? It hurts to talk loudly. I went over to get some of Rose's linen to initial for her. And then— Did you pick it up?"

"The linen? Yes, I brought it in," Linda said soothingly. "It isn't hurt."

"Silly of me to think about that—Dewey had been with Rose but he'd left. He was going to stop in to ask after Anette. So I missed him and started back alone.

"Of course I walked past Earl's house, which is nearest the garage. I happened to look that way and I thought I saw a light. It was a foolish thing to do but I wondered—I walked toward the garage and then I heard the door, creaking in the wind.

"Lovett always saw that the garage was locked, so I thought perhaps whoever was last in there hadn't closed the door. And I thought I had better do that."

"And you didn't have any light?" Andy said.

"No. You see, I'd expected to come back with Dewey. And there was no light in the garage as I approached it. I was close to the door when I . . . ."

"Yes?"

Mrs. Hobart closed her eyes. She touched the wet compresses Moody had put about her throat. Linda said: "Aunt Bertha, if it hurts you too much to talk . . ."

"I only wanted to be certain it really happened. I was close to the door," Mrs. Hobart said, looking steadily at Andy, "when I heard someone say: 'Before I'll let that happen, I'll kill you.' It was a whisper: a stage whisper, I suppose you would call it. But if there was any answer, the other person spoke in a lower voice. Then the first speaker said: 'I'm ready, if necessary, to take that risk.'"

"And you didn't recognize the voice?"

"No. How could I? A whisper like that . . ."

Andy looked at her doubtfully but he did not press the point. Anyone could see that if she had thought she recognized that voice she wasn't going to admit it. And perhaps she wasn't certain she had recognized it. He said:

"What then?"

"I heard that as I was trying to reach the door without making any noise. But I must have." Mrs. Hobart smiled ruefully. "It's hard to walk silently on a gravel driveway. I didn't think anyone heard me. The door was swinging a little open and I listened and couldn't hear anything. There are doors—"

"The garage used to be a barn and there is a side door and back doors," Linda said. "They lock from the inside with bolts. It would be easy to get out."

"I noticed that. Only," Andy said, "when a person got out he'd have to wait. I mean: before he dared to sneak into—well, back into one of the houses, with you at the front of the garage."

"I suppose you're right. I decided that whoever had been in the garage was gone. So I pulled the door open because I was going to slam it shut. And then someone got his hands around my throat and dragged me into the garage. And—I suppose—when he thought I was helpless, threw me off so that I fell and my head hit against the running board of one of the cars."

"You don't think he had any idea of killing you?"

"There was nothing to prevent his doing it, was there? I suppose, as you suggested, he wanted time to get away. And for the other person there to escape. It was really an accident that I hit my head and was unconscious for a while."

"Well, it was about a quarter of ten when we found you."

"And it was about nine-thirty when I left Rose. If that is important."

"I have to check up," Andy said apologetically. "But I won't bother you any longer."

Linda sprang to her feet as a deep angry voice made itself heard from the hall. "Oh dear, after all the pains we took, Aunt Lucilla has waked up."

Miss Lucilla entered the room, more square and formidable than ever in a padded green robe with a black silk handkerchief tied over her head. She said:

"Why am I to be let sleep when something like this happens? I just got it all out of Moody. Why haven't you called a doctor?" Then, more gently: "Bertha, you and Linda between you will give me heart failure with your wanderings around in the dark. What good does a guard do?"

Andy, before she could turn her attention to him, muttered "Good night" and backed hastily from the room.

"So none of them could prove an alibi?" Rocky said.

"No. Dewey Stinson was in the house when we carried Mrs. Hobart in. He said he must just have missed her: that he left Earl Graydon's place before she left the Hadleys'. But he didn't see anybody but the maid and she doesn't know exactly what time. Earl and his wife were supposed to be in bed: separate rooms."

"And Miss Lucilla slept through ever'thing. What about Hadley?"

"He was in bed. He wasn't feeling well. I talked to him and he certainly didn't look very well. Miss Hadley says Stinson left there about ten after nine and Mrs. Hobart came in about five minutes later and didn't stay more than a quarter of an hour.

"I couldn't help thinking," Andy went on, "how sometimes a guilty person manages to fake an attack on himself. But—"

"Mrs. Hobart couldn't strangle herself? No," Rocky said. "Or fall to cut her head the way you say hers was. That don't necessarily mean she wasn't up to somethin' more 'n she told you."

"And I think she at least *thought* she recognized that voice. Linda only heard a word or two outside the library door but Mrs. Hobart heard whole sentences. And she said, telling about it: 'someone got *his* hands around my throat.' She said that without hesitating and kept on saying 'he' and 'his.'"

"It may have been a slip. Or she may have said it deliberately because she didn't want to say 'she.' Or just because the masc'line pronoun is generally used in cases of doubt. At any rate, as you've said, she isn't goin' to tell any more than she already has."

Andy leaned on the desk, waiting for additional questions, but Rocky apparently had none to ask. He did not seem very interested in what had happened while he was gone, Andy thought indignantly. But then, he must be tired. He hadn't even changed the suit he'd worn to San Francisco.

Rocky was thinking that, while sentimentality was a waste of time, nevertheless you couldn't help feeling it was hell when a woman didn't have anything but a dog to love. And she'd been just childishly hurt by the idea that someone had wanted to kill her. He'd felt like he'd been run through a washing machine by the time he and Eleanor left Molly Harris.

Then something had made him examine the chocolate he had dashed out of Eleanor's hand. Before he put it in the box, to give to Pat McCarthy, he was quite certain it had been tampered with. A rather clumsy job, but people weren't in the habit of examining pieces of candy closely before they ate them.

And of course he hadn't been able to fool Eleanor; she'd asked him about it after they went to bed. "Oh well," she murmured finally, "it will make a thrilling story to tell to my friends—sometime."

"It's nothing to joke about."

"That's why I am." She burrowed her head deeper into his shoulder. "I'm not anxious to die young. Or have you do it. And you might have taken another piece—I'm not hysterical: just cold. That's why I'm shivering."

"It is cold since the fog came in." But he held her close and, after an instant, said: "In case I don't mention it often enough—I love you. Only please try not to have nightmares tonight."

"Not one nightmare," Eleanor said firmly. "Not with two of us in one twin bed. Oh, I hate to think of getting up at six o'clock."

Neither of them had slept well and for at least an hour out of Alameda it was poor flying weather, with a swirling wall of fog blotting out the wing tips. But they had landed safely and he was here in his office again with Joshua Graydon's will in front of him and a coldly angry determination to make someone pay for that box of poisoned chocolates.

He began to read through the will again with Andy looking over his shoulder. There were two pages of it; ordinary 8 by 11 sheets of white paper. Rocky muttered:

"Maybe she might have got it on one sheet if she hadn't double spaced and left such wide margins."

"Is that important?"

"The fact that there are two sheets of paper is damned important. None of this probably would've happened if there had been just one."

"Oh! Well, the will itself . . ." Andy read it, lips moving in silent concentration:

I, Joshua Albert Graydon, resident at The Stockade, Brookdale, California and being of sound mind, do hereby make and declare my last will and testament, as follows:

I give to George Martin, an old and faithful employee, the sum of $1000.

I give to Leif Hanson, who has served us faithfully for many years, the sum of $1000.

I give to Lily Hale, in appreciation of her services to us, the sum of $1000.

I give to my old friend Michael Riordan, of Westwood, California, the sum of $1000.

I give to Thomas Elsey, for his willing and faithful service, the sum of $1000.

I give and bequeath to my son, Earl Graydon, all my stock in the Graydon Lumber Company and the sum of $5000.

I give to Samuel Arney, as a token of esteem, the sum of five hundred dollars.

I give, devise and bequeath all my other property, real and personal, to my daughters, Lucilla Graydon and Bertha

Hobart, and my granddaughter, Melinda Graydon, share and share alike.

I hereby appoint my daughter, Lucilla Graydon, executrix of this my last will, to act without bond.

Andy put his finger on the initials J.A.G. scrawled on the margin of the first page. "Why, this is the original, isn't it?"

"Yes, and a hell of a time I had gettin' it from Oscar. But I had to have this or nothing. I think," Rocky said slowly, "that the old man meant this to be the end of his will. But then he thought of some unimportant bequests."

"Yes, they are unimportant," Andy said, reading on:

I give and bequeath to Prof. Warren Blake of Reno, Nev., my collection of Indian relics.

I give and bequeath to Frederick Roche, of the Spanish River Lumber Co., any 100 volumes to be chosen by him from my library.

Signed by me in the presence of witnesses this 9th day of July 1931 at The Stockade, Brookdale, Calif.

(Signed) JOSHUA ALBERT GRAYDON

Witnesses:

(Signed) DEWEY STINSON

(Signed) ELLIS HADLEY

"Well," Andy said finally, "there's certainly nothing wrong with those signatures, is there?"

"No. I never thought there would be, when I knew there were two pages. Those initials—what about that microscope of yours, Andy? Is it in workin' order?"

"Sure. What do you want me to look at?" Andy said eagerly. "The initials? I'll set it up right now and—"

"Well—we'd have to consult an expert and probably that wouldn't be enough to prove anything in court," Rocky said vaguely. "And as the will stands, it don't eliminate anyone. But if you take a look at it and find anything queer, that should help."

"Well, do I or don't I?" Andy said impatiently.

"Let's step down the street and talk to Arney first."

Although he was the only lawyer in Brookdale and—of any standing—in the county, Samuel Arney always said that his legal practice never interfered with his reading. He put down *The Way of All Flesh,* pushed his glasses up on his forehead, and looked at them questioningly.

"Now what? I've devoted a good deal of quiet thought to this business," he said. "Not to what the man on the street knows—though I warn you *he* is beginning to wonder—but what *you* may know. What do you want me to tell you—that I can."

Rocky grinned wearily. "Without violatin' professional secrecy? Don't worry. What did you think of Joshua Graydon's will?"

"There was nothing wrong with it. He knew the law and he liked to do things for himself—"

"Yes. But was there anything about it that surprised you?"

"That," Arney said, "was what surprised me. There wasn't. I wondered why he had bothered to make another."

"It was just like the ones you'd made for him?"

"Except for two provisions. Thomas Elsey had been with him for years and Graydon was very fond of him. He left him ten thousand dollars in the last will I drew for him."

"Well, Elsey was dead too. That's fine."

"It didn't matter," Arney said, "because Elsey predeceased him. As he wasn't related to Graydon, his heirs had no claim."

"I hadn't thought of that. And I wouldn't be certain without askin'—lots of people wouldn't. Did ever'one know how Graydon felt about Elsey?"

"They must have. But I doubt if he ever stated the exact sum he was going to leave him. In the first will I made for Graydon, Elsey received only five thousand. The second will I drew up predated his third and final one by about nine months. He had given up the management of the mill and wanted Earl to have his stock."

"I know. What other provision surprised you?"

"His leaving me five hundred dollars in the third will. I hadn't ever detected any great signs of his esteem for me," Arney said dryly. "Perhaps he had five hundred dollars worth."

"His esteem usually came higher, didn't it? Well, why waste good money? Nothing wrong about the other small legacies?"

"Not that I know of. Old friends, employees and servants. Lily Hale was the cook; she'd been with them a long time. The clauses regarding the Indian relics and books weren't in his earlier wills. I suppose he had a sudden impulse toward generosity."

"Do you think they all knew what to expect from his will?"

Arney hesitated. "No reason not to answer that, I suppose. He told me he'd let everyone know what his arrangements were."

"He always intended Miss Lucilla to be executrix?"

"Yes—well, that is, she was so named in the second will I made for him. The first one was made when he was much younger and Earl was named executor."

"But he had a chance, between the first and second wills, to find out Miss Lucilla was a better man than Earl?"

"Perhaps," Arney said cautiously. "There was a lapse of perhaps ten years—"

"Well—thanks. He'd deeded the houses over to Hadley, Earl and Miss Lucilla, hadn't he? I was told that— Have you anything he ever initialed for any reason?"

"Initialed? He usually signed letters to me with just his initials. I think I can find a letter for you in the files. Just a minute."

Rocky read the letter, a scrawl regarding several mortgages held on property in Indian Valley. "This is fine. Thanks a lot," he said again. And to Andy, when they were outside: "Here, try this under your microscope along with the initials on the will. I'm going to call up The Stockade and tell that gang to get together so I can talk to them."

"But, Rocky—is there anything about that will, except maybe the initials—"

"Oh," Rocky said unsatisfactorily, "nothing you can prove anything by. But there are—discrepancies. And the—arrangement is interestin'."

II

Linda half closed her eyes and tried to identify sounds without looking at the people or things that were making them. The cracking noise of the fire when a lump of coal broke in two, people breathing—that would be Moody, sniffing unpleasantly and indignantly, standing behind Aunt Bertha's chair.

Mr. Allan hadn't asked Aunt Bertha to come downstairs but he might as well have dragged her down by her heels, the way Moody was acting. She had a bottle of smelling salts in one hand and the air of one who expects the worst to happen—and rather hopes it will.

At nerve-rackingly regular intervals Earl cleared his throat. He always did that when he was angry—or disturbed about something. The dry, rasping sound irritated Linda. Why couldn't he be quiet, as everyone else was? Dewey was even smiling his usual half-mocking smile. He looked as if he might be admiring the set of Mr. Allan's coat.

He did look different in that dark blue suit when you were used to seeing him in high boots and corduroys. And anyone with shoulders like his and no hips to speak of . . . Linda wondered if Mrs. Allan picked out his clothes. Very likely. Someone should tell Andy that, with his red hair, light gray was not the best color for him to wear.

It was really funny—Linda stifled an impulse to giggle hysterically—that they should all be here together at two o'clock in the afternoon simply because Mr. Allan had given orders to that effect. Particularly because he didn't seem to realize that it *was* funny.

Aunt Lucilla had only rumbled a little—probably unprintably—when Dewey gave her the message. But Earl had objected vehemently, until Dewey turned on him with unprecedented impatience.

"If, as Mr. Allan told me in his softest and most Texan accents, you prefer to have him drag you into his office for questioning, go right ahead! Also, he tells me that there are reporters in town."

So Earl was here: angry, resentful—but here. And Anette, looking as if she would take the center of the stage at any moment with a beautifully executed burst of hysterics. She would like that. But, Linda admitted, she was really pitiably nervous. That was another sound; the click-clack of her long, painted nails against the arm of her chair. Thank heaven, Rose and her father were always quiet. And why didn't Mr. Allan begin? There was really no excuse for his taking so long.

He said: "I've had plenty of time to listen to your stories and you've had plenty of time to decide to tell the truth, if you'd wanted to. Now I'm going to tell you a story about an unimportant person."

Maud Evans couldn't be called anything but that, he said. A nurse companion, poorly paid for the tiresome work she did. But Joshua Graydon had liked her; perhaps because he was old and tired and liked to talk of a past that was new and interesting to her.

Because she was always interested in the lives of those about her. And she kept a diary and, since almost nothing happened to her, she filled it with surmise and facts about those people.

On June fifteenth, for example, she had recorded a quarrel between Miss Lucilla and her father. And whatever she had written on the next two days had been considered important, because it had been cut out of the diary. On the eighteenth she had remarked that rich people were not quite as one expected them to be.

Then four entries, those from June twenty-sixth to twenty-ninth, inclusive, were missing. On the third of July she had spoken of a disagreement between Joshua Graydon and his son. And on the fourth she had devoted some space to Mr. and Mrs. Hobart and Anette Graydon.

Those entries were the last anyone would ever see. One would naturally conclude that the next three pages, which covered six days and had been cut out of the diary, contained some definite and perhaps startling information.

Because one of those days was the ninth of July and on that day Joshua Graydon dictated his will to Maud Evans. A will signed and witnessed; a seemingly unnecessary will since it differed in no important points from his last one.

"But," Rocky said, "I don't imagine he was given to doin' things he thought unnecessary. Something happened—that Maud Evans put down in her diary—that made him decide to change his will. He died the next day without bein' able to talk. And she died before he did, which left the way clear."

Left the way clear for someone else who knew what change Joshua Graydon had made in his will to creep down to the library in the dark hours after he died. And there to type a new first page to that will, which made its provisions those everyone had always expected.

That person was aided by the chance circumstance that there were two pages to the will; that all important provisions were on the first page while the second page bore the three necessary signatures that would have been difficult and dangerous to forge.

True: Joshua Graydon had initialed the first page, but—Rocky nodded to Andy. He gulped and flushed under the intent gaze of nine pairs of eyes.

"I'm no expert—but I'll bet," he added as Earl Graydon laughed harshly, "that an expert will say the same thing. That those initials were traced. You see— well, shall I be technical?"

Rocky smiled. "Not very—if you don't mind."

"Well then, the main strokes have too many serrations. I mean: under a microscope they look— wavery. And the terminal strokes don't taper like they do when a person's writing and not tracing. In tracing they're apt to stay thick to the end. Sometimes they end in a knob. Those things are true about the initials on the will but not of the ones he wrote himself. The typing doesn't do us any good because Maud Evans wasn't a touch typist and there's the same unevenness of pressure on both pages."

"Thanks. O.K.?" Rocky said to the room in general "I want you to get this foundation."

"Surely," Dewey objected, "one set of initials presumably traced and the fact that there was no apparent need for that will to be made are not very much to go on."

"Maybe not. But," Rocky said—and Linda thought that he was almost purring now—"there was another unimportant person in the house that night Mr. Graydon died."

That person was Molly Harris, who had gone into the hall and so heard what she thought must be ghostly fingers pecking laboriously away at a typewriter in the library. Maud Evans was dead, so she could not have been in the library. But someone else was.

And Molly knew what the one working feverishly against dawn did not: that Maud Evans made carbon copies of everything she typed for Joshua Graydon and kept them in her room. Molly had learned that fact more or less by accident and no one else paid any attention to Miss Evans' activities. So, when she was dead, those carbons were included in her belongings by Molly and shipped away.

Supposedly to her brother, but there another woman stepped into the picture. A woman who thought she might as well have whatever Maud Evans had left, since Cooper would be gone for some years. And who, being lazy, had not destroyed papers and a diary that seemed worthless to her.

So more than five years passed. Molly Harris, who knew one important fact without understanding it, had been discharged and was in San Francisco. But Cooper had finally come home, and his coming set the wheels in motion.

He was shrewd and unscrupulous and needed money. His sister must have talked to him most of one afternoon about the people at The Stockade.

So he had been interested, reading her diary. And, almost certainly, he had discovered some facts or story in it that he believed might be the material for blackmail.

He hadn't been certain at first. He had said he must investigate; had gone off and spent half a day "reading newspapers." Something that he read had sent him back to search frantically for the carbon copy of Joshua Graydon's will that he had tossed aside as valueless.

Finding those two sheets, he had read certain pages of the diary again and said: "Well, there's something wrong with the setup. This may be bigger than I hoped. It means money if I'm right, and it's worth taking a chance to find out."

"Wait a minute," Dewey said. "If you don't mind?"

"Not a bit. I want you all," Rocky said pleasantly, "to get this perfectly straight."

"Molly testifies to hearing someone typing in the library after Mr. Graydon died. And that Miss Evans made and kept carbons of everything."

"Put them away in Manila envelopes," Rocky said helpfully. "And Molly remembers packing two or three of them with Miss Evans' things. And the woman at the hotel remembers receivin' the papers that way."

"Yes, that's another link," Dewey said impersonally. "And this woman can swear Cooper examined the papers? But not that one of them was the carbon of a will?"

"Not one: two pages. She knows he put two pages into his pocket very carefully. And Oscar Finch, at the courthouse, will swear that on Thursday mornin' Cooper got a copy of Mr. Graydon's will, read it, lookin' like something pleased him, and took some notes. And then he came out here."

"So you argue his trip had been worthwhile: that he found what he had suspected was true. Yes, I suppose you're right."

"I don't understand," Anette said fretfully. "If he found a carbon of the will why didn't he know at once that it was valuable?"

"The carbon was of the *real* will," Rocky said. "What he read in his sister's diary about it would naturally agree with what he read in the carbon. If someone should have been disinherited but wasn't, because of a substituted first page, he didn't know that—then. But he hoped to use some items in the diary for blackmail. He said right away that there might be money in it. And he cut out entries for the middle and end of June. Well, isn't it true that Mr. Graydon decided very suddenly to make that will?"

"No use denying that," Miss Lucilla said. "I thought he was up to something that day, wanting Dewey and Ellis in the library. But I didn't know what, until they told us."

"We were the witnesses, you know," Hadley said. "He asked us not to speak of it for a day or two."

"Well, whatever caused him to make the new will probably happened only a day or two before he made it. So I'd guess those earlier missing entries had nothing to do with the will. Cooper thought, though, that he'd better get some information on you all first. For instance, if he was intendin' to get money from Mrs. Graydon it might be wise to find out, if he could, whether she and Mr. Graydon were still married."

He smiled unsympathetically at Earl Graydon as he half rose from his seat with strangled sounds of indignation.

"I'm just usin' you for an example. My guess is that he found something in your activities as described by the newspapers—and you know the Brookdale *Sun* couldn't get along without you all—that didn't fit in with what Joshua Graydon provided in his will and Maud Evans put down about it in her diary.

"Again for instance: he might know Mrs. Hobart had been disinherited but found out she still

had money enough to do anything and go anywheres she wanted to. Or that you, Mr. Graydon,
are still president of the Graydon Lumber Company, when your father's will provided otherwise.

"We're checkin' up on him at the library. They
may remember him there. Or he might've gone to
the Mining Bureau. They keep newspapers from
the mountain counties. Reading over the papers
ourselves, we still can't be exactly certain what
it was that started him thinkin'. Also, I imagine
there are times when your names and faces appear
in the city papers."

"You are frank, at any rate," Mrs. Hobart said.
"Please, Moody, don't jiggle my chair."

"You ought to be in bed," Moody muttered with
a hostile glance toward Rocky.

"I don't mind admitting a gap or two," he said.
"I want to know who made the changes in that
will only because I think, then, I'll know who
killed Cooper and Lovett. And tried to kill Molly
Harris. . . . Let's get back to Cooper. Didn't he
come here and introduce himself as Miss Evans'
brother?"

Mrs. Hobart nodded. Anette said: "And then
Bertha asked him to stay to lunch. I had nothing
to do with that."

"No, certainly you didn't," Mrs. Hobart said
evenly. "And I was the first person to talk to him,
alone, before Dewey came back for lunch."

"And I took him over to the mill, enjoying a private chat with him on the way," Dewey said cheerfully.

"It's funny you both mention talkin' to him alone. What interests me is that by Friday mornin'— or say Friday noon—if not earlier, you'd decided Linda and Miss Hadley wasn't to be told who Cooper was. The servants . . ." Rocky frowned; looked toward Moody. "Were you told who Cooper was?"

"No—sir. Why should I be?"

"I reckon you all wouldn't bother to explain. Well, Miss Graydon did see Cooper at dinner Thursday night but, aside from that, her opportunities for talkin' to him was limited. But I suppose she was told who he was."

"Naturally," Miss Lucilla snapped. "I wasn't interested in him; hadn't ever paid any attention to his sister. But something seemed to be called for. I supposed he'd leave Friday morning. But some people can't take a hint."

"And, not seein' him again till Friday night, you didn't have a chance to give him one? And shortly after that, Mr. Cooper went out on his ear. Well, since becomin' slightly acquainted with you, Miss Graydon, I conclude you threw him out. Therefore, he didn't come here to deal with you as a fam'ly. Or if he did, you didn't know about it, because he'd have been kicked out as soon as you did."

"Right! I would have—and did."

"Well, you didn't talk to Linda before Friday night. I can believe you didn't happen to mention who he was durin' dinner, since she'd never known Miss Evans. She didn't talk much to Mrs. Graydon Friday afternoon, the only time she saw her after Cooper came, or see Mr. Graydon at all. The same goes for Miss Hadley. So we don't know whether Mr. and Mrs. Graydon kept still about Cooper purposely or accident'lly. But certainly you'd expect Mrs. Hobart and Mr. Stinson to introduce Cooper as Miss Evans' brother. Instead, they kept still about it. And I take it Mr. Hadley didn't bother to enlighten his daughter."

"No," Hadley said quietly, "I didn't."

"Well, there *was* some reason to keep still after Cooper was killed. But you didn't want Linda an' Miss Hadley to know who he was before he was dead. Why?"

III

Dewey said, smiling: "What do you think?"

"Me? I think Cooper came here knowin' one person would almost have to pay him blackmail. That person bein' the one who changed the will. That little peccadillo could hardly be confided to the whole fam'ly," Rocky drawled. "So Cooper would know, too, that to collect his money the business must be between him and one person. Call that one X.

"X knew he was goin' to kill Cooper, either because he couldn't pay or didn't trust him. Thinking ahead, X saw that when Cooper's death was investigated the trail mustn't lead back to Maud Evans or Milly Harris. But X couldn't tell the real reason why Cooper's identity must eventually be hidden.

"And it wasn't safe to wait till after his death and then expect you, as a group, to hide that. You might have, just to avoid publicity, if it could've been done like that," Rocky said cynically. "But it couldn't. And if Miss Hadley or Linda knew who Cooper was, they couldn't be counted on not to tell, even after he was dead.

"X was in a position to order Cooper to keep still. But some excuse had to be given or suggested in some way why you'd all better keep quiet about Cooper's relationship to Maud Evans. Well, why not appeal to the fam'ly pride and dislike of scandal *before* his death. Say: 'He's hinted he knows something about us and wants money to keep still. Better not let Linda know about it. She's too young and wouldn't be tactful.'"

Linda giggled involuntarily and rather hysterically. Rocky smiled at her and went on: "'And we must handle this tactfully. So don't tell Lucilla, either. Because she'll lose her temper and throw him out.'

"Now, something like that must've been in X's mind. On the other hand, Cooper may've played into X's hand by bein' something of a hog. He had more 'n one string to his bow: he may have approached more than one person. And that person got panicky and played into X's hands by insisting y'all must be very careful. I think that's more likely, from what I've learned of Cooper. And also because he must finally have talked out of turn or Miss Graydon wouldn't have kicked him out. But something like what I've outlined must've happened to account for all your plain and fancy lying—unless you formed a kind of syndicate among you to dispose of Cooper, Lovett and Molly Harris. Which seems improbable."

"It might," Dewey said with mild regret, "have been simpler to tell the truth in the beginning."

"And I'm telling the truth right now!" Anette sprang to her feet with a dramatic fluttering of georgette ruffles. Then "no one can kill me to keep me from telling. I'm not going to be the goat any longer. There wasn't a word of truth in that story. Cooper didn't insult me."

"Give him time and you opportunity and he would have," Miss Lucilla remarked.

Anette looked at her venomously. "Well, he wasn't thrown out because of that and he didn't leave of his own accord! But no one told me anything till they needed my help. Oh no! Then Earl came home Saturday morning and said Cooper had read a lot of stuff in his sister's diary and said her relations with the old man weren't what they should have been. And him past seventy-five!"

Anette laughed shrilly and Miss Lucilla's hands tightened on the arms of her chair. Mrs. Hobart's face was no longer pale. Earl Graydon caught at his wife's elbow and she struck his hand aside.

"That's what you said: as much as you told me. And you said you'd found out that Cooper had been killed, so you weren't going to admit he was Maud Evans' brother. Because then someone might not only uncover a good motive for murder but they'd blacken your father's name. What do I care about a dead man's name? You and your family pride!"

"Just a minute," Rocky said gently. "When they put this proposition up to you, why did you agree?"

"Because," Anette said viciously, "I've been waiting fifteen years to get all of them in a position like that! I could afford to grant a favor. And I didn't have time to think it out."

"Yes, I can see why you did what they asked."

"You do see?" Anette's eyes were suddenly those of a wounded doe. "I knew you would see."

"Yeah. It would give you such a nice little hold over the rest of 'em. And you could always tell. Don't," Rocky said wearily, "expect your husband to throw *me* out for insultin' you. Why should he? Of course you know there's no reason Cooper couldn't have been blackmailin' you."

"He could not! I never saw the man alone. And I've got no satisfaction from anyone else as to what may have happened."

"You ungrateful little fool!" Mrs. Hobart said clearly. "It was your name Earl was trying to protect." She leaned back and closed her eyes, brushing the dark hair back from her white forehead. "I'm sorry, Earl. I didn't mean to say that."

"Me? Protect my name?"

"Miss Evans might have said a few things about the young fellow from Spanish Mill that came here too often for a while and then stopped comin' at all," Rocky said reflectively. "That was in June of '31."

Anette's mouth sagged and the rouge stood out triangularly on her cheeks. She sat down suddenly. Rocky went on:

"I'd like to have some connected story. Can you tell me one, Stinson?"

Dewey shrugged. He would try, he said. They had made the best of Cooper for a day. But on Friday the man showed no disposition to accept the offer of a ride into Brookdale.

"So," Mrs. Hobart interrupted, "I asked Dewey to see if he and Earl couldn't get rid of the man—tactfully."

"But Earl," Dewey said, "wasn't tactful. He didn't bother to hide his dislike of Cooper when the man appeared at the mill that morning. And finally Cooper had smiled unpleasantly and said:

"'You had better be polite to me, Mr. Graydon. I know too much about this family. Remember, your father thought highly of my sister. And she noticed things.'"

Dewey stopped to ask: "Is that right, Earl?" and Graydon, staring at his linked hands, nodded mutely. No tact or consideration could prevent Dewey, as he went on, from drawing the picture of a man foolishly frightened at the idea that they might be made to appear ridiculous.

"I didn't mind finding out what the man's game was," Dewey said. "Once he had declared himself, we had him for attempted blackmail. I thought that threat would be enough to settle him. We went to Ellis—as we always do—and he agreed with me, although we were both inclined to think

Cooper might only want to be disagreeable. But Earl didn't."

"All right: I didn't," Graydon said thickly. "I heard him: you didn't. I persuaded you and Bertha to try to—bear with him. And I did say we'd better not tell Lucilla. Or Linda. If we told her who he was he was quite capable of throwing out hints—really meant for the rest of us—"

"And how," Rocky said, "did you stop him doin' just that?"

"I—I talked to him. That is—he talked to me. More than I told the others."

"More than you wanted to tell them about? Didn't he say enough to make you go in to the bank in a hurry?"

Miss Lucilla said: "You damned fool!" and Mrs. Hobart: "Oh, Earl! You promised me you wouldn't. We agreed we wouldn't pay him, no matter what he might say."

"I—Bertha! I told *you* it was—was about Anette. But he had these four entries, beginning the twenty-sixth of June. And you know what a row there was."

His eyes were clinging desperately to Bertha Hobart's: he reminded Linda, suddenly, of a small boy asking comfort and pardon from someone older and wiser. A slow, hot flush crept over her face. There wasn't much that Mr. Allan wasn't learning today about the Graydons. Anette and Earl—and Aunt Bertha's contemptuous dislike of Anette . . .

"I didn't even want one of you to see what she—Miss Evans—had said. Because I—I'd tried to forget—I didn't want to be reminded—"

"I knew about that little episode, Earl, though you thought I didn't," Miss Lucilla said. "How could I help it, with Father shouting at Anette as well as Whatever-his-name-was from Spanish River? And what could Cooper have done with those entries? Printed them in the newspapers? I don't think so."

"He could have showed them. To people in town perhaps. And I didn't want—Linda or Rose to see them."

"That would have hurt your pride. Noble!" Anette jeered. "You weren't thinking about me. It was your father who made a row about a perfectly harmless friendship with a man who was far more entertaining than you ever were. You didn't mind saying Cooper had insulted me as long as you said that for once you'd acted the heavy husband and tossed him out."

"That was my idea," Bertha Hobart said coolly. "After Mr. Cooper was killed, we knew we'd have to give some excuse for his sudden departure if anyone learned of it."

"So I have you to thank!"

"It was a quite plausible story, wasn't it? Dewey and I persuaded Earl—and Mr. Allan, after meeting you, was undecided whether or not to believe it."

"Yes, it was perfectly reas'nable," Rocky said. "Did you pay him, Mr. Graydon?"

"No. I—my checking account—"

"I suppose," Mrs. Hobart said pleasantly, "that Anette has been ordering clothes again."

"Why not? You've always had everything you wanted! Yes, and I think you'd murder to keep it. Both of you!" Anette's smoldering eyes included Miss Lucilla in her accusation. "You got the money and we got the mill—which doesn't bring in any great income even under Ellis' very expert management."

Rose Hadley sat erect. Her slim shoulders stiffened. "I don't like you," she said deliberately. "I never did. Someday I'm going to slap your face. If it hadn't been for my father the mill wouldn't have gone on running. And if we can live within our income, there's no reason why you shouldn't. But you think you have a right to everything you want, just because you're *you*. Heaven knows what your mental image of yourself is, but it certainly can't be what the rest of us see."

She stopped: drew a deep breath. For the last half hour she had forgotten to push hairpins back into place and her hair was loosened and curling about her forehead. Her eyes were bright with anger; her mouth, scornful.

"For that matter," she said, "you're all of you like that. I wonder if Mr. Allan hasn't spoken so much of 'unimportant' people because he realizes your attitude. No one matters to you except yourselves and what you want and think you're entitled to. There! I've finished—for another ten years."

She looked at Dewey defiantly. He smiled and touched her hair gently. For once she seemed quite unembarrassed: her hand went up and caught his. And Rocky Allan was watching them with an odd look on his face: as if something had given him a new and disturbing idea.

Ellis Hadley said, "Doesn't it occur to any of you that you are doing exactly what he has been hoping you would do someday?"

"When the ice on a river breaks up, it goes out with a bang," Rocky said, unabashed. "However, let's get back to facts. You didn't pay Cooper, Mr. Graydon?"

"I said I would try to have the money by Saturday. But I couldn't bring myself to ask anyone to lend it to me. I hadn't told them the truth about what Cooper had said to me. And if I did . . . My sisters—don't like Anette," Earl said without looking at either of them. "They think I'm a—fool about her. I am."

"O.K.," Rocky said quickly. "Did Cooper do any more—hinting to the rest of you?"

"He—smirked when I happened to mention our father," Mrs. Hobart said. "And remarked that he knew a great deal about him and that his sister had known more, not only about him but about the rest of us."

"I was there at the time," Dewey said. "But when I tried to draw him out—because I wanted him to declare himself—he only smiled and wouldn't talk."

"I think he was shrewd enough to pick his man," Miss Lucilla said. "That is—Earl. He didn't tackle Anette instead, you notice. But he did talk—too much. At dinner on Friday I found him still here. When we were alone in here: Bertha, Dewey, Cooper and myself, I suggested he'd find it convenient to have Lovett take him into town in the morning.

"Not too politely," she added casually. "Cooper said: 'You ought to be glad to have me here. Glad I don't make public what my sister knew about your father and his affairs.'"

"But he hesitated before he said 'affairs', Lucilla. I've remembered that now," Mrs. Hobart said. "He might have been intending to say something else but changed his mind."

"So you may've jumped at conclusions?" Rocky said.

Mrs. Hobart nodded. Miss Lucilla said: "I suppose so. I asked him if he were insinuating there had been anything between my father and his sister. It's easy to think now that he may have been startled by that. Then he grinned and said: 'You knew your father better than I could.'

"Then I lost my temper and threw him out," she said unregretfully. "I remembered how Earl was always saying Miss Evans might worm her way into Father's affections. His term. And that he confided in her too much. But catch me paying blackmail to that skunk! Out he went!"

"I'd like to 've been here to see it. Was he mad?"

"That's putting it mildly," Dewey said. "I showed him to the door. He had some harsh things to say about our peculiar brand of hospitality but Lucilla shouted him down. You think, in spite of being very angry, he kept his bargain with this person you've so originally called X?"

"He had to, didn't he, to collect his money? So you shoved him out into the rain?"

Dewey looked sidewise at Miss Lucilla. "When I saw how hard it was raining I offered to drive him into town. He said to hell with it and me too. So I let him go."

"You always were a softhearted fool," Miss Lucilla grunted. "After he was gone they told me all about it. Except that it seems now that Earl had told the whole truth only to Bertha—and not quite all of it to her. But I agreed there was no use telling Linda and Rose unless he did make trouble and we had to. Earl reproached me next morning: said I'd spoiled their chances of finding out what he knew and then frightening him off. Then Ellis brought word the man was dead."

"It cert'nly is nice to have you all tellin' the truth— for a change," Rocky said blandly. "Our friend X must've had some uneasy minutes before Cooper decided to keep still. Once he was gone, it was all for the best. It was much better for him to die at the hotel than here. We might never find out who he was since we found nothin' on his body to identify him. We had just his name—Miss Lucilla helped overcome the difficulty of killin' him here and avoidin' investigation. Maybe on purpose."

"Certainly," Miss Lucilla said, unmoved. "He could easily have talked to me privately in my room, and the other could have been an act on my part—and his."

"I thought about that. Well, that ends the story. Cooper decided, I suppose, to hide some of the entries from his sister's diary in the library Thursday night. When your cook saw him comin' out and Linda told about it, X could guess what he might've done. Saturday night he found the things and burned 'em, except the one scrap Linda found. I know now that that was part of a page from the diary. The writin' agrees. But we'll never see the rest of the pages Cooper cut out or the carbon of the will.

"Linda and Miss Hadley mentioned his questions to them about them bein' here at the time of old Mr. Graydon's death. So that date was called to my attention. And if I followed that through, I might end up talkin' to Molly Harris. So that box of choc'lates was sent off to her Saturday night. Very logical," Rocky said grimly. "Unfort'nately, Molly burned the wrappings, so we don't have them to go on.

"Lovett took the package out to the Junction. It wasn't on the table with the rest of the mail, so someone either gave it to him or put it where he'd see it. Anyway, it was something he wouldn't forget. He'd found something in one of the cars."

He stopped; turned to Hadley. "You wouldn't like to take your turn tellin' the truth, would you?"

                              IV

Hadley hesitated, then: "Why not?" he said with his slow, tired smile. "Obviously a car was used. I went to the garage early Saturday morning."

"Why?"

"Oh well—I don't sleep well and from my bedroom window I can see the driveway to the gates. I heard nothing, but I was looking out and I thought

I saw a car drive out about midnight. The lights went on for an instant at the gates. I was curious enough to watch to see if the car came back. It did, in about forty minutes.

"At that time I supposed it was Lovett. I was going to speak to him; point out the muddy car before he could clean it. I didn't," Hadley said, "because I found one of the dustclothes I carry in the car pockets lying near the garage doors, marked with blood. Not much; enough for some-one to have wiped his hands on it. I burned it."

"Well, someone did almost certainly search Cooper's pockets. And he bled a good deal. Was the steerin' wheel clean?"

"Why—yes. You mean the cloth might have been used to wipe off that after someone whose hands were—not quite clean had driven the car back? Yes, that's reasonable. But why leave it?"

Rocky shrugged. "Probably dropped it. It was dark and, bein' in a hurry . . . Go on."

"Then I found some ashes in the car. Traces—but not cigarette ashes. They were like—well, I thought someone had burned papers."

"Someone must have. A private bonfire in the woods on the way home would've been wisest. But it was important to get back quickly. If I did it in a car, I'd hold on to each sheet till I had to let go and then throw it out the car window. And then a few flakes might drop off— I suppose you cleaned that up?"

"Yes," Hadley said. "But I was in a hurry to get the car out before Lovett came, so I didn't think to look under the cushions. I was worried, remembering Cooper was at the hotel—so I drove to Spanish River."

"Well, when Lovett took the cushions out, he found something. Then, I think, he tried a little blackmail himself. But he got scared or didn't get the response he hoped for—or both. So he called me and—exit Lovett."

"You've explained how everything has happened. But not who was responsible. Where do we stand; all of us?" Dewey asked.

"Under suspicion," Rocky said. "Anyone named in that will—Miss Graydon, Mrs. Hobart or Mr. Graydon—might've altered it. Or Mrs. Graydon, to keep her husband's inheritance. Yes, I know— you weren't here that night. But there wasn't anything to prevent you comin' back. I leave Linda out of it because she wasn't here and she was only fourteen. Also, there were two witnesses."

"But we didn't read the will," Dewey said. "We simply signed it. Unless Ellis was asked to read it afterward . . ."

"I wasn't."

"Well," Rocky said, "either one of you is lyin', both of you are lyin', or you're both tellin' the truth. If the last is true there's still a possibility Cooper thought you read the will when you signed, and gave himself away to one or both of you.

"Remember: there were two people in the lib'ary Saturday night. Either they came together, or they came one after the other and for the same purpose. Or one came to find what Cooper had hidden and the other stumbled on him by accident. But kept still! One of the words Linda heard was 'witness.' I thought then it referred to one person bein' witness to murder. I don't now. And Mrs. Hobart overheard two people talkin'.

"The possibilities seem to be endless. Mr. Graydon may 've innocently started the business of hidin' Cooper's identity or simply covered up the really serious piece of blackmail Cooper had in mind by callin' attention to what I've called his side issues.

"Ordinarily, in a murder case you check up on people's activities. It took me too long to find a motive for Cooper's death to be able to do that right away for the night he was killed. It's too late now to find out which one of you may have had wet shoes and clothes. However, you can do one thing for me. Andy, have you got that pad of paper? And the pencils?"

"Sure." Andy got up and began to distribute small sheets of paper and beautifully sharpened pencils.

"Ready? This is a letter," Rocky said, "to Montgomery Ward and Company."

Linda giggled and Dewey grinned. "For a copy of the family Bible?" he murmured.

"It's that, among other things, to some people up here. Go on: write it. 'Montgomery Ward and Company, Oakland, California.'"

Miss Lucilla muttered: "Damned foolishness!" but she wrote. Anette crushed her sheet of paper into a wrinkled ball.

"I won't! It's some trick."

"Give the lady another sheet of paper, Andy," Rocky said imperturbably. "It's no trick, unless your conscience—or whatever it should be called— is botherin' you."

Anette chewed at her full lower lip, watched her husband reluctantly set pencil to paper, and finally said: "Oh, all right! What else?"

"Oh—'Gentlemen.' Then: 'Kindly send to the Graydon Lumber Company, Brookdale, California, one hundred folding chairs. I enclose check for $100 in payment.' That's all. Sign your names please; and gather 'em up, Andy."

"And do you expect," Dewey said politely, "to solve this case by an analysis of the way in which each of us has written this extraordinary composition?"

"It might help. I'll have to study the will a little more in connection with this 'extraordinary composition.' And I talked to Molly Harris, you know. She didn't know—enough. She didn't have Miss Evans' opportunities for observation. Still, she made sev'ral suggestions. . . . By the way, how many bedrooms are there in this place?"

"Bedrooms? Eight—if it's any of your business," Miss Lucilla said.

"It is. I figured eight would be about right. Well, I'm havin'—shall I say your fam'ly history —checked on. That may take time. Also, Cooper didn't bring ever'-thing with him. He left a few interestin' pages in his sister's diary and the letters she wrote for old Mr. Graydon. I haven't had time to look over ever'thing together and I've got to wait to hear from the city.

"Unfort'nately," Rocky added, "there are other affairs not connected with you all that have to be tended to this afternoon. I'm sorry about the reporters."

"Why did they suddenly decide it was worth while to come up here?" Dewey asked.

"I didn't talk to any in the city, if that's what you mean. They're just a nuisance to me: I've been dodgin' them since late this mornin'. They came in by way of Reno. I reckon some ambitious young journalist in the county tipped them off Lovett was your chauffeur."

"They didn't get in here," Miss Lucilla said with grim satisfaction. "Moody slammed the door in their faces."

"But I talked to them at the mill," Hadley said. "It seemed better to do that."

"Much better. They aren't bad guys; kind of disillusioned, which is better 'n being young and smart, so far 's I'm concerned. Well, do as you like about talkin' to them. I'll be back tonight and you'll all be safe enough, anyway, if you use some sense about wandering aroun' in the dark."

The telephone rang. Rocky, stretched flat on Lovett's bed, glanced toward it, smiled and did not get up. He looked at his watch: twelve-fifteen. Andy was on time to the minute.

Damned thoughtful of old Graydon to put a telephone in this guest cabin. Well, of course, it was the natural thing to do, since it was quite a distance from the house. And it was very convenient now, unless—he frowned—the whole thing was too obvious? Because he'd used the telephone, after he came here, to call all three houses. He remembered exactly what he'd said: "Better take your upstairs phones off the hooks tonight if you don't want to be waked up. Andy had to go to Merton this evenin', about a body they found on the railroad tracks, and he may call me about it, no matter how late he gets back."

That was all right, if the reaction was what he hoped: if the innocent believed he was telling the truth and the guilty that he might not be—and didn't dare risk knowing. If Andy played his part convincingly it might work. It was all he could think of—and the telephone had rung long enough.

He said: "Hello. . . . Oh, Andy? I was dead for sleep. What about that business in Merton? Is it serious?"

"No. Just a hobo that fell off a freight. Pretty messy, but it's clear that's what happened. . . . No; it isn't that. I just got back and had something to eat. Then I went to the office and Cy Rand had left a message on your desk."

"What was it?" Rocky could imagine how Andy would look at this minute, his freckles standing out on a pale excited face. His voice had a slight tremor in it, but that was all right.

"McCarthy called up, late. Cy left word that McCarthy wouldn't tell him anything definite: said you'd told him to handle this particular angle carefully. But he finally gave Cy this message he said you'd understand, since Cy didn't know where you were. He said: 'Tell Allan situation as he suspected about money angle and everything else. Seems Graydon investigated too.' He said you'd understand that. Do you?"

"Um-hum. Taken with what I've put together tonight from the letters and things I've got here, that about cinches it."

"But, Rocky—"

"I can't tell you about it over the phone, kid. Wait till tomorrow. You know more than McCarthy does."

"Then he knows just nothing at all!"

"He don't need to and he don't ask questions. You go to bed. Come out early in the mornin' if you want to and I'll be systematic and let you make me some notes. . . . Thanks. I'm goin' to try to get a few more hours sleep myself before I make the rounds again. 'Night."

He sat down on the edge of the bed. Andy had done his part very nicely and not at all as if he had rehearsed it. But, as a matter of fact, Andy's perplexity and indignation were sincere enough. And he had had to go to Merton, though he must have been back in Brookdale for a good many hours.

The important thing now was to do exactly what would be expected of him if he were here for no other reason than to keep an eye on the place. The door was locked; to leave it open would be a too obvious invitation. "Will you walk into my parlor . . ." No; no one but a fool would go to sleep with that door open.

And he didn't think they considered him a fool— quite. He did hope someone thought him blind to his own danger and suffering slightly from a sense of omnipotence. And perhaps he was. Eleanor had said that he resembled the Duke of Wellington.

But having Andy with him here tonight might ruin everything. As for trying to justify his own suspicions to Andy—well, even if he could and did, the kid had such an expressive face. He wasn't able, yet, to treat a suspected murderer like a casual acquaintance.

Rocky looked at the pile of papers on the bedside table. They were useless, of course: the carbons of Joshua Graydon's letters and what was left of the Evans diary. Nor had Molly Harris been able to give him any information he hadn't made public.

There was one paper there, though—he found and read it again:

Montgomery Ward and Company,
Oakland, California.

GENTLEMEN:

Kindly send to the Graydon Lumber
Company, Brookdale, California, one
hundred folding chairs. I enclose check
for one hundred dollars ($100) in pay-
ment.

It was, as Dewey had intimated, a ridiculous
document. But—he stared at the precise handwrit-
ing—taken in connection with the will, a signifi-
cant one. As legal proof—well, it would probably
be laughed out of court.

He put the papers back on the table, turned off
the light and lay down again. He had said he was
going to sleep, so sleep it should be—if possible.
He had already made a circle of The Stockade,
about ten o'clock, very ostentatiously. In a few
more hours he would do that again: it would look
odd if he didn't.

He closed his eyes. He hadn't been lying when
he told Andy he needed sleep. No one could unlock the door without first knocking the key out
of the lock and that would wake him.

He sat up, blinking at the darkness. He was
a damned fool, after all. He had a picture of it

before his eyes now; the window shade that had stuck when he tried to pull it down. And that window was on a line with the bed.

He got up reluctantly; moved the largest chair into a corner and sat down. It was a poor substitute for a soft and comfortable bed but perhaps a safe one. Gun and flashlight on the floor beside him; he was ready for whatever happened.

And probably nothing would—here. If someone wanted those carbons and the mutilated diary, it would be common sense to wait until he'd left the cabin. Still, anyone who sensed the danger of a trap would know he might be expecting that. Besides, he thought cheerfully, as long as he was alive he could always tell what he—alone—knew or was supposed to know.

Of course, a gun used outside would be heard more easily than one fired inside this cabin. In any case, he could do nothing but wait. He did not look forward with any great pleasure, however, to making another circle of The Stockade. He had a distinct aversion to being shot at from the back, and there were too many convenient and dark corners in the place.

He dozed finally: woke so suddenly that his head had already jerked erect before he realized he had been sleeping. The silent blackness of the small room still closed about him unbrokenly. But something had wakened him or he would not have this strained sense of groping; of trying to remember something that now seemed part of a dream. Someone trying the door? Probably: the knob rattled a little when you turned it.

Slowly, because he was still cramped and stiff, he reached toward the floor and got his fingers about the flashlight. Then glass tinkled suddenly onto the floor, he heard the harsh bark of a gun, and his nostrils were filled with the smell of powder. Instinctively he ducked; then hesitated, hand tightening about the flashlight. If he showed it now . . . No; better wait. Cooper had been shot three times and Lovett twice.

But there was no other shot. Rocky sprang to his feet, snatching at his gun. He stumbled against a chair, kicked it savagely aside and unlocked the door. He shouldn't have waited. No use trying to move silently now.

Just beyond the white swath of light from his torch the darkness moved. The night was all black shadows, but shadows wouldn't run. This one was heading for the trees about the garage, where two people might play hide-and-seek and one of them manage to slip safely away. Or into the garage and a car.

Rocky stopped running. He shouted: "Stop, or I'll fire!" The words—which sounded to him

foolishly melodramatic—echoed back to him un-
answered. He jerked his gun up and, as its roar
died away, a piece of the darkness fluttered to the
ground like a huge bird with a broken wing.

V

Rocky straightened up and stood, there at the corner of the garage, for a moment of indecision. The
wound did not look to be a serious one but it was
still bleeding under the clumsy bandage he had
fashioned. The man's eyes were closed: that was
probably shock. But something had to be done for
him and there was nothing to work with in the
cabin.

He went back to the cabin, gathered up the
papers there and put them and the diary in his
pockets. Returning, he stooped and lifted the
limp figure over one shoulder. He went past Earl
Graydon's house and on toward the Hadley's. A
light showed there in an upper window. The man
he was carrying began suddenly to struggle, trying
to free himself.

"Damn it! Must you take me in here? Anywhere
else."

"They're awake here," Rocky said. "And no danger of hysterics. Hold still!"

"What difference does it make?" But Dewey relaxed against his shoulder. "What nice cheese you baited that trap with," he muttered. "And I ran into it."

"Never mind that. Can you stand up so 's I can ring the doorbell? I've got my hands full— Oh, Mr. Hadley!"

"I was awake," Hadley said. "I thought I heard— Good God! What . . ."

He stood aside to let Rocky in. "You'd better put him on the couch in the living room," he said in a flat, dead voice. "And be quiet. Rose—"

"This wasn't my idea." Dewey tried to sit up, winced and lay flat again. "He would bring me here." His bloodless lips twisted into a brief smile. "Anxious that I shouldn't cheat the hangman."

Rocky ignored him, starting for the telephone. "Get some towels or rags and give him a drink. I'm going to call the doctor."

The operator rang dutifully but briefly. She said, curiosity impregnating her voice: "The doctor isn't home. He was called out on a baby case near Juniper Lake. I don't think they have a phone where he went. Shall I—"

"Never mind: I'll call again."

Juniper Lake was at least twenty miles from Brookdale, but Dr. Bradley went, grumbling, to attend a few old patients there. Rocky returned to the living room.

"God knows when the doctor'll be back. I'd better see what I can do. Have you got any iodine? And some cotton?"

"I think so," Hadley said. "Upstairs. I'll . . ." He turned quickly; stepped closer to the couch. "Rose! Please, go back to bed. This is nothing you need—"

"What are you trying to hide?" Rose said steadily. "I heard you say something about iodine. Who . . ." Her voice changed; she cried: "Oh—my darling!" She pushed her father aside, sat on the edge of the couch and lifted Dewey's head against her breast. "Mr. Allan, can't you do something? The doctor—"

"He was starting to do something when you appeared. It's only a scratch," Dewey said lightly. "Listen, dear—if you love me—"

"If?" She kissed him deliberately and as if there were no one else in the room but themselves.

Rocky looked quickly away for an instant. Something had seemed to break in Dewey's face when she did that; his good arm tightened convulsively about her waist. The pleasant, sardonic voice was suddenly harsh and strained.

"Then go upstairs and stay there. Tomorrow—later on—we'll talk about it."

"Of course. As soon as we've made you comfortable."

He looked at her, then toward Rocky, and closed his eyes, shrugging one-sidedly. "You see?"

"Um-hum. Just like all women. . . . Hot water," Rocky said. "And iodine—and cotton, if you have any."

"I'll get it." They heard her running lightly upstairs.

Rocky said casually: "We won't talk about it now. This isn't so bad: a clean hole, with no bullet to get out."

"I forgot," Dewey said, "to congratulate you on your marksmanship—hitting a running man in the dark."

"I didn't want to hurt you—much. It was luck, getting you through the top of the shoulder, because I couldn't make out arms and legs. . . . All right, Miss Hadley. Hold that water for me."

He was applying iodine when the doorbell rang hysterically. "Better see who that is, Miss Hadley. Tell 'em Stinson and I collided in the dark and he got the worst of it. And to go back to bed."

Rose released Dewey's hand, stopped to pin back the heavy hair that fell over her shoulders and nearly to her waist. The silk of her yellow negligee clung to the fine slim lines of her figure that were so successfully hidden by her dark loose dresses. Dewey's eyes followed her. When she was gone, he said:

"It will have to be talked about sometime, Allan."

"Not now. It's after two-thirty. I'll get the doctor here soon 's I can."

"There's no hurry," Dewey said between clenched teeth. "You're doing very nicely."

"So are you. I know I'm clumsy as hell—but that does it? Now: where's the best place to put him to bed?"

"What?" Hadley started nervously. "Oh—bed? There's a downstairs bedroom. If you're going to stay here—"

"Don't you reckon I'd better?" Rocky bent and lifted Dewey; said to Hadley: "Show me where the room is. Then you'd better calm down Mr. Graydon. I think that's him on the doorstep."

In the small room at the end of the hall he laid Dewey on the bed and began to unfasten his shoes. "You are being—very solicitous," Dewey said with a pale smile. "I have pajamas on underneath these trousers. Or did have, until you ripped the jacket off."

"Relax, will you? Where'd you drop that gun?"

"Not very far from the cabin window. It's mine," Dewey said casually.

"Thanks for tellin' me. It saves time."

"Am I to sleep now?"

"You will."

"The condemned man ate a hearty breakfast," Dewey murmured. "Yes, I think I will sleep. My eyes won't stay open."

Rocky straightened up and stood looking down at him. "In some ways," he said gravely, "I like you as well as anyone I ever met. And—though you can tell me it's none of my business—why didn't anyone ever bother to tell me you—you really love Rose Hadley?"

"I told Linda. Perhaps she didn't really believe me. But she wouldn't discuss that with you. Besides"— Dewey turned his face into the pillow, stifling the groan that Rocky's rude surgery had not wrung from him— "what does it matter—now?"

"It might matter—a lot. One more question. You don't have to answer it. You did know that will was a fake, didn't you?"

Dewey said, without looking up: "Need you ask that? Yes, I knew."

Rocky hesitated; then: "I'll put out the lights," he said. "And come back soon as I find that gun and see if everyone is all right. Sounds like the maid might be havin' hysterics now."

Dewey was still sleeping when Rocky tiptoed from the room a little after seven o'clock. The sun was hidden by a cold gray veil of clouds, and frost still silvered trees and house roofs.

He went into the cabin, stepping carefully through the broken glass beneath the window. Only one of the large panes was broken, but that gap was space enough for a hand and wrist. The bed was on a straight line from that spot. Even in the dark, if you knew its location and how to handle a gun, the danger that you'd miss someone lying in bed was very slight.

He found the one bullet that had been fired buried in the mattress near the pillows and dug it out with his pocket knife. Outside, he picked up an ejected shell near the window. The ground was hard underneath a slippery coating of needles from the pines close to the cabin. The needles had been scuffed up by the pressure of feet but there was no mark there that you could call a footprint.

Rocky went back to the cabin and the telephone. It took five minutes ringing to rouse Dr. Bradley, but after a good many words, all of them censorable, he admitted that he could be at The Stockade in ten minutes. In less than that time he drove his old car jerkily through the gates Rocky had opened for him.

"What now?" he growled as Rocky jumped to the running board. "Can't you stop these people killin' each other? Twins last night—and they couldn't afford even one brat—and then you get me out at this time of— Is it Hadley that's sick? He's got a bad heart."

"He don't look very well but it's not him. And nothing really serious." Rocky suddenly released his hold on the car door; stumbled and recovered his footing.

The doctor roared: "Damn fool! Are you trying to kill—" Then, abruptly, he stopped his car. Rocky ran on toward the old cannon and the girl who was leaning against one of them, hands pressed tightly against her forehead.

She gasped: "I didn't scream, did I? I didn't hear anyone scream—I had to get outside. And find you—it's Aunt Bertha again. But she's dead this time."

"Then she didn't—"

"She didn't kill herself. That would have made everything very simple, wouldn't it? But people who take poison don't have time to throw away a glass and wash out a vacuum bottle, do they?"

"No." Fatigue and a sudden sense of failure brought lines to Rocky's face that made him look, for once, older than his twenty-nine years. "No,

282   VIRGINIA RATH

they don't. It looks like I—guarded the wrong person. Well—you'd better come in here first, Doc."

"I can't tell you anything else," Bradley said.
"She's probably been dead about two to four hours.
Cyanide, I suppose."

"You're definite?"

"Definite as I want to be. I'll go take a look at
Stinson."

"That round mark on her temple . . ."

"What about it? You said she fell the other
night, and I see the side of her head is cut a little.
She has the kind of skin that bruises easily. Beautiful woman—too bad. Can't be helped, though.
See you later."

Rocky walked aimlessly about the room. Nothing out of place, according to Moody. Nothing
missing, except a glass that should have stood on
the bedside table beside the wide-mouthed vacuum bottle.

The bottle had held hot Ovaltine, Moody said,
between hiccoughing sobs. She had been awake
after midnight and thought she heard a shot. So
she got up to see if anything was wrong. By the
time she got into the kitchen Miss Linda came
running in to investigate.

Then, of course, Miss Lucilla and poor Mrs.
Hobart woke up and Miss Lucilla discovered Mr.

Dewey wasn't in his room. After that Mr. Earl came running over with a gun to see if they were all right. When he found they were, he started for the Hadley's house. He said he might find Mr. Dewey and Alr Allan somewhere outside.

They were all in Mrs. Hobart's room and Miss Lucilla returned to her own for some brandy. She and Miss Linda had some but Mrs. Hobart said it would only keep her awake and would Moody mind making her some Ovaltine?

So Moody went downstairs, made the Ovaltine and put it in the vacuum bottle that Mrs. Hobart always kept on her table. But she had just reached the upstairs hall when the doorbell rang, because Mr. Earl had forgotten his keys.

So she put the vacuum bottle on the nearest hall table and went downstairs to let Mr. Earl in. And Mrs. Earl, who was hysterical and wouldn't stay alone with the maid. And they all crowded into Mrs. Hobart's room to talk about it, Moody said, and she had stood at the door.

But she forgot about the Ovaltine until she was just getting into bed. Then she went back upstairs and took it in to Mrs. Hobart. But she said she already felt quite sleepy and wouldn't drink it until later—if she needed to. And Moody had gone out and left her.

That was Moody's story. Linda's: She hadn't been able to sleep so she had risen earlier than usual and decided to go down to the kitchen for coffee. Miss Lucilla had called out to her to see if Mrs. Hobart was all right: if she wasn't feeling better this morning they would call a doctor.

Linda had opened the door cautiously. The shades were drawn and she could not see the room clearly. But almost at once she had felt that it was empty; cold and deserted. That was why she called her aunt's name; finally went over to the bed. And touched an icy hand.

She hadn't screamed; only backed toward the door and when her outflung hand touched the light switch she had pressed it automatically. Then in an instant she turned the lights off. But she had a clear picture of the bed, the woman in it and the bedside table.

There had not been any glass on that table or on the floor or bed. She had thought about that; wondered: what did she drink from? Not the vacuum bottle; she would never do that. Of course it wasn't a trivial question but it had seemed so at the moment.

Then she called Miss Lucilla. She had gone close to the bed; stayed there a long time, looking down at her sister. She said, finally:

"There's no glass here but there's a little stain on her gown. It looks like that stuff Moody brought her last night." She turned and examined the vacuum bottle; said tonelessly: "Someone's washed this out." And then to Linda: "Don't stand here, child. Go find Allan."

Everyone, Linda told Rocky steadily, had an opportunity to poison the drink in that vacuum bottle. And they all knew it was Mrs. Hobart's. Miss Lucilla never took hot drinks at night; neither did Linda.

Anette had been alone in the hall; at least, she had said she was going to the bathroom and been gone for a few minutes. Miss Lucilla had come over from her own room when Earl came back the second time. And he had left them to look for matches in Linda's room.

That ended the evidence. The glass was gone and the vacuum bottle had been washed clean. Rocky walked over to the bed and stood looking at the fresh round bruise on Bertha Hobart's temple.

PART FIVE
"THE COURT PRONOUNCES—"

I

They came in through the kitchen door and Rocky looked instinctively at the clock and then, quickly, at his own watch.

"Your clock's ten and a half minutes slow, Clara," he said, with an ex-railroader's habitual regard for fractions of minutes.

"Is it now?" Clara said comfortably. "Well, I'll tell Moody. They're all in the living room, sir. Moody just told me Mr. Dewey came over. I'm making him some nice chicken broth."

"That's swell," Rocky said grimly. "I know he'll enjoy it. You might make me some nice strong black coffee."

They went on through the dining room and into the hall. Rocky took the wire Andy had just brought out from his pocket and read it again. TALKED TO FIRM AND OLD FRIENDS CONFIRM YOUR GUESSES GRAYDON INVESTI-

GATED. MCCARTHY. Well, he thought, last
night's fake message had come pretty close to it,
after all.

As Clara said, they were waiting, on this gloomy
afternoon that was so much like the one on which
he'd first met them. Even the smells were the
same: burning coal, Anette's heavy perfume, dry
old timbers. Andy sat down beside Linda. Rocky
put the two pages of Joshua Graydon's will on a
small table; said gravely:

"I'm sorry to have to go through this right now
but waitin' won't help matters any and those newspaper men are roving aroun' outside and getting
mighty suspicious." And, without further preamble: "There are some discrepancies between the
first and second pages of this will; due, I imagine,
not to carelessness but habit.

"When an expert typist is copying anything the
job is more or less mechanical. But a person who
isn't a touch typist depends a lot on mem'ry. He
gets two or three words or a sentence in mind before he types it because he has to look at the keys
as well as the copy.

"So, even in a job like this, when carefulness
meant ever'thing, the person who was copying the
first page of the will and changing one part couldn't
help lettin' his way of writing creep in. Probably
without realizing it, since he had so many things

to watch out for. And if he did, he still didn't have time to go back and do the whole thing over for a little matter of abbreviations and numbers.

"Because Maud Evans did abbreviate, in her diary and when she addressed a letter. And on the second page of the will you have 'professor', 'Nevada', 'company' and 'California' abbreviated and 'one hundred' written in numerals. But on the first page 'California' is twice spelled out as well as the word 'company.'

"All the sums of money mentioned on the first page are written with numerals and the dollar sign except in one clause; that relatin' to Arney. Which we'll take up right now.

"That clause gives him five hundred dollars and it's important because Arney was very much surprised by it; because it hadn't been in any of Mr. Graydon's previous wills and because it takes up two lines.

"Disregard all of this will but the last five clauses on the first page. The first one devotes two lines to Thomas Elsey. The next one, three lines to Earl Graydon. The third gives Arney those two lines. The fourth takes up four, dividin' the residue of the estate between Linda, Mrs. Hobart and Miss Lucilla. And the fifth clause takes three lines to appoint Miss Lucilla executrix.

"Now, so far 's side margins go, the first and second pages of the will are the same, with a left-hand margin of one and three-quarters inches and a right-hand margin—uneven, of course—of about one and a half inches. Miss Evans also left a top margin of one and a quarter inches on the second page so she certainly left at least that much at the top of the first page. Those top margins, like the side ones, had to be the same on both pages if a substituted first page was goin' to pass inspection.

"If she left a wide top margin on the first page, you'd naturally suppose she left as wide a margin at the bottom. But that bottom margin could not be *too* wide, because she took a second page to begin on the will's last two clauses, and that page, with its signatures, had to be used without alteration. Neither could the bottom margin on the first page be too narrow, when Miss Evans had plainly indicated she was leavin' wide margins all aroun'.

"That means there had to be almost the same number of lines on the substituted first page as in the original. If too much was added, it might look crowded. Since it don't, we'll argue nothin' was added but something was changed or cut out. Well, if only a change in wording was made, there would be no difficulty. But if an entire clause was cut out, something had to be put in to take its place and fill up that space.

"Now you see why that clause regarding Arney is so important. And consider its position: stuck in between the one relatin' to Earl Graydon and that naming the residuary legatees, when Graydon had presumably finished with his minor bequests and begun on the fam'ly.

"And in that clause five hundred dollars is written out in full. Because that was an original composition and habit cropped up again, just as it had when it came to writing California out in full. When you're used to doin' that, even when you're trying hard to copy exactly, it's hard to remember a little thing like that.

"The clause relatin' to Elsey was almost certainly altered, because he'd always been given more 'n one thousand dollars in the other wills. But all that had to be done, there, was to leave off a zero. It was a mistake, because Elsey died before Mr. Graydon, so his heirs had no claim, while his legacy being lowered from ten grand to one looked suspicious. But lots of people wouldn't be certain Elsey's heirs would not get what he was supposed to have.

"Joshua Graydon knew the law. He knew, then, that if you disinherit a child you must, to be safe, mention him specifically in your will. If you just omit his name there'll be trouble. There must be some clause like: 'I leave to my son, John, the sum of ten dollars.' A clause that would take up about two lines, so that when it was cut out, the clause regardin' Arney filled that space—and was cheap at five hundred dollars.

"But Earl Graydon is specifically mentioned in the will. He has three lines to himself. As it was always understood he was not to be one of the residuary legatees, he had to, whether disinherited or not, have one clause to himself. And as long as he did, even if those three lines disinherited him in the will as Maud Evans typed it, he had only to change the wording and he wouldn't have to add anything to fill up space. Also, he abbreviates 'company' and 'California' and don't write out numbers. And if you're eliminatin' him, that also lets out Mrs. Graydon, since her only interest in the will was in what he would get by it.

"But when you come to the clause dealin' with the three residuary legatees, you find it takes up four full lines, but that the omission of one name wouldn't change the number of lines. But if there had been originally only *two* names mentioned in that clause, the name that did *not* appear in it had to be specifically mentioned in another clause or the will wouldn't hold.

"The name of a person who'd get less than a third of the estate or be entirely disinherited. If that third name was *added* to the clause dealin' with the residuary legatees, then that other clause had to be cut out and something put in to take its place—and space.

"A will—a lawyer—Arney. I reckon that's how her mind worked. Because the two residuary legatees—leavin' Linda out of it—are women. That always seemed reas'nable enough: that it was a woman responsible for all this. Because Cooper and Lovett, who both certainly knew they were in danger, did let someone into their rooms. And it seems they'd be less apt to fear a woman than a man. However, that's just an idea.

"Getting back to the will: the last provision, regarding an executor, was there, whoever was to be executor, and one name could be easily substituted for another."

Miss Lucilla raised her square grizzled head, her black eyes fixed unwaveringly on Rocky. "Well?" she said steadily.

"That was misleadin'. There's an old poem people used to recite years ago," Rocky said slowly. "I remember the last line of it: 'The court pronounces the defendant—dead.'"

Linda spoke first. "Aunt Bertha! But she is—she *is* dead!"

"That complicates things but it hasn't anything to do with this. If you're goin' to accept my argument that one of the two residuary legatees, excludin' yourself, forged that first page and killed Cooper, it's got to be Mrs. Hobart. Miss Lucilla can't type."

"But neither could Aunt Bertha—really."

"I should've said: Miss Lucilla has never even tried to use a typewriter. She said so and I checked on it. I can't believe any person could sit down to a typewriter for the first time and manage to turn out a new first page to that will."

"N-no," Linda said. "Of course not. You make the most fearful mistakes. And Aunt Bertha was at least familiar with a typewriter. Only why didn't she just destroy that will? That would have been so much easier."

"You're not being very bright," Rose said. "Dad and Dewey had witnessed a will and knew there was a new one. If it couldn't be found, the first question would be: why was it destroyed and by whom? Scandal, investigation—perhaps publicity. And very likely more danger than there would be in substituting a first page that would pass without question."

"That about covers it," Rocky said. "To go back: while I said Cooper'd be more apt to let a woman than a man in to talk to him, I couldn't see him feelin' too safe with you, Miss Lucilla. Unless your throwin' him out was just an act. But if it was, it almost had to have been staged with his consent. I didn't think it had been, because I knew he was really mad that night.

"And when I went over what you all wrote to my dictation yesterday, Mrs. Hobart was the only one who'd written out everything: numbers, dollars, the words 'company' and 'California.' The men abbreviated and used numerals: wrote reg'lar men's business letters. Miss Lucilla abbreviated 'California' and wrote 'one hundred' in figures.

"There are still a lot of gaps you'll have to fill in for me. I'll tell you, though, what I thought about Mrs. Hobart. She'd always had ever'thing she wanted: she was the fam'ly beauty and her father's favorite. People like that get in the habit of thinkin' they have a right to whatever they want. And even bad luck—if you want to call her marriage that—don't always make them think diff'rently.

"And even if she was her father's favorite that didn't mean he'd forgive her anything and ever'thing. Just the opposite's sometimes true about a father and his fav'rite child, once he does turn against her.

"No one blamed her because her marriage hadn't turned out well. They said her husband drank, was very jealous, and probably had once taken his firm's money. And Joshua Graydon was supposed to have refused to do anything at all for him.

"But he changed his mind a little before he died and I wondered why. Also, after talkin' to Molly Harris and findin' out how many bedrooms you have here, it was easy enough to subtract and see that if there were two extras when Mr. Graydon died, Mr. and Mrs. Hobart occupied separate rooms. I may be old fashioned but that don't seem to fit in with the picture people had of Mrs. Hobart always being more than willing to forgive him and go back to him. I'll bet her father had old-fashioned ideas too.

"Most people think Miss Lucilla rules the roost here. I think"—he smiled at Miss Lucilla—"that your bark is worse 'n your bite. There was a remark you made about being willing to play the part of the dowager who has an iron hand in a velvet glove. Only, you said, *you* didn't wear the velvet glove. Or did you say it with just that emphasis?"

Miss Lucilla nodded. "I suppose I did. Meaning that it was Bertha who hid her iron hand with velvet gloves, not I."

"I wondered. Also, I kept on wonderin' why your father changed his mind about Hobart. Suppose he investigated, decided the situation had been no more Hobart's fault than his wife's and that the man deserved a chance?

"Well, your father did do that. He found out Hobart had taken some of his firm's money. And that his old friends blamed your sister's extravagance for drivin' him to it. I only got the results of that investigation this mornin'."

"You're right," Miss Lucilla said. "She always got what she wanted without—blustering. And credit for being a perfect lady at the same time. I thought she was greatly to blame for what Hobart did. But I didn't carry tales to Father.

"Earl and I together paid the company off and hushed the matter up. Hobart didn't have any force of character, of course. But he was mad about her until the day he died. But don't make any mistakes: she wasn't a—a passionate woman. Hobart never had any real cause for jealousy."

"I thought," Rose said, "from what little I saw of him, that it was a case of 'she smiled, no doubt, whene'er I passed her; but who passed without much the same smile?' Only Mr. Hobart wasn't the Duke of Ferrara and he couldn't give commands."

"But it is true he was jealous?" Rocky said.

"Unreasonably," Miss Lucilla admitted. "Oh, she liked admiration. She thought it was her right and she valued her—beauty for its own sake. But she liked power even more. And money meant

power—we'd been taught. Also, the matter of pride
must have entered into it. Not to share equally
with me and Linda when everyone had supposed
she would . . . Well, I was always afraid, after
Cooper was killed. But I didn't know and I didn't
want to.

"But I hadn't the least suspicion there was anything wrong with that will. Only, the evening it
was made, my father spoke to me about Hobart.
He said he didn't want to leave him any money
because he wasn't certain he was fit to handle it.
But if he should die, he wanted me to see that Hobart had a chance here. Well, I should have known
then that something was wrong, but I didn't give
it another thought. And he didn't live very long
after that."

"Well, there was no reason I could see why the
fake message I had Andy give me over the phone
last night about investigatin' Hobart in the city
should mean anything to you," Rocky said. "It was
ambiguous enough that it might have meant somethin' to Mr. Stinson—maybe. But no one tried to
remove me till I said that that message, with what
else I knew, cinched my case.

"And Mrs. Hobart took Linda to Hawaii after
she graduated and after giving her a dance at the
Fairmont. That was written up in the Brookdale
Sun with all the details. That it was her present

to Linda and how they took the best boat and—well, went in style. That may've been the item that int'rested Cooper, because he wondered how Mrs. Hobart had that kind of money. Anyway, with what else he had, from his sister's diary, he'd figure it was worth his while to come up here to find out. If that didn't come to anything, he could just try blackmailin' Mr. Graydon.

"Well, that brings us to—call it an accomplice. Because the fact that there were two people in the library that Saturday night pointed to one who knew something important he wasn't telling. The word 'witness' made me think of the witnesses to the will—when I knew about the will. And that made me rule out Earl Graydon as his sister's accomplice, though I must admit that wasn't an airtight reason for doin' so.

"Then the other words: 'you wouldn't dare' and 'regretted'—'murder'—'again'—'armed' were suggestive of two people who didn't dare give each other away. And that one regretted his part in the business and was warning the other he would be on his guard.

"Well, Mr. Hadley and Mr. Stinson were the witnesses to the will. And Mr. Stinson was always the most likely suspect of the two, because of his situation here in the house and bein' more intimate with Mrs. Hobart. He certainly was, after what happened last night. He's admitted he knew that will was a fake, but he doesn't say when he knew it."

Dewey eyed him warily. "What do you think?"

"A very Stinsonian answer," Rocky said, smiling. "Well, if you want the works—"

"I don't see why it matters," Rose said. "You've solved your case."

"But Mr. Allan is a seeker after the truth," Dewey drawled. "And in this case I think the exact truth will benefit all of us. Go on."

"For about one minute it occurred to me you were a party to the substitution or, at the very least, kept still about it because it was on your account Mrs. Hobart had been disinherited."

"That seems to me a very reasonable and natural solution," Anette said with her irritating laugh. "Why discard it so quickly—or at all?"

"I doubt if you'd understand. I can easily imagine Mr. Stinson committing murder if he thought it necessary. But I can't see him havin' an affair with the daughter of a man to whom he was indebted and when he was living under his roof. And not just because it'd be a very dang'rous thing to do, either."

Dewey murmured: "Three cheers!" but there was nothing facetious in his tone. Rose laughed unexpectedly.

"No; Anette wouldn't understand," she said sweetly. "Remember how you took it on yourself to warn me, dear?" Her "dear" was a slap in the face. "And what I told you? To go straight to hell, wasn't it?"

II

Linda glanced at Andy; began to giggle hysterically at his expression of mild discomfort. Dewey's grin was one of pure joy.

"Thank you, dear," he said. "I see I can depend on you. Which is a relief, because my dear mother brought me up to be kind and courteous to all women."

"And that's just what got you in a jack pot, isn't it?" Rocky said. "It occurred to me you weren't necessarily keepin' still just because you'd been party to forgery or—purposely—accessory to murder. Or even because you'd been Mrs. Hobart's lover and didn't want that known.

"It was perfectly possible Cooper gave himself away to you. So many people think witnesses read the wills they witness. As a matter of fact, they very seldom do. Cooper saw you before he did Mr. Hadley, so you could've steered him away from Hadley. But if Cooper did jump at such a conclusion, you're smart enough to have drawn him into tellin' you all about it by pretendin' to know more than you did.

"And—since Hobart was jealous—he may've been jealous of you and that would probably have been noted down in Miss Evans' diary. And strengthened Cooper's notion you knew about the will.

"Miss Lucilla says you've always been a 'soft-hearted fool.' You wouldn't give Mrs. Hobart away, because you wouldn't know she meant to kill Cooper—though you should have. But once she'd done it, she had you between the devil and the deep, havin' used your gun.

"Also, she could claim you were or had been her lover if she wanted to give that reason why you'd helped her. It would be her word against yours on all points. A jury would be apt to accept her word against yours. If I thought for an instant that such a situation was possible, a lot of people would have the same idea—permanently. Especially as you have no reputation for havin' been a plaster saint.

"You'll excuse my sayin' this, Miss Hadley, but for a while I thought of your engagement to Mr. Stinson as just one of these fam'ly affairs. When I saw it was such a serious business with him, I saw how Mrs. Hobart could've kept him in line just by threatenin' to tell that kind of story."

"I wouldn't have believed it!"

Rocky looked at Rose admiringly. "I don't b'lieve you would. But other people might have. I really should arrest you, Stinson, but I'm soft-hearted too. I can imagine you've sweat blood over this—and known, besides, that your own life might be in danger.

"I'll let you off if you'll fill in the gaps. I still don't know why Joshua Graydon changed his will. The only thing I can think of is that I was told he couldn't forgive a liar or a person who didn't pay his debts."

He looked at Miss Lucilla as she made a sudden sharp sound of understanding. But she shook her head. "I'm guessing. Let Dewey tell you."

"Oh, I'll tell. And glad to. And very thankful you spent last night watching over me, Allan. Because if Bertha wasn't dead, I'd hardly dare talk. You've covered that very well.

"And you guessed right about Cooper thinking I'd read the will and been a party to the forgery. Also, there was some—twaddle in his sister's diary. I gathered Miss Evans thought the natural gallantry of my manners a trifle uncalled for. Hobart did and told me so one day in the hall. That woman seemed to hear everything.

"I got it all out of Cooper. I doubt if he believed me when I said Ellis hadn't read the original will, but he did agree not to bother him, as the price for my keeping still.

"Bertha admitted the whole thing to me. She'd run up bills—staggering ones—and made the mistake of trading on her relationship to Joshua when she did it. They were hounding Hobart and he told Joshua, at about the time one firm sent him a polite query regarding his possible responsibility for his daughter's debts.

"He'd already been pretty well displeased with her when he decided to give Hobart a chance, though he didn't discuss that with anyone else. He'd suspected her of at least misrepresenting the facts all along. When he found out about her debts, he knew she'd lied. That was one of his weak points and he flew into one of his famous rages and made that will. I suppose you guessed that, Lucilla? Well, you would, knowing her—and Joshua.

"He left her three thousand dollars with the terse remark that he'd paid her debts. That was down in the diary; also the fact that the will had been signed and witnessed. Also some fairly shrewd reflections of Miss Evans' to the effect that it must be a shattering blow to Bertha's self-esteem and her ideas regarding the future. My words: not hers.

"I didn't intend to give Bertha away. I thought Joshua had been rather harsh. Of course he told her about it: said it might 'tone down her grand ideas.' That is what she told me and it sounds characteristic. But if he'd lived a few months more he might very well have relented. You couldn't even begin to question his sanity, but his illness certainly had not improved his temper.

"And she had—in her way—a temper too. She could have counted on Lucilla's generosity—as Joshua very well knew—but she didn't. Besides, there was that matter of pride. Call it that for want of a better name. And if Hobart suspected anything when the will was produced, she was quite able to control him.

"Well, I saw nothing for her to do but pay Cooper. She couldn't, at once. She would have had to sell some securities. It seemed natural for her to be panic stricken, but it never occurred to me she would kill Cooper. Earl played into her hands, but I should have known why she was so anxious Cooper's connection with Maud Evans should be hidden while it was still possible to do so.

"When Lucilla threw him out, I said I would try to deal with him in the morning. That was going to be difficult, I knew. He said he would keep still, when I showed him to the door, because he 'had to, to collect.' But that he'd 'add it onto the bill.' He said he thought it might be safer to walk into town. He didn't seem to trust me."

"Odd! I reckon," Rocky said, "another reason he was mad was because he had to leave some of his belongings here."

"The papers in the library? I hadn't thought of that. But he did put the most important entries from the diary there and kept the carbon of the will and the pages relating to—Earl on him. Which seems to prove that, from a purely practical standpoint, Bertha was doing the wise thing to kill him. He might have made her pay more than once.

"Of course I guessed she had killed him. But I couldn't prove that. And I knew nothing of the cyanide or those chocolates because I didn't know much about Molly Harris. Bertha omitted telling me about her until it was all over.

"And I didn't know Lovett was in danger. He'd found her cigarette lighter—monogrammed—in Ellis' car. She almost never used it but she'd put it in her pocket that night and used it to burn those papers. Somehow, it slipped down behind the cushions without her missing it—until Lovett told her about it.

"And she'd given him that candy, out at the garage, just before he left with the other mail. Of course he was going to remember that, if Molly Harris died and they traced the chocolates back here.

"She would admit all these things when I charged her with them but told me—truthfully—that I had nothing to back up any accusation. And that if I did, she could accuse me. She'd taken that gun of mine. I hadn't used it for years but it had my initials on it. Thoughtful of her— Well, she was right: she had me tied hand and foot.

"The final touch was her threat to say we'd been lovers for years, as a good reason why I would be involved even if I could prove I had no interest of my own in Joshua's will. Well, you've covered that item—I wasn't watching the night Lovett was killed. I really did fall asleep in here and didn't know she listened in on the telephone in the lower hall.

"After that I did watch; as I'd been doing all along, so far as my own safety was concerned. But I didn't catch her until—"

"This mornin'? I thought you must've," Rocky said. "That message shouldn't have meant anything to you. And there was only one shot. You had plenty of time to get away if you'd fired just once, because I was expectin' the usual two or three an' waited. But if you caught her and disarmed her—"

"That's what I did," Dewey said. "She jerked away and ran for the house and I dropped the gun and, like a fool, stopped to look for it. She was wearing gloves, of course. I'd been expecting trouble because"—he smiled—"it was fairly obvious you wanted us to think you knew more than you did."

"It was pretty obvious," Rocky said, unoffended. "Only it's true I have a had habit of keepin' things to myself. Ask Andy. And murderers are apt to be scary."

"Yes. I knew that. I thought you could take care of yourself but I meant to be on guard. And I would have liked some definite proof—of attempted murder, at least. But I haven't had any too much sleep lately. She must have heard the downstairs telephone ring and listened in on it. All I know is that I woke and found her gone from her room. Then I ran out and managed to catch up with her. With the results that you know," he added, moving his bandaged shoulder cautiously.

"And what'd you do the night Linda caught you in the lib'ary? Take it on the lam?"

"I'm not very proud of that—but, yes. I'd decided to look things over in the library and caught her there. We had an—interesting conversation that showed me where I stood. Well, I had no key to the front door with me but she was prepared with one. When we heard Linda she pushed me out the side door and said she would come in an instant. When she did finally come and explain about Linda, I—well, I was—"

"Never mind," Linda said. "You did come back to let me out if you had to, didn't you?"

"Yes. I dodged down the hall when I heard you put the key in the door."

"There's one other thing," Rocky said, "that seemed to point to Mrs. Hobart's havin' an unwilling accomplice. You haven't mentioned your talk in the garage, Stinson."

"Our . . . No, I hadn't. I didn't really mean to hurt her."

"But you were a little—overwrought by then? You wanted to warn her things had to stop where they were? That you were willin' to take what risks you had to, to see that they did."

"You mean—she told the truth about what she heard?" Linda said.

"Why not? Wasn't it the easiest thing to do, when she had to tell some reas'nable story in a hurry? She repeated what had been said to her and left out her answers, claimin' she could hear only one person. But if she heard two full sentences she should've heard at least a few words from the other person in the garage."

"Then that had nothing to do with the other murders?" Linda said. "But she is dead. And she was murdered."

"Yes. But it don't make sense," Rocky said. "Not the way it was done. I can alibi Stinson, who had the best motive for killing her. Well, who gets the money?"

"Earl says she left it to him—and me."

"But I didn't— Of course that's a motive," Earl Graydon said. "And I suppose I had the opportunity to get some of that poison before Duncan took charge of it. But I—I was very fond of her."

His long chin shook a little. "He's telling the truth about that," Anette said briefly. "She always babied him. He confided in her but I can't imagine her confiding in him."

"Besides," Earl said, "someone had to take the glass—didn't you say there should have been a glass?"

"There was one on the table when Moody put the vacuum bottle there. And it looks like she drank some of the Ovaltine and spilled a little on her nightgown. An autopsy will show if she did drink the Ovaltine. But she had to take the poison *in* something. Someone did—between about four and eight—have to remove that glass and wash out the vacuum bottle. And—"

"I am the most likely person to have done that?" Miss Lucilla suggested. "I had the best opportunity. And I might have thought that was the best way out if I suspected her—and I did."

"Yes, but it wasn't the best way out—with that setup," Rocky said. "Makin' it look like murder wouldn't do you any good. Quite the opposite. What you'd want to do was to make it look like suicide. So why take away the glass and wash out the vacuum bottle?"

The old clock on the mantel gave out three tinkling chimes. Rocky glanced at it automatically; then at his watch. He closed his eyes suddenly. The clock ticked on, its flowered pendulum swaying between pink and green shepherdesses. He said at last:

"Stinson, didn't you remark once that Moody is a human time clock?"

"Moody? Perhaps I did. She is—"

"Andy! Go get Clara and Moody. Right now."

Clara came in, wiping her hands on her apron, followed by Moody, eyes and long nose still red and swollen.

"The coffee's all hot and—"

"Never mind the coffee, Clara. What time did you get up this mornin'?"

"The alarm went off at seven. We take turns making the fire. This was Moody's time, so she got up and built it."

"And how long after that did you get up?"

"Oh, no time at all, sir. In about ten minutes after Moody did. Just time for the fire to get going good."

"How do you know it was just ten minutes? Did you look at the alarm clock?"

"Well—no. Because it won't run except lyin' down on its face. But it was only seven-fifteen when I got in the kitchen. Moody called me."

"And that clock is always right because Moody sees that it is. But it was ten minutes slow a while ago. Why," he said softly to Moody, "didn't you set it right?"

"I didn't notice it was wrong—being upset and all."

"It's pretty hard to upset a habit like that. Clara, were you in the kitchen all day?"

"Every minute of it, sir. I never stepped out at all."

"So you didn't have a chance to change the clock back, did you, Moody? Not without Clara seein' you do it, and you were afraid she'd ask you how it came to be runnin' slow, or remember about you doin' it." Rocky drew a deep breath. "I haven't been able to help noticin' that you were very fond of Mrs. Hobart."

"Mr. Allan!" It was Linda, her blue eyes wide with sudden remembrance. "You couldn't know, because I didn't tell you—but you did love Aunt Bertha, Moody! And you did say to me once that suicide is the worst disgrace that can happen to anyone! You took away that glass and washed out the vacuum bottle when you went up to her room, as soon as you got up, to see how she was."

"The first thing that came to your mind, I suppose. You didn't stop to think what a—dumb thing it was to do. I suppose you didn't know enough about what's been going on to realize that. Then you set the clock back ten minutes so Clara wouldn't think you'd taken too long to build the fire. But suicides write notes," Rocky said implacably. "Come on—where is it?"

Moody thrust her hand into her flat bosom; drew out a folded sheet of heavy cream-colored paper. "It's here. I didn't mean any harm." She gulped, licking tears from her long upper lip. "She was the best of the lot of you and I couldn't stand the idea . . . I didn't stop to think. And I didn't read this till after I'd taken the glass and washed out the bottle. I still don't believe it's so but after I read it I was afraid to say what I'd done or you'd have said I killed her myself."

"Never mind: we all have some funny ideas," Rocky said perfunctorily. He unfolded the paper. "This is what should've been here—and wasn't." He read it, slowly:

"'This is to confess that I killed Walter Cooper and Charles Lovett. I also sent the box of chocolates to Molly Harris. I alone was responsible for these killings. I had no aid from anyone. The motives for the murders are already known to Mr. Allan.'"

Rocky straightened his shoulders wearily. "Signed—and that's that," he said. "This will have to be made public, of course. I'm sorry, but there's no way out of it. And I might as well show it to those reporters now and get it over with."

III

"Do you think," Eleanor said, "that the state of crime in Brookdale will permit us to spend a pleasant New Year's Eve together?"

"I don't see why not." Rocky yawned and settled himself more comfortably on the couch. "What kind of hilarity are you plannin'?"

"Well, after all, Brookdale is somewhat lacking in bright lights and night life. I suppose we can sit up to let the new year in—if you can keep awake that long. Well"—she looked approvingly at the richly embroidered Chinese robe she was wearing—"it was a nice Christmas. Thank God, you've never given me a washing machine."

Rocky grinned. "You're goin' to want one after the Christmas surprise you gave me."

"Only it wasn't a surprise and I was very much disappointed. I had the very silly idea that you would clasp me to your chest and say in reverent accents: 'My wonderful little—'"

"Honey—come here! If you don't mind." He drew her down against his shoulder. "Look: you *are* wonderful. I always said so. Only you aren't unique. And I've never been able to understand why a man's always expected to be knocked in a heap when he finds out he's due to walk the floor in a hospital waitin' room in six or seven months. Or never guess it till about the twentieth time his wife coyly waves a tiny garment in front of his eyes."

Eleanor giggled. "I spared you that."

"And you should've noticed I hired that kid to keep your wood boxes filled so you won't ever have to run out for a load of wood, because sometimes you haven't got much sense."

"Darling! That long ago?"

"Why not? This isn't somethin' you thought up all by yourself, is it? I thought I had something to do with it?"

Eleanor smiled at him. "Oh, was *that* man you? Well . . . Somebody at the door. Maybe we're going to have company this evening, after all. . . . Oh, Dewey!"

"I come to announce," Dewey said, "that we are starting the new year right. We are moved into our house and have enough chairs to sit on and Rose wants you to come over. I have some superfine benedictine, Eleanor, and various other things that Rocky may like. And Linda is there and Andy will be."

"To say a last fond farewell?"

"Poor kids," Dewey said tolerantly. "I hope they have sense enough to stick it out."

"Poor kids—nothing!" Rocky said, sitting up. "The only good deputy I ever had and he's got ambition and goin' back to college."

"Who's lending him the money?" Eleanor said.

"Well—what else could I do? Since he thinks he'll make a better doctor than detective—and I agree with him."

"Only something must be done about Linda," Dewey said. "Lucilla says she is too old to pull up roots and Linda doesn't want to leave her. But it's no place for her with"—he smiled wryly—"Anette and Lucilla not speaking and Earl torn between two fires. Well, after a while we'll see."

"Do you like your new house?" Eleanor asked.

"Like it! Rose is like a kid out of school. She's going to join—things. Whatever it is that women join." He stopped, fumbling for a cigarette. "I'm just talking to gain time," he admitted. "Rocky, how much do you tell your wife?"

"Oh—what I don't tell her, she worms out of me."

"This is serious. I—I made up my mind to start the new year right in more ways than one. I followed your lead that last afternoon out at The Stockade, though I nearly bobbled it. Since then I've been asking myself how much you did know. And now—"

"Now that Hadley's dead you can tell me?" Rocky said. "Well, you had sense enough to keep still and agree with me. I knew it couldn't have been you in the garage with Mrs. Hobart. You didn't have to sneak out there to talk to her. But I did think she reported part of the conversation that took place there acc'rately. Only what was said to her could easily have been said by Hadley. Or by Rose, but they'd just been alone together, so why go to the garage to talk?"

"Hadley was willing to do anything for Rose's sake. And I thought he might have guessed her happiness was threatened. For one thing, you said once that you all always took your troubles to him. Did *you?*"

Dewey hesitated. "I—hinted. Ellis had—I always thought—such a level head and had always been a balance wheel to all of us. And I was pretty much on edge that night, after Andy Duncan

reported that affair of the chocolates to us. And
since Lovett had been killed the night before—I
did throw out some hints while Rose was out of
the room. Then Ellis went upstairs."

"Maybe he already suspected Mrs. Hobart?"

"He never liked her," Dewey said. "And of
course he knew something dangerous was going
on under the surface."

"Well, it's possible, you know, that Cooper
double-crossed you and did talk to Hadley about
the will."

"Yes, he was quite capable of doing that. But
if he did, Ellis kept still about it and never did
speak to me of it."

"And I didn't ask him that day we finished
things up. I was afraid to. But whether or not
Cooper sounded him out, too, he'd heard what
Linda had to tell about hearin' you and Mrs. Hobart in the library. That could have suggested to
him, as it did to me, an unwilling accomplice.
And then if your hints confirmed his suspicions
and made him think she might have you pretty
well involved in the mess, there was nothin' to
keep him from following her that night. Telling
her to come into the garage where they could talk
privately and warnin' her to be careful.

"Even threatening to kill her and sayin' he was
prepared to risk anything to shield you—which

meant Rose. Afterwards, he wasn't well—Andy told me. That pointed to some unusual exertion when Doc Bradley told me he had a bad heart.

"He may 've been afraid she'd try to kill you or, at least, that she'd make you the goat. Especially after I carried you in there after catchin' you outside the cabin. If she was dead she couldn't accuse you. He knew all of you so well it wouldn't take him long to figure out the situation.

"I suppose he knew he couldn't live very long. If he got Mrs. Hobart out of the way and made it look like suicide, ever'thing would be all right for you—and Rose. He had a key to the house, so he could sneak over there and get in—while I dozed in that back room, lookin' after you.

"And he told me to put you in that room instead of upstairs and found out if I was goin' to stay there. I didn't pay any attention to that at the time. I was too much embarrassed at havin' caught you in a trap I'd set for Mrs. Hobart.

"I don't think I ever really said she killed herself. I said the setup was wrong. If it looked like murder, what good did it do to kill her? What was needed was a suicide note."

"A suicide note when it wasn't suicide—Rocky, talk sense!"

"Honey, I am. There was a round bruise on her temple. Her skin bruised very easily. That mark hadn't been there the day before. It could have been made by a gun pressed very hard against her head. But she didn't do that herself; she had no gun. If he pressed a gun to her head and gave her the choice of takin' poison or havin' the side of her head blown away—well, what would you do?"

"I'd prefer to look well in my coffin," Eleanor said. "And she was beautiful, wasn't she? And valued her beauty. Yes: it's reasonable enough."

"If he was willing to risk anything, the only choice she had was how she was to die. Because she must've been able to tell he wasn't bluffing. So she wrote the note—and then that fool maid almost ruined ever'thing.

"Then Hadley was sick again that mornin'. I suppose he had a heart attack after he got back. I asked the doctor later how bad his heart was—and found out. He'd warned him, more than once, to be careful."

"Well, he wouldn't take a thing like that—lightly. He never got over it," Dewey said. "But he died so suddenly that he didn't have time to say much—to me privately. Just: 'In garage that night: warned her.' And then: 'Want you to know, if Allan not satisfied. I made her kill herself. Gave her her choice.' That was all."

"And Rose?"

"I don't know. If she guessed, she will probably never speak of it."

"I'd make her, if I were you," Rocky said soberly. "Get it out of the way. Because she's too smart not to 've guessed. So is Miss Lucilla. Good Lord! How could they ignore it? You admitted she had you in a nice mess. Why should she give up and kill herself? What evidence did I have that would hold in court?

"She did get panicky and run into a trap, thinkin' I knew more than I did. But *you* got caught and that was duck soup for her. When she thought it over that night, she must have seen she had a good chance if she threw you to the wolves. A jury would have thought her a very much injured woman. No; I couldn't see her killin' herself at that stage of the game.

"And that confession—it's so plainly dictated. Short businesslike sentences. 'Gentlemen: this is to inform you . . .' Not her style but Hadley's. If she had all night to write it in, wouldn't you expect something a little more flowery? Some attempt to justify herself?"

"Women," Eleanor admitted, "do insist on justifying themselves."

"But you kept still," Dewey said.

"I suppose I could've kept plugging away and got together proof that Hadley made her kill herself," Rocky said slowly. "As a matter of fact, I think he'd have confessed if I'd started askin' him questions. But he saved me a lot of grief—and you. And he wasn't goin' to live long. The truth is, I liked him and I was thinking as much about Rose as I was him."

"Well, I'm glad you did," Eleanor said. "I know it's the first time you've ever done a thing like that. Sonetimes I've wondered . . . Of course you're usually right: there isn't any justification for murder. But I don't want you to be—be too narrow minded."

"Isn't that a woman for you?" Rocky said. Dewey smiled and shook his head.

"I don't care. You were right, under the circumstances. You would have been even if Mr. Hadley were still living. Because she was better off dead."

"Casuistry! Yes, I read a book once," Rocky said. "Well, let's go over to your place, Dewey, and get a little cockeyed. Not uncomfor'bly—just pleasantly."

COACHWHIP PUBLICATIONS
CoachwhipBooks.com

VIRGINIA RATH

DEATH AT
DAYTON'S FOLLY

COACHWHIP PUBLICATIONS
CoachwhipBooks.com

MURDER ON
THE DAY OF
JUDGMENT

VIRGINIA RATH

COACHWHIP PUBLICATIONS
CoachwhipBooks.com

VIRGINIA RATH

FERRYMAN,
TAKE HIM ACROSS!

COACHWHIP PUBLICATIONS
CoachwhipBooks.com

VIRGINIA RATH

THE ANGER
OF THE BELLS

COACHWHIP PUBLICATIONS
CoachwhipBooks.com

SAMUEL ROGERS

YOU'LL BE
SORRY!

YOU LEAVE
ME COLD!

www.ingramcontent.com/pod-product-compliance
Lightning Source LLC
Chambersburg PA
CBHW032242010726

47494CB00002B/591